HARDCASTLE'S CONSPIRACY

HARDCASTLE'S
CONSPIRACY

Graham Ison

This first world edition published in Great Britain 2005 by
SEVERN HOUSE PUBLISHERS LTD of
9–15 High Street, Sutton, Surrey SM1 1DF.
This first world edition published in the USA 2005 by
SEVERN HOUSE PUBLISHERS INC of
595 Madison Avenue, New York, N.Y. 10022.

British Library Cataloguing in Publication Data

Ison, Graham
    Hardcastle's Conspiracy
    1.   Hardcastle, Detective Inspector (Fictitious character) - Fiction
    2.   Police - England - London - Fiction
    3.   Detective and mystery stories
    I.   Title
    823.9'14 [F]

    ISBN-10 : 0-7278-6264-2

Typeset by Palimpsest Book Production Ltd.,
Polmont, Stirlingshire, Scotland.
Printed and bound in Great Britain by
MPG Books Ltd., Bodmin, Cornwall.

One

The knock at the door came just as Alice Hardcastle had started to wash up the breakfast things. Young Walter had gone to school, and Kitty and Maud, having only recently mastered the intricacies of shorthand and typing, had left for work at their respective offices. These were only a short walk from where the Hardcastle family lived in Kennington Road, Lambeth, not far from where the famous Charlie Chaplin had once resided.

Muttering to herself about the lack of help in the house that the absence of her two working daughters had caused, Ernest Hardcastle's wife shook the water from her hands and wiped them on a tea towel.

'Good morning, ma'am.' The young policeman who stood at the door, his oilskin cape shiny with rain, looked apologetic. 'Sorry to bother you, but—'

'If you're wanting the inspector,' cut in Alice, 'he left for work about ten minutes ago.'

'Oh!' The policeman fumbled beneath his cape and produced a message flimsy. 'He's wanted at the station, er, Cannon Row, that is,' he said, glancing down at the form.

'Well, it's no good telling me, lad,' said Alice. 'Anyhow, he should be nearly there by now. If he was in time to catch his tram,' she added, half to herself. As usual, her husband, claiming that he could not go to work on an empty stomach, had insisted on a good breakfast: fried eggs, bacon, two pieces of fried bread and a couple of sausages followed by two slices of toast and marmalade, washed down with three cups of tea. And that often made him miss the tram he normally caught.

'Ah, yes, right then.' The constable stuffed the message back into his pocket. 'Sorry to have bothered you, ma'am,'

1

he said again, as he sketched a salute made more difficult by his encumbering cape, and departed.

Divisional Detective Inspector Ernest Hardcastle, as head of the CID for the A or Whitehall Division of the Metropolitan Police, had his office at Cannon Row police station off Whitehall, and immediately opposite the forbidding edifice of New Scotland Yard. Fittingly, both buildings had been erected from Dartmoor granite hewn by convicts.

Far from missing his usual tram – it had been delayed by an overturned milk float – Hardcastle had been obliged to wait in Westminster Bridge Road for about twenty minutes. In the pouring rain. Although his umbrella had kept his shoulders reasonably dry, his shoes, socks and spats were soaked. And he was in a foul mood.

The officer in charge of the police station, his four stripes proclaiming him to be a station-sergeant, had his back to the main door searching for a form in the huge stationery cabinet, and did not hear Hardcastle enter.

The DDI deliberately let the flap of the counter fall with a resounding crash; he did not care to be ignored.

'All correct, sir,' said the station officer, turning hurriedly, 'and you're wanted, sir.'

'What is it *this* time?' asked Hardcastle crossly. 'Not the bloody suffragettes been at it again, I hope.' Just over a month previously, some of Mrs Pankhurst's followers had caused a minor explosion in Westminster Abbey, slightly damaging the Coronation Chair. But fortunately for the DDI, Special Branch had relieved him of what promised to be a futile enquiry. Nonetheless, these aggressive women were continuing to conduct a campaign of malicious damage throughout the capital.

'No, sir. Male body found in the park, sir.' The sergeant fingered a piece of paper that lay on his desk. 'We sent a message to Kennington Road nick for them to send a PC round to your house to fetch you out.'

'Which park? St James's, Green Park or Hyde Park?' snapped Hardcastle.

'Er, St James's, sir.'

'Well say so, man. I'm not a bloody mind-reader.' And with

2

that caustic reproof, Hardcastle marched through the charge room and upstairs to his office.

'Reckon he got out of the wrong side of the bed this morning, Sergeant,' commented the constable on station duty.

'You watch your bloody tongue when you're talking about the DDI, lad,' responded the station-sergeant, 'or you'll find yourself out on the streets again.'

The constable, not wishing to lose his coveted post inside a dry, warm police station, lapsed into silence.

Hardcastle flung open the door of the detectives' office and glared around. 'Well, what's this about a body in St James's Park?' he demanded.

Detective Sergeant Charles Marriott, the first-class sergeant in charge of the office, rose to his feet. 'Man's body found in the lake, sir. About an hour ago. Mr Rhodes is out there with DS Wood and DC Catto.'

'What is it, Marriott, some drunken sot fell in and drowned himself?'

'Don't rightly know, sir, but Mr Rhodes sent for the divisional surgeon not half an hour ago, and he's asked if you'd attend the scene.'

'We'd better go and have a look then, Marriott. Grab your hat and your gamp. It's raining cats and dogs out there.'

Despite the weather, the two detectives walked to the park, striding into Derby Gate, across Parliament Street, through King Charles Street and down the Clive Steps.

A small group of police stood around a body at the side of the lake. Some distance from it, and prevented from venturing closer by another policeman, a knot of sightseers craned their necks in an attempt to see what was happening. A wheeled stretcher – what the police called a hand-ambulance and which they normally used for conveying drunks to the police station – was parked in the nearby road, its attendant policeman hunched beneath his waterproof cape.

Hardcastle immediately singled out his deputy, Detective Inspector Edgar Rhodes, the man in charge of the sub-divisional CID.

'Good morning, sir.' Rhodes raised his bowler hat.

'Well, Mr Rhodes, and what have we here?' asked

3

Hardcastle. 'I hope you haven't called me out for a simple drowning.'

'No, sir, there's a bit more to it than that. Looks as though the deceased had a good wallop over the head, and it might have been that's what did for him. But I s'pose we'll have to wait for the pathologist's report to be certain.'

Hardcastle grunted. 'Who found him?'

Rhodes pointed to a constable standing next to a uniformed park-keeper. 'PC 419 Wilkins, sir. He hadn't long come on early turn, five beat, when he was called by the park-keeper who'd seen this stiff face down in the lake. By the time we got here, they'd fetched the body out.'

'Any idea who he is?'

'Not yet, sir. He hadn't got a wallet or nothing like that on him. Looks like a robbery. Knocked over the head and pushed in the lake, like as not.'

'What did the divisional surgeon have to say?'

'Certified death and went on his way, sir.'

'Just stayed long enough to earn his fee, I suppose,' muttered Hardcastle as he stepped across to the body. 'Why are you holding your brolly over him, Catto?' he asked, staring at the DC.

'Keeping the rain off of him, sir.' Detective Constable Catto, somewhat mystified by the DDI's query, had thought the reason obvious.

'No bloody point in that, lad. You've just dragged the bugger out of the lake. He's soaking wet already.' Hardcastle stooped to inspect the man that the police had found. There was a wound on his head some three inches in length that must have bled quite copiously until stemmed by the victim's death and immersion.

'Reckon he must have gone in off there, sir,' said Rhodes, pointing to the iron suspension footbridge that crossed the lake and connected The Mall to Birdcage Walk.

'Not likely to have fallen, not over those railings,' mused Hardcastle. 'Better chance he was shoved over. And he could have bashed his head on something on the way down, I suppose.'

'Might have hit the concrete bottom, sir,' said Rhodes. 'The lake's only four feet deep.'

4

'Unlikely, Mr Rhodes. The water would have slowed him down. I reckon he was clobbered before he went in.' Hardcastle stood up. 'Had a look round, have you?'

'I had the men search the whole area, sir,' said Rhodes. 'There was nothing. No hat anywhere, and no sign of a weapon.'

'Well, that's a bugger and no mistake. More than likely got tossed in the lake by whoever done for him. If it wasn't an accident, that is.' But as he said it, Hardcastle knew it was an untenable theory: the wound and the absence of a wallet gave the lie to that. 'Better get him off to the mortuary, Mr Rhodes. There's nothing more to be done here.'

It was three o'clock that afternoon, Wednesday the fifteenth of July 1914, before Dr Bernard Spilsbury, the Home Office pathologist, was able to tell Hardcastle the results of his findings.

'I estimate the time of death at around midnight, Inspector, and the blow to the head fractured his skull. There's no doubt he was dead before he went into the lake. No water in the lungs, d'you see. And before you ask, it wasn't vagal inhibition.' A little under a year later, Spilsbury was to demonstrate his expertise in determining the cause of such deaths when he testified in the 'Brides in the Bath' case at the Old Bailey. 'You'll be looking for a blunt instrument very likely.'

Hardcastle had no idea what Spilsbury had meant when he talked of vagal inhibition. 'Anything else, Doctor?'

'Yes, he'd had a few glasses of brandy. Quite a few, and not long before he died.'

'Well, it's murder and no mistake,' said Hardcastle when he and Marriott were back at the police station. 'And we don't even know who he was.'

'I think we might, sir,' said Marriott.

'Oh, and how might we know?' Hardcastle picked up his pipe and teased out the old ash.

'I had a good look at the clothes he was wearing, sir. Black jacket and striped trousers. It's possible he was in service. Anyhow, there was a label inside his jacket marked with the name of Joseph Briggs.'

'Good work, Marriott,' said Hardcastle.

5

Marriott smiled at the rare compliment. 'And the name of the tailor was Burroughs, sir. Got a place in Tottenham Court Road.'

Hardcastle put his pipe in the ashtray and stood up. 'In that case, Marriott, we'll have a word with them. See what they can tell us about this Mr Briggs.' He lifted his bowler hat and umbrella from the hatstand and paused as a thought occurred to him. 'But if he's in service, what's he doing having his whistle made by a tailor, eh? Might be a city gent for all we know.'

'Perhaps he's got a rich employer, sir.'

'We shall see, Marriott, we shall see. Better bring that jacket with you.'

The manager at Burroughs, attired in similar fashion to that in which the victim had been dressed, examined the jacket that Marriott placed on the counter.

'Yes, sir, that's one of ours,' said the manager, whose name, he told the detectives, was Martin. 'It's wet through,' he added, raising his eyebrows.

'Probably on account of us having pulled the dead body of its owner out of a lake early this morning, Mr Martin,' said Hardcastle without a trace of irony.

'Ah, I see,' said Martin, and nodded as though such an occurrence was commonplace. He turned and thumbed through a ledger that rested on a shelf behind the counter. 'Ah, yes, I thought so.' He turned to face Hardcastle again. 'This jacket was part of a suit we supplied to Kendall's for Mr Briggs.'

'What, Kendall's the Pall Mall club?'

'The same, sir,' said Martin with a satisfied smile. 'We undertake all the tailoring for their staff. Mind you, we shall be busy on uniforms if there's to be a war.'

'War!' exclaimed Hardcastle. 'There ain't going to be a war.'

'I'm not so sure about that, sir,' said Martin. 'Some of my clients reckon there's a bit of sabre-rattling going on in the Balkans after the archduke was assassinated.'

'Bloody twaddle, all this talk of war, Marriott,' muttered Hardcastle as they left Burroughs. 'But more important than that, we'd better go and have a chat with the powers-that-be at this here Kendall's.'

*   *   *

6

The head porter at Kendall's, one of many similar gentlemen's clubs in Pall Mall, prided himself on knowing every one of the members by sight. And he knew immediately that the two men who had just entered did not belong to the club.

'May I help you, sir?' he asked, addressing Hardcastle.

'We're police officers and we need to see whoever's in charge.'

'That'll be Major Carmichael, sir, the club secretary.' Determined not to allow these two 'strangers' into the inner sancta of the club, the head porter flicked his fingers at a boy in page's livery. 'Tell the major there's a couple of gents from the police what wants to have a word with him, lad. Quickly now.' And turning to Hardcastle again, said, 'Won't keep you half a mo', gents.'

The man who appeared in the entrance hall a few minutes later was short and stocky. Probably about fifty years of age, he had a guardee moustache and iron-grey hair, brushed flat. 'I'm Major Carmichael, gentlemen. How may I help you?'

'Divisional Detective Inspector Hardcastle of the Whitehall Division,' said Hardcastle, 'and this here's Detective Sergeant Marriott. We want to talk to you about a member of your staff, Major. Well, we think he's a member of your staff.'

'I see. You'd better come along to my office then, Inspector.' Carmichael looked beyond Hardcastle and gave a brief nod to a tall man in evening dress. 'Good evening, Chairman.'

'Evening, Carmichael,' replied the chairman affably.

'Sir John Webster, the club chairman,' whispered Carmichael in an aside, and turning abruptly on his heel led the two detectives across the smoking room and through a door in the far corner.

The walls of the club secretary's office were oak-panelled and hung with traditional military prints. That part of the wooden floor not covered with a Persian carpet was highly polished, and across one corner was a heavy oak desk with an inlaid leather top.

'Take a seat, gentlemen.' Carmichael waved a hand towards two deep, leather club armchairs. 'May I offer you a drink? A glass of whisky, perhaps?'

'Very kind,' murmured Hardcastle. 'Thank you.'

Once Carmichael had dispensed liberal measures of

Glenlivet into crystal tumblers, he sat down behind the desk, placing his own glass in the centre of a leather-edged blotter. 'Well now, one of my staff, you say? What's he been up to?'

'If, in fact, Joseph Briggs is a member of your staff, Major.'

'Yes, he is. What about him?'

'He's dead,' said Hardcastle, and took a sip of his malt whisky.

Carmichael expressed no surprise at the demise of one of the club's employees, but Hardcastle assumed that, being a major, sudden death was not unique in his professional experience. 'What happened to him? Get run over, did he?' But then, realizing that so high ranking an officer was investigating the matter of Briggs's death, added, 'No, I suppose not.' He brushed his moustache and took another mouthful of his whisky.

'We are treating his death as murder, sir,' said Hardcastle before taking another sip of his drink. 'I have to say this is a very good drop of Scotch, Major,' he added, raising his glass to peer closely at the contents.

'Only the best at Kendall's, Inspector,' said Carmichael with a smug smile. 'And that includes the staff. I handpick them myself.'

Hardcastle described how the body of Joseph Briggs had been found that morning, and then asked, 'When was the last time that Briggs was seen here in the club, Major?'

'Eleven o'clock last night.' Carmichael spoke without hesitation. 'I was here myself until then, and saw him leave. He was the late-duty smoking-room steward, you see. If there are any members left here after that, decanters of whisky, brandy and port are left out, and the members sign a chit and leave it with the night-duty porter.'

'Putting a bit on trust, isn't it?' asked Hardcastle with a smile. He certainly wouldn't have put policemen on their honour where alcohol was concerned.

'Kendall's is a *gentlemen's* club, Inspector,' said Carmichael sharply, as if to imply that cheating was unthinkable.

'Why is it called Kendall's?' Hardcastle asked. Most of the clubs in Pall Mall had names that gave some indication of the members' interests, like the Army and Navy, the Travellers, the Oxford and Cambridge, the Reform and the Royal Automobile.

'It was named after Major John Kendall,' Carmichael began,

'an officer of the Royal Sappers and Miners. He was killed in the Crimean War. One of his brother officers, a Colonel Charles Ingram, founded the club and named it in Kendall's honour. It's primarily a club for army officers, serving and retired – originally for those who had fought in the Crimea – but these days we also admit gentlemen of substance and good standing.' He paused. 'Provided, of course, that they're not engaged in trade.'

'Very interesting,' said Hardcastle, wishing he had not asked. 'I take it that Briggs did not live in, Major.'

'No, he didn't. I think I have his address here, if that's of any use to you.'

'That would be helpful, yes.' Hardcastle turned to his sergeant. 'Make a note, Marriott.'

Major Carmichael turned to a book on his desk and flicked through the pages. 'Yes, here we are. According to my records, Briggs lived at twenty-seven Hatfield Street, wherever that is.'

'It's a turning off of Horseferry Road, Major. Just a short stride across the park,' said Hardcastle. 'How long had he been in the club's employment?'

Carmichael glanced down at the book again. 'Just over two years, and we paid him fifty pounds per annum, if that's of any interest.'

'Was he married, d'you know?'

'No, I'm afraid I can't assist you there, Inspector.' Then, as a thought crossed his mind, Carmichael asked, 'Is this likely to get into the newspapers, d'you think?'

'Wouldn't be at all surprised,' said Hardcastle, tiring of the club secretary's somewhat patronizing attitude. 'There's not a lot you can keep from them Fleet Street hacks when they get going, Major, and that's a fact.'

Marriott turned back a page of his pocket book. 'Is there any chance that Briggs could have helped himself to a few glasses of brandy when no one was looking, Major?' he asked.

'Certainly not,' said Carmichael, a little too hurriedly. 'That sort of behaviour would result in instant dismissal.'

Based on what Dr Spilsbury had said, Hardcastle decided that the club secretary was not as clever as he thought he was. 'There's the question of identification, Major,' he said. 'Perhaps you could make yourself available to come to the Horseferry Road mortuary tomorrow morning.'

9

'Well, I don't know about that, Inspector. You see I'm rather—'

'Shall we say ten o'clock,' Hardcastle put in. 'Me and my sergeant will meet you there.'

'Well, I don't know, Marriott,' said Hardcastle as the pair strode down Pall Mall. 'Strikes me that the bold major back there was more concerned about the reputation of his precious club than he was about the fate of his smoking-room steward. And I don't reckon he knows half as what goes on, neither.'

'Reckon he's hiding something, sir?'

'Hiding something? Him?' Hardcastle scoffed. 'I doubt it, Marriott. I've met army majors before. Too full of their own piss and importance. But that's not to say we won't have a quiet word with the head porter, just to see if what Major Carmichael said was true about when Briggs left the club.'

'Is he likely to come across without Carmichael's say-so, sir? He does seem to rule the roost in there.'

Hardcastle tapped the side of his nose. 'Don't you worry about that, Marriott my lad. When Ernie Hardcastle decides he's going to put a few questions to someone, it'd take more than the Major Carmichaels of this world to stop him.'

'What's next, then, sir?'

'Number twenty-seven Hatfield Street.'

'What, now, sir?' asked Marriott, glancing at his watch.

'It's only eight o'clock, Marriott, and for all we know there might be a *Mrs* Briggs sitting there wondering why her old man hasn't shown up since last night.'

TWO

Number 27 Hatfield Street proved to be a public house called the Rising Sun.

'So, Marriott,' said Hardcastle, as he pushed open the door of the saloon bar, 'our Mr Briggs lived in a pub. He can't have been all bad.'

'Evening, gents.' A ruddy-faced man gave the top of the bar a cursory wipe with a cloth. 'What's your pleasure?'

'Two pints of best bitter,' said Hardcastle.

'Two pints it is.' The man took glass tankards from the shelf behind him and slowly pulled on the pump handles to fill them. 'There we are, gents,' he said, placing them on the bar.

Waiting until Marriott had put a shilling down, Hardcastle addressed the man who had served them. 'Are you the landlord here?'

'That I am. Jed Parsons is the name. And you're Mr Hardcastle, I believe.'

'How d'you know that?' asked Hardcastle suspiciously.

Parsons grinned. 'Anyone who keeps a pub makes it his business to know the local law, guv'nor,' he said, pushing Marriott's money back towards him.

'What d'you know about Joseph Briggs, then?'

'Got a room upstairs. Works across at Kendall's in Pall Mall. Why, what's he been up to?'

'And what makes you think he *might* have been up to something?' asked Hardcastle, taking the head off his beer.

'Well, with you coming in here asking about him, I thought you might've got him locked up somewhere.'

'We have,' said Hardcastle. 'In the mortuary.'

'Blimey! What happened to him, then?'

'That's what I'm trying to find out,' said Hardcastle, 'but we pulled him out of the lake in St James's Park early this morning. He'd been murdered. Last night, around midnight most like.'

'Strewth!' said the landlord. 'Who'd've wanted to do for old Joe?'

'How long's he been living here?'

Parsons pondered the question for a moment or two. 'About a year, I suppose,' he said eventually.

'How did he come to fetch up here, then?'

'Had a bit of wife trouble, I think,' said the landlord. 'Leastways, that's what he said. To be honest, guv'nor, I never had much to do with him before he lodged here. He used to come in for a drink – midday mostly – and then one day he asked me if I'd got any rooms on account of his wife having chucked him out.'

'Any idea why she threw him out?' Hardcastle asked.

Parsons grinned. 'Dunno, but I do know he was a bit of a ladies' man, if you know what I mean. As a matter of fact, his missus come round here one lunchtime demanding to see him. Had a couple of kids with her, an' all. I told her there wasn't no one here of that name, and I'd never heard of him neither. She started kicking up a hullabaloo at that, and gave me a right mouthful, so I threatened to call the law. She pushed off then, and I never saw her again. Don't do to get between husband and wife in my experience.'

'D'you know where she was living or where Briggs was living before he came here? Be the same place, I suppose.'

'No idea, guv'nor,' said Parsons as, unprompted, he refilled the detectives' tankards. 'But he did say he'd been working at Kendall's for about a year before he fetched up here, so I reckon it wouldn't have been far away.'

'Didn't you think it was a bit odd that he never came back here last night?' asked Marriott.

The landlord glanced at the sergeant. 'Wouldn't have been the first time,' he said. 'He'd done it before. Had a fancy woman, see. As a matter of fact he brought her in here one time. About six months ago.' He paused in thought. 'Polly, her name was. Pretty little thing, about twenty-three, I s'pose. Bit of a tart, mind.'

'What was her other name?' asked Hardcastle.

'Dunno, but . . . no, hang on a minute. I remember now, Francis – Polly Francis – that was it. We had a joke about it because I asked her if she lived in Francis Street, not being far away from here, but she said no, she lived in Malacca Street.'

'So he stayed out quite often, then, did he?'

'Two or three nights a week, I reckon, usually when he was on earlies at the club. But I couldn't say for sure. I gave him a key, see, and he'd let himself in the back door if he was late. Really late, I mean.'

'What time d'you pack up then?'

'Half after midnight, guv'nor, but he only ever come in through the bar if he was in need of a wet.'

'We'd better have a look at his room, then,' said Hardcastle, draining his beer.

'Right you are, guv'nor.' Parsons glanced across at the

12

barmaid. 'Keep an eye on things, Queenie love. I'm just taking these gents up to Joe's room.'

At the top of two flights of stairs, Parsons opened the door into a garret, which had bare wooden floorboards.

'These rooms is meant for the living-in staff, but I had this one spare when Joe asked,' he said.

The furnishing was minimal: an iron bedstead, a washstand on which stood a chipped porcelain ewer in an equally chipped enamel bowl, and a cheap wardrobe, the door of which was hanging open.

Parsons slammed it shut, but it swung open again. 'Dunno what he's done to that,' he said. 'And I won't be able to charge him for it now, neither,' he added with a chuckle that lacked any sympathy for the late Joseph Briggs.

'Well, get to it, Marriott,' said Hardcastle.

It did not take long. In the space of about five minutes, Marriott had emptied the pockets of the few items of Briggs's clothing and searched the drawer beneath the wardrobe. Under the mattress was a five-pound note, but at the finish, the only items likely to be of use to the detectives were three letters, one of which Marriott had found screwed up under the bed.

Hardcastle glanced through the two of them that were addressed to Briggs, care of Kendall's. Each was from a Kate Briggs at an address in Gillingham Street, and lacked the endearments customary between husband and wife. Both missives, in places badly misspelled, alluded to their two starving children – the word 'starving' being heavily underlined – and made demands for money.

'Well, that'll save us a bit of time, Marriott. At least we know where Briggs's trouble-and-strife lives.' Hardcastle shot the sergeant an arch smile. 'And Malacca Street ain't that long, so Catto should be able to track down this Polly Francis a bit *tout de suite*.'

'I'll get him on to that first thing tomorrow, sir.'

'Ah, it seems we might have stumbled on a motive here, Marriott.' Hardcastle, having smoothed out the third letter, read it aloud: '"*I know what your game is, so you'd better come across with the cash or you know what'll happen.*" Not what you'd call an educated hand, Marriott,' he said, folding the letter and putting it in his inside pocket.

'Sounds like someone was putting the black on him, sir.'

'You could well be right there, Marriott,' said Hardcastle, 'but in the meantime, we'd better pay this Mrs Briggs a visit.'

Although Gillingham Street was little over a mile away, it was now nearing a quarter to nine, and Hardcastle hailed a cab.

Despite it being mid-July, and a warm evening, the careworn woman who eventually answered the door wore a shawl over her head and shoulders. Scooping up her apron and wiping her red-raw hands on it, she stared suspiciously at the two policemen.

'Mrs Kate Briggs, is it?' asked Hardcastle as he raised his hat.

'If you've come for the rent, I ain't got it,' she announced truculently. 'And if it's the debts, you'll have to ask me husband, 'cos I ain't got no money.'

'We're police officers, madam,' said Hardcastle.

'Well if it's Joe Briggs you're after, you won't find him here. And if you do find him, you can let me know where the bugger is. He owes me.'

'It's about Joseph Briggs we've come,' said Hardcastle.

'Nicked him, have you?'

'I think it might be better if we came in, madam,' said Hardcastle.

'Please yourself,' said Kate Briggs. But as she opened the door wide, a frisson of concern crossed her face, as if she was anticipating bad news.

The parlour was in squalid disarray. A basket of washing stood in the centre of the table that, like the rest of the sparse furniture, had seen much better days. The ashes of the last fire of winter were still in the cast-iron grate. And an over-riding odour of boiled cabbage pervaded the air.

'What's this about Joe, then?' demanded Kate, standing with arms akimbo. 'What's he been an' done?'

'I'm sorry to have to tell you that he's dead, Mrs Briggs.'

'Oh my Gawd!' Kate sank on to the only chair that was not laden with clothing and a few rough, home-made children's toys. 'It'll be the workhouse now, then,' she muttered despairingly, looking up at Hardcastle, 'and Gawd only knows what'll happen to the little 'uns.'

14

It was obvious that the woman was upset at the news the police had brought her despite being estranged from the late Joseph Briggs, and a few tears rolled down her lined face. But Hardcastle presumed her distress to be the result of losing the breadwinner of the family, not that he appeared to have done much to support them in recent months, certainly if the tenor of her letters to him was anything to go by.

'What happened to him?'

'He was robbed and murdered last night, Mrs Briggs,' said Marriott.

'Robbed?' The woman stared at Marriott with a tear-stained face. 'I dunno what they got, but he always reckoned he never had nothing. What did they want to murder him for?'

'I understand that he left you about a year ago,' said Hardcastle, 'and went to live at a pub called the Rising Sun in Hatfield Street.'

'The lying sod,' said Kate, her face a mask of anger.

'I can assure you he did,' said Hardcastle. 'I've been there today.'

'I'm not talking about Joe. I mean that bugger of a land-lord, Jed Parsons. I went round there once, and he told me he'd never heard of Joe. He threatened to call you lot if I didn't clear off.' Kate paused for a moment or two. 'What'll happen now, mister? I ain't got no money to bury him with.'

'I daresay the parish'll take care of that, Mrs Briggs,' said Hardcastle, producing the five-pound note that Marriott had found beneath Briggs's mattress. 'We found this in his room at the Rising Sun. You'd better have it. It might help.'

'Where the hell did he get that much from?' Kate Briggs snatched the money and held it tightly, as if fearful that Hardcastle might change his mind. 'It'll buy a bit of food for a week or two,' she said. 'It's the most I've ever had from him, and that's a fact.'

'Why did Mr Briggs leave you?' Marriott asked.

Kate snorted. 'Went off with some doxy, didn't he. Got ideas above his station, that's what. He was a drayman with Simcock's when we got married, five years back. But a couple of years ago he got this job at some swish club up Pall Mall, and a bit later on went off with this tart. I dunno who she was, and I don't care. Welcome to him she was, bloody cow.'

Hardcastle and Marriott left the grieving widow, but, the DDI surmised, her grief probably stemmed less from the loss of her man than her hope that he may eventually have been persuaded to part with some money.

'This is a rare do and no mistake, Marriott,' said Hardcastle as he and his sergeant walked into Vauxhall Bridge Road in search of a cab. 'He had a fiver under his mattress, and we know from the bold major that he was getting about nineteen bob a week and, no doubt, a few tips to boot. But it looks like he was being blackmailed over something. If this letter's anything to go by,' he added, tapping his breast pocket.

'Be interesting to know what he was being blackmailed about, sir,' said Marriott.

A taxicab pulled into the kerb. 'New Scotland Yard, cabbie,' said Hardcastle, and in an aside to Marriott, added, 'If you tell 'em Cannon Row, half the time you'll finish up at Cannon Street in the City.'

'Yes, I know, sir,' said Marriott, who had heard this little homily every time he and Hardcastle returned to the police station by cab.

After meeting Major Carmichael at Horseferry Road mortuary the following morning – where he had positively identified the murder victim as Joseph Briggs – Hardcastle and Marriott returned to Cannon Row.

'I've tracked down this Polly Francis, sir,' said a triumphant DC Henry Catto.

'I should hope you have, Catto,' said Hardcastle. 'That's why you're paid to be a detective. So, whereabouts in Malacca Street is she at, eh?'

'Number twelve, sir. The house is owned by a Mr and Mrs Winston, but they take in lodgers. Polly Francis has got a single room there.'

'Any idea what she does for a living?'

'No, sir. I didn't make any enquiries at the house. It was a neighbour what told me that's where she lived.'

'No time like the present, Marriott. We'll have a stroll round to Malacca Street and see what she's got to say for herself. Anything about this killing in the linen drapers this morning?'

'There was a bit in the *Daily Mail*, sir, but it didn't say who the deceased was. Just that a man had been pulled out of the lake in the park.'

Hardcastle grunted. 'No doubt they're thinking he fell in and got drowned. Well, that'll suit my book for the time being.' He pulled out his watch, glanced at it, and wound it a few times before returning it to his pocket.

When Hardcastle announced who he was, the woman who answered the door of Polly Francis's lodgings glanced nervously up and down the street. 'You'd better come in,' she said hurriedly.

'It's Polly Francis I've come to see, Mrs Winston,' said Hardcastle. 'Is she here?'

'She's up in her room. What d'you want her for?'

'That's between me and her, Mrs Winston. It's official police business.'

'Is she in some sort of trouble?' The tone of Mrs Winston's voice, and the expression on her face, implied that, at the first sign of scandal, her 'paying guest' would be looking for somewhere else to live. But her concern later proved to be for an entirely different reason.

'Is there somewhere we can talk to her in private?' asked Hardcastle, declining to answer the woman's question.

'You'd better come into the parlour,' said Mrs Winston, somewhat frostily, as she opened a door off the small hallway, 'and I'll call her.'

As Hardcastle and Marriott entered the fussily furnished front room, they heard Mrs Winston shouting up the stairs.

'Polly, there's a couple of gentlemen from the police here to see you. They're in the parlour.'

The young girl who entered the room moments later certainly seemed to be about twenty-three years old, as the landlord of the Rising Sun had suggested, and was dressed in a plain white blouse and a black skirt that fell to within four inches of the ground. Her rich auburn hair was taken up and carefully coifed. Nonetheless, there was a coarse allure about her overall appearance.

'Miss Polly Francis?' asked Hardcastle.

'S'right. What's this all about?' Polly asked in rich cockney tones.

'Perhaps you'd better sit down, Miss Francis,' said Hardcastle.

Polly sat down and carefully arranged her skirt to give a glimpse of trim ankles above a pair of black, glacé-kid court shoes.

'You're acquainted with a Mr Joseph Briggs, I understand,' Hardcastle began.

'What of it?' the girl demanded truculently.

'I have to tell you that he was murdered on or about midnight on Tuesday. That'd be the fourteenth of July.'

Polly stared at the detective, a stunned look on her face. 'He can't've been,' she said eventually.

'I'm afraid it's true,' said Hardcastle. And after a suitable pause, asked, 'How well did you know him?'

'We was walking out. Going to get married, we was.' Suddenly the girl started to cry. 'Oh, it's too awful,' she mumbled through her tears. 'Who can have done such a thing?'

'You say you were walking out?' Hardcastle asked. 'Is that all?'

'Wotcha mean by that?' The tears stopped as quickly as they had started, and Hardcastle immediately became convinced that Polly Francis would 'walk out' with any man who was willing to spend money on her. And for that matter, she may even have been a prostitute, if only an amateur one. 'If you're asking if he ever shared my bed, the answer's no. I'm a respectable girl, I am.'

Hardcastle reserved judgement on that claim. 'Where d'you work, Miss Francis?'

'Behind the bar at the Albert, across in Victoria Street. Why? What business is it of yours?'

'According to my information' – Hardcastle had no intention of identifying the landlord of the Rising Sun in Hatfield Street – 'Mr Briggs often stayed out of his lodgings all night. Now, if he wasn't with you, he must have been with someone else.'

Polly shot Hardcastle a glance laden with malice. 'All right, mister, so he and I enjoyed each other's company. So what? Like I said, we was going to get wed.'

'Don't you think his wife might have had something to say about that?' asked Marriott.

Until then, Polly had occasionally smiled at the good-looking sergeant, but now that smile changed to an expression of malevolence as she turned her gaze on him. 'Wife? What wife? What are you talking about?' she demanded.

'He'd been married for five years,' observed Marriott mildly. 'And his wife was none too happy that he was seeing you.'

'And a few others, I shouldn't wonder,' added Hardcastle.

'I don't believe it.' But Polly was clearly stunned by this news.

'Well,' said Hardcastle, 'I would suggest you went and saw Mrs Briggs – she'd confirm it all right – but she'd probably scratch your eyes out. When she'd finished putting her children to bed, that is.'

'Children!' Polly obviously had great difficulty in taking in these revelations about her fiancé. 'You mean he had kids as well?'

'Two of them.'

'Well, a right sod he's turned out to be.'

'Were you aware, Miss Francis, of anyone threatening Mr Briggs? Demanding money from him. I'm talking about blackmail.'

'He never said nothing about that. Why should anyone have wanted to put the bite on Joe?'

'That's what I'm trying to find out,' said Hardcastle. 'When was the last time you saw him?'

'Last Monday,' said Polly without hesitation. 'We was supposed to meet on Tuesday an' all.'

'But he was working late that night,' said Hardcastle. 'Finished at eleven o'clock.'

'Well, I know that,' said Polly. 'Course I knew.'

'So, what were you going to do at eleven o'clock at night?' asked Hardcastle, well knowing the answer.

'The landlord of the Albert lets us have a room, on the QT like, so's we can have a chat in private.' Seeing Marriott smile, Polly tossed her head. 'You've got a dirty mind, you have,' she flung at him.

'But in fact, he didn't keep the appointment.'

'No, he never. But now you've told me he got hisself topped, that explains it, don't it?'

'Where were you supposed to meet him, Miss Francis?'

'Down Palmer Street, the side of the pub. It's where we always met, just by the door to the side bar, the one they call the Music Room.'

'How long did you wait there?'

'About half an hour, I s'pose. He always said not to wait any longer, 'cos he might've been held up at work. It happened sometimes, specially if they had some function going on.'

'How did you meet him?'

'Wotcha mean, how did I meet him?'

'When did you first make his acquaintance?' asked Hardcastle, certain that the girl was being deliberately obstructive.

'He used to be a drayman, delivering beer to the Albert pub. But then he got this better job at some club in Pall Mall. He said as how he was getting more money then and could afford to take me out. T'weren't long after that he proposed.' Polly held out her hand to display a cheap engagement ring. 'Might as well hock it now,' she said. But there was no trace of sadness in her voice.

Three

'It wouldn't surprise me if that Polly Francis hadn't done for Master Briggs herself, you know, Marriott,' said Hardcastle as he and his sergeant were finishing a mutton pie and a pint of ale at the Red Lion just outside Scotland Yard.

'D'you reckon so, sir?'

'Well, look at it like this, Marriott. She admits to being less than half a mile from where Briggs got topped, but we've only got her word for it. And if she *was* there, she won't have an alibi. Hanging about at gone eleven in Palmer Street waiting for Joe Briggs is all my eye and Betty Martin if you ask me.'

'But why tell us she was there if she wasn't, sir?' said Marriott thoughtfully. 'On the other hand, she might have been hanging about somewhere else for a different reason that she didn't want to tell us about.'

'It had crossed my mind,' said Hardcastle. 'When we get back to the nick, get Catto or Wilmot to make a few enquiries at surrounding stations – and our own here at Cannon Row, of course – and see if she's ever been nicked for hawking her mutton. Not that it'll help much,' he added gloomily.

'But what would be her motive for topping Briggs, sir?' Marriott asked.

Hardcastle rubbed his thumb and forefinger together. 'The age-old motive, Marriott,' he said. 'Money.'

'But why kill the goose that lays the golden egg?'

'That's supposing he was the goose,' said Hardcastle. 'If he was being blackmailed, he could have been on his uppers. On the other hand, Polly might've found out that he was seeing some other doxy and, what with being engaged to him – for what that was worth – she didn't fancy it too much. Nothing like that for getting a woman's dander up.'

'But could a slip of a girl like her have done for Briggs, sir? That was a pretty heavy blow that was struck.'

'Slip of a girl be buggered, Marriott. A weight from a sash window or a case-opener up her sleeve would have taken care of it.'

'But could she have heaved him over the side of the bridge, sir?'

'She's a tall girl, is that Polly Francis,' said Hardcastle, 'and a barmaid would develop some fair old muscles pulling pints all day long and, no doubt, heaving the odd barrel. Yes, the more I think about it, the more I fancy her for this job.' He paused. 'Get some of the Uniforms doing a search of the lake, Marriott. Whoever topped Briggs might have slung the weapon in there after he was done for.'

'Right, sir.'

'Good. I'll let you buy me another pint, Marriott, before we go back to the nick so's you can get that organized, then we'll pay another visit to Kendall's. See what the head porter's got to say for himself.'

'If you're wanting Major Carmichael, sir, he's gone to the bank,' said the head porter.

'No,' said Hardcastle, 'it's you I want to talk to. I understand that you're the head hall-porter.'

'Yes, sir, but I'm called the sergeant-porter. It's a tradition
of Kendall's, being a military club, you see. So I'm known
as Sergeant Lucas. Lucas being my name.'

'Very interesting,' said Hardcastle. 'And were you a
sergeant?'

'No, sir. As a matter of fact I was a corporal in the Royal
Marine Light Infantry.'

'Well, I'm glad we got that sorted out,' said Hardcastle
drily. 'Were you on duty the night before last? That'd be the
Tuesday evening.'

'Yes, until midnight, sir.'

'That's when the night porter comes on duty, is it?'

'That's correct, sir,' said Lucas.

'I understand that Joseph Briggs finished duty at eleven
o'clock. Did you see the going of him?'

'No, sir, not at all.'

'But according to Major Carmichael, that's when he went
off duty. So surely you must have seen him leaving.'

'If that's what Major Carmichael said, then I daresay that's
the case, sir.' The sergeant-porter gave a disdainful sniff. 'But
the staff don't use the main entrance. Be most improper, that
would. The main entrance is for members only. The staff goes
out the back door and through the gardens.'

'Major Carmichael also told me that those members that
stay on past eleven o'clock help themselves to drinks and
leave a chit with you or the night porter.'

'Quite right, sir,' said Lucas.

'What happens to those chits?'

'I take them to the secretary's office first thing the following morning. Soon as I come on duty. The major's very particular about that.'

'So Major Carmichael would have a record of those
members who left chits on the night of Tuesday the fourteenth, would he?'

'Of course, sir,' said Lucas, 'but so have I.' He ferreted
among a pile of papers on his counter and produced a small
book. 'Now let me see. Ah, here we are. The fourteenth. Sir
John Webster – he's the chairman – General Lord Slade, Major

Henry Groves and Colonel James Fitzpatrick was all in the smoking room. And Mr Victor Dawson, Mr Horace Davenport, Mr Geoffrey Hunt and Captain Peter Reilly was in the card room playing cards, like they do almost every night.' The sergeant-porter looked up. 'Very keen on a hand of *vingt-et-un* is them four, and for pretty high stakes an' all. Nothing under a sovereign a stake, so I've heard.' Casting the book aside, he added, 'But they was the ones who had drinks, sir. There could have been others there that weren't drinking. Leastways, not alcohol. There's always coffee on the go, but they don't pay for that.'

'I suppose the night porter would have seen them leaving,' said Hardcastle, once he was satisfied that Marriott had recorded the names in his pocket book.

'Of course, sir. They're usually all gone by one, except for Captain Reilly. He lives in the club, being widowed, like.'

'Ah, Inspector. Waiting to see me?'

Hardcastle turned to see Major Carmichael standing in the doorway, a frown on his face.

'No, Major, I was having a word with Mr Lucas here, the sergeant-porter.'

'Really? I'd deem it a favour, Inspector, if any enquiries about the club were directed to me.'

Hardcastle took a step towards the club secretary. 'When I'm making enquiries into a murder, Major,' he said, loud enough for Lucas to hear, 'I'll speak to anyone I think may be able to assist me in those enquiries. And I would regard anyone who tries to stop me as obstructing me in my duty. I hope that's clear.'

'Well, yes, of course, Inspector. All I meant was that I may be in a better position to—'

'Marriott, give me that book of yours,' said Hardcastle, cutting across what Carmichael was saying. 'Now, Major, I have here a list of some of those members who was here the night that Briggs was murdered. I shall need to interview each and every one of them.'

'But really, Inspector—' began Carmichael.

'At their own convenience, of course. I shall also need to speak to the night porter. What are his hours of duty?'

'Er, I'm ...' Carmichael glanced at Lucas. 'Sergeant,

perhaps you can assist the inspector.' And cowed by his confrontation with Hardcastle, he retreated to take refuge in his office.

'I don't think the major liked that very much, sir,' said Lucas, a half smile playing around his lips.

'Then he'll have to lump it, won't he,' snapped Hardcastle. 'Now then, the night porter. What's his name and what are his hours of duty?'

'He's called Hicks, sir, George Hicks, and he comes on at midnight, like I said, and goes off at nine the following morning when I come on again.'

'Good,' said Hardcastle. 'Perhaps you'd warn him, when he turns up tonight, that I'll be here at nine o'clock sharp tomorrow morning to have a word with him.'

'Er, he'll have to get permission from the major, sir,' said Lucas hesitantly.

Hardcastle leaned closer to the sergeant-porter. 'You heard what I said to the major just now, Mr Lucas. And you can tell Hicks that I'll be talking to him tomorrow morning. Either here or down the nick. There, that plain enough for you?'

'I'll tell him, sir,' said Lucas, secretly delighted that Major Carmichael had been put in his place.

It was gone four o'clock by the time that Hardcastle and Marriott returned to Cannon Row police station.

Henry Catto was waiting outside the DDI's office.

'Well, Catto, what've you got to tell me?'

'I found a record of Polly Francis, sir.'

'A record of what, Catto? I ain't got the time for riddles.'

'Arrested for soliciting, sir, in Hyde Park, and weighed off at Great Marlborough Street police court.'

'And when was this?'

'Fourteenth of June last year, sir. Nicked on Saturday night, in court on the Monday.'

'And that's it, is it?'

'Yes, sir,' said Catto. 'Couldn't find anything else against her. Not on any of the inner divisions.'

'Well, Marriott,' said Hardcastle, having dismissed Catto, 'it looks like our Polly Francis was on the game after all. But I wonder why she only got nicked the once.'

24

'Maybe she travelled further afield, sir,' said Marriott.

'Yes, maybe. But I think we'll go and have another chat with her. She's beginning to rise to the top of the heap.'

'Oh, it's you again,' said Polly Francis's landlady.

'Yes, Mrs Winston, it's me again. Is Miss Francis in, or has she gone to work?'

'You'd better come in, Inspector.' But Mrs Winston went no further than the end of the hall before turning to face the two policemen. 'She's gone,' she announced. 'And she owes me two weeks rent. A right liberty, I call it, and I want to know what you're going to do about it. As good as stealing, that's what it is.'

'Yes, but it's not stealing, Mrs Winston. It's what's called a civil matter. If you want to get your money, you'll have to take her to the county court and get your remedy there. If you can find her, that is.'

'Well, really, I don't know. Why should I be put to all that trouble? It's her that's welshed on me, you know, not the other way round.'

'What makes you think she's gone for good, ma'am?' asked Marriott.

'I know she has. It wasn't long after you left here this morning. About an hour after, I suppose. I was in the kitchen getting dinner for my Cyril – he works round the corner and comes in for dinner every day – and she called out like she always does.'

'Yes, but did she *say* she was leaving for good, or was she just going to work?' asked Marriott, patiently attempting to extract the facts from Mrs Winston's somewhat diffuse narrative.

'Well, I *thought* she was going to work,' said Mrs Winston. 'It was her usual time. Anyway, "Cheerio, Mrs W," she shouts, bright as you like. That was just after Cyril had gone back to work, about half past two it must have been. I went upstairs to do the bathroom and her door was open. So I glanced in and all her stuff was gone. And she hadn't even made the bed. Downright disgraceful, I call it. I've never had a paying guest do that before.' She paused and primped her hair. 'But I thought something was up when you came here this morning.

Florence Winston, I said to myself, the police don't come round to speak to a young girl unless there's something a bit shady going on. Leastways, not you plainclothes lot.'

'As a matter of fact, we'd come to tell her that her fiancé had been murdered,' said Hardcastle mildly.

'*Murdered!*' Mrs Winston put her hand to her mouth. 'Oh, the poor dear child. She couldn't have known what she was doing, and there's me saying all those awful things about her.'

'If she should return, Mrs Winston, perhaps you'd ask her to come round to Cannon Row police station. There's something important I wish to talk to her about.' But Hardcastle had no great hopes that Polly Francis would return or, for that matter, go anywhere near a police station. Unless she was arrested again.

The Albert public house stood on the corner of Victoria Street and Buckingham Gate and, in Hardcastle's opinion, sold the finest ale in London.

The landlord spotted the DDI as soon as he and Marriott entered. 'Nice to see you again, Mr Hardcastle. The usual?'

'Yes, please, Jim.'

'You doing that murder in the park?'

The news had been splashed across the front pages of the midday editions of the *Evening Standard*, the *Evening News* and *The Star*. Hardcastle had known all along that he had little hope of keeping it from the press, and assumed that someone – probably Sergeant-porter Lucas at Kendall's – had earned a few shillings for the information.

'Yes, I'm doing that one, Jim,' said Hardcastle, as the landlord pushed two pints of best across the counter, and waved away Marriott's money. 'And there's a tie-up with this here pub of yours.'

The landlord looked worried and leaned forward. 'What's that then, Mr Hardcastle? You know I run a proper house here. I don't want no trouble.'

'I know that, Jim. But one of your barmaids reckoned she was getting spliced to this Joe Briggs, him what got topped. Mind you, she never knew that Briggs was married already.'

'Was she, be damned? Which one was it? Got a name, have you?'

26

'Polly Francis. She says she met Briggs when he was working for Simcock's as a drayman and delivering here.'

'Someone's been throwing you the dummy there, Mr Hardcastle,' said Jim. 'I've never heard of a Polly Francis, and my ale comes from Young's. I've never had Simcock's in the ten years I've been here.'

'I thought that was the case,' said Hardcastle gloomily. 'When me and Marriott here spoke to her this morning, she told this tale about her benevolent employer – she meant you – always letting her have a room so's she and Briggs could have a bit of nookie without freezing to death in the park.'

'Cheeky young bitch,' said Jim. 'Where's she live? I'll sue her.'

'She did live at twelve Malacca Street, but after we spoke to her there this morning, she scarpered owing two weeks rent.'

'You reckon she's up for this topping then, Mr Hardcastle?'

'I don't know, Jim, but I have to say she's looking a bit favourite.'

'I think you'd better have another pint, Mr Hardcastle,' said Jim, refilling the detectives' glasses, 'because it don't look like you're having a lot of luck.' And with that, he moved away to serve another customer.

'If she went out the same time every day, sir,' said Marriott, placing his elbow on the bar, 'I wonder where she *was* going. Must have had a job somewhere.'

'Yes, Marriott, and I think we know what sort of job it is. But how come she's never been caught? I reckon the coppers round here are getting a bit slack.'

'Polly Francis was nicked the middle of June last year, sir,' said Marriott.

'What about it?'

'That was about the time Joe Briggs split up with his missus and moved into Hatfield Street, according to Jed Parsons. Maybe the two of them were working some fiddle somewhere. I can't believe that if she was still on the game she wouldn't have got herself nicked for a whole year.'

'That's all very well, Marriott, but how do we find out until we find her?'

'I'll have her details put out to divisions on the telegraph, sir,' said Marriott, 'saying that we want to interview her.'

27

'You know how that thing works, then, do you?' asked Hardcastle, casting a sceptical eye in his sergeant's direction.

'No, sir,' said Marriott with a grin, 'but the PC who works it does.'

It was exactly five to nine the following morning when Hardcastle and Marriott entered Kendall's.

'I'm Divisional Detective Inspector Hardcastle of the Whitehall Division, and this is Sergeant Marriott. You're Mr Hicks, I take it?'

'Yes, sir. The sergeant-porter told me as how you'd be coming in.'

'Right, for a kick-off, how well did you know Joseph Briggs, him what was murdered last Tuesday night?'

'Not at all, sir,' said Hicks. 'I always work nights, midnight to nine, and he works mornings and evenings, alternate weeks like, as smoking-room steward. I've never set eyes on him.'

'Well, that's a good start, I must say,' muttered Hardcastle. 'Show him that list of names, Marriott.'

Pulling out his pocket book, Marriott opened it to the page where he had recorded the names of those members who had signed chits on the evening of Briggs's murder.

'Have a look at that list, Mr Hicks,' said Hardcastle. 'Is them the members who was in here last Tuesday?'

Hicks glanced down the list. 'That's right, sir, as far as I can recall. At least, them as had drinks and left chitties.'

'What time did they leave?'

'The last three – them's what we call the card school – went about ten to one. Except for Captain Reilly, sir. He lives in and I s'pose he went upstairs at the same time.'

'And the others?' Hardcastle pointed to the names of Webster, Slade, Groves and Fitzpatrick. 'What about them?'

After a moment's thought, Hicks said, 'The general – that's Lord Slade, sir – went about quarter past twelve. I was a bit surprised really, because he's getting on a bit and don't usually stay that late. But the other three all went together at about one. As a matter of fact, I went out and called a cab for them.'

'Where were they going, any idea?'

'I did hear Sir John Webster tell the cabbie Piccadilly, sir, but your guess is as good as mine. Mind you, I do know that he's got rooms at Albany, so I s'pose they might all have been going there for a night-cap.'

'Was there anyone else in the club at that time, apart from the ones on that list?' asked Hardcastle, prodding Marriott's pocket book with his forefinger.

'Not that I know of, sir. Mind you, one or two of them sometimes goes out the back door, especially them as lives in St James's Square, or off of it. Saves a bit of time, particularly if they wants to avoid paying for a cab.' Hicks lowered his voice. 'There's one or two here what's got deep pockets and short arms, I can tell you, Inspector.'

Four

'I think this evening might be as good a time as any to interview some of those members at Kendall's who were there on Tuesday, Marriott. See what they've got to say for themselves. You never know, we might even find something out. Something useful, I mean.'

But on their arrival at the Pall Mall clubhouse, Hardcastle and Marriott were met with disappointment.

'It's Friday evening, sir,' said Sergeant-porter Lucas. 'Most of the members are away to the country. There's hardly anyone here.'

'Off killing grouse wholesale, I suppose,' grumbled Hardcastle.

'Not until the Glorious Twelfth, sir.' Lucas smiled condescendingly. 'That'd be the twelfth of August, sir,' he explained, in case Hardcastle was unfamiliar with the convention that grouse may only be shot between that date and the tenth of December. 'I think Monday evening would be your best bet to catch 'em here. They'll have spent a weekend with the missus and'll likely be dying to get away from her. The place is usually quite crowded of a Monday evening.'

'Oh bugger it, Marriott,' said Hardcastle, as the pair made

their way back to the police station, 'we'll call it a day and have the weekend off, same as them toffs back there.' He cocked a thumb in the direction of Kendall's. 'There's nothing we can do this side of Monday.'

But when they reached the station, Hardcastle found a jemmy on his desk. Half guessing what it was, he examined it closely, but did not touch it.

Crossing the corridor to the detectives' office, he flung open the door. 'Who left a crowbar on my desk?' he demanded, scowling at the assembled officers.

'Me, sir,' said Catto, hurriedly struggling to his feet.

'Well, what's it doing there, lad?'

'Found in the lake this morning, sir, by the Uniform men who were searching. Sergeant Marriott gave the instruction for the search to be done. Could be the murder weapon.'

'God Almighty, Catto, you know the drill. You should have wrapped it in paper and put a label on it. You don't just leave important bits of evidence lying about. I hope no one's put their fingers all over it.'

'Oh, no, sir,' said Catto, 'I wore gloves.'

'I should bloody well hope so,' muttered Hardcastle. 'Well, lad, put your gloves back on and *then* wrap it in paper – clean paper, mind – and take it across to the Commissioner's Office. The Fingerprint Bureau is on the top floor. See Inspector Collins and ask him if he can find any fingerprints on it. Once you've done that, find the science inspector, or whatever he calls himself, and ask him if there's any blood on it.'

'But won't the water have washed it off, sir?'

'We won't know till we ask, Catto. But water don't necessarily clean off blood. You want to have a read of Hans Gross's *Criminal Investigation*, my lad. Might teach you a thing or two about the job you're s'posed to be doing.'

'But will Mr Collins be there now, sir? Or this science inspector? It's gone six.'

'How on earth d'you expect me to know? Go and find out.'

'Yes, sir,' said the chastened Catto.

Hardcastle shook his head. 'And I suppose you're hoping to be an inspector one day, Catto,' he said.

'Yes, sir.'

Hardcastle grunted. 'Well, on your present showing, you'll be lucky to make third-class sergeant. Now get on with it.'

Detective Constable Henry Catto was waiting outside Hardcastle's office when the DDI arrived on Monday morning.

'Well?' asked Hardcastle, entering his office without breaking step.

Still wearing his gloves, Catto followed Hardcastle and placed the crowbar – now shrouded in clean, white wrapping paper – on the edge of the DDI's desk. 'Inspector Collins says there's a thumbprint on this, sir, but that it don't match any of those in his collection. And he said that there was other fingerprints on it, but none as he could identify.'

'Just my bloody luck, that is,' grumbled Hardcastle.

'And the science inspector said there's definitely blood on it, sir, but he says he'll need some of Briggs's to compare it with before he can tell if it's the same group. And not necessarily then.'

'Right, lad. Leave it there. I'll have to have a word with Dr Spilsbury. I s'pose this inspector has produced some sort of report about the blood, has he?'

'Yes, sir. Sergeant Marriott's got it, sir.'

'Is he in the office?'

'Yes, sir. He's reading the paper.'

'Good grief! What's in the linen drapers that's so important?'

'I don't know, sir.'

'Well, ask him to come in.'

'What's all this about the newspapers, Marriott?' asked Hardcastle.

'It's the Balkans, sir. Things are getting a bit nasty out there. The *Daily Mail* seems to think there'll be a war. And the Irish question's hotting up too.'

'Bugger the Irish, Marriott. We've got more important things to deal with than a few foreigners shouting at each other, and the Micks getting all of a bust. Now then, does that report you've got from the science inspector say what blood group was on this here crowbar?'

'Yes, sir, it's type "O".'

'Good,' said Hardcastle. 'Get up to St Mary's a bit *jildi* and see Dr Spilsbury. I want to know what blood group Joseph Briggs was. If it's the same, this might just be the weapon that was used to kill him. On the other hand, seeing as how it's the commonest group there is, it might not mean anything. Except that there could be another body lying about in St James's Park that we haven't found yet.' He gave a humourless cackle and began to fill his pipe with his favourite St Bruno tobacco. 'On second thoughts, you'd better take that with you' – he gestured at the crowbar with the stem of his pipe – 'because Dr Spilsbury might be able to tell you if it's likely to be the weapon that did for Briggs. But take care of it. Charlie Collins in the Fingerprint Bureau reckons there's a thumbprint on it. Never know, might solve this little job for us. And this evening we'll have another go at the members of Kendall's.'

Marriott returned at midday with the crowbar.

'Dr Spilsbury says that the blood type matches Briggs's, sir, and he's pretty sure that it was the weapon used. He reckons it tallies with the wound. As far as he can tell, sir.'

'That's good enough for me, Marriott,' said Hardcastle. 'So all we've got to do now is find out who's lost this crowbar.'

Hardcastle's next call was at 12 Malacca Street.

'Mrs Winston, I wonder if you can spare a moment to look at this here.' Hardcastle gestured at the parcel Marriott was carrying.

'Whatever is it?' Florence Winston opened the door wide to admit the two detectives and was about to lead the way into the parlour when Hardcastle spoke again.

'Might be better to use the kitchen table, Mrs Winston,' he said.

Mrs Winston raised her eyebrows in mock surprise. 'As you wish,' she said, changing direction and opening the kitchen door.

Marriott put the parcel on the table and unwrapped it.

'Did you ever see this in Polly Francis's room, Mrs Winston?' asked Hardcastle. 'And please don't touch it.'

'What is it?' Polly's former landlady took a step closer and peered at the jemmy that now lay exposed on her kitchen table. 'I mean, I can see what it is, but why are you asking?'

'We think it was used to kill Joseph Briggs who, as I mentioned before, was Miss Francis's fiancé.'

'Holy Mary, Mother of God!' Mrs Winston took a pace back and quickly crossed herself. 'D'you mean that Polly—?' She broke off as the full implication of Hardcastle's question became apparent.

'I'm not jumping to any conclusions, Mrs Winston,' said the DDI, 'and I advise you not to either. I just want to know if you've ever seen it before.'

'No, I haven't.' But Florence Winston was sharper than she looked. When two detectives showed her the murder weapon and asked if she'd ever seen it before, there could be only one conclusion that she could draw: she had been harbouring a murderess in her house.

Marriott carefully wrapped up the crowbar again.

'Perhaps we could have a look at her room, Mrs Winston,' Hardcastle said. 'Or have you let it again?'

'No, not yet, but a commercial gentlemen came this morning and he's moving in tomorrow.'

'Well, see if you can find anything, Marriott,' said Hardcastle, once the three of them were upstairs in the room that Mrs Winston said had previously been occupied by Polly Francis.

Marriott knew what his chief meant and, taking a magnifying glass from his inside pocket, began to examine all the surfaces in the room. 'Nothing, sir,' he said once his search was completed.

'What are you looking for, Inspector?' asked a puzzled Mrs Winston from the doorway.

'Fingerprints.'

'Well, you won't find any in here,' said Mrs Winston with a laugh. 'I spent all Saturday afternoon cleaning and polishing this room.'

Major Clive Carmichael, the club secretary, had resigned himself to frequent visits from Hardcastle, and was noticeably less hostile when the DDI and Marriott arrived at Kendall's later that evening.

'Ah, Inspector, we meet again. And what may I help you with this time?'

'When I was here last Thursday, Major, I showed you a list of members who were here on the Tuesday evening. That's the night that Briggs was murdered.'

'Yes, Inspector, indeed you did.'

'And you may also remember that I said I'd need to have a word with them.'

'Of course.' Carmichael was unlikely to forget his last abrasive interview with Hardcastle.

'Are any of them here now?'

'Possibly. Perhaps you would be so good as to refresh my memory.'

Hardcastle took Marriott's pocket book, opened it at the requisite page and handed it to Carmichael. 'Those is them, Major,' he said.

Carmichael skimmed rapidly down the list of eight names. 'Sir John Webster is here and so is Captain Reilly. They're both in the smoking room.' He returned the book. 'Perhaps you'd care to use my office,' he added, with an uncharacteristic display of generosity, 'but the club is almost empty this evening.'

'The smoking room'll do,' said Hardcastle. 'I'm not anticipating arresting any of them.'

Unsure whether Hardcastle was joking, Carmichael gave a sickly smile and led the way into the vast smoking room. Contrary to Sergeant-porter Lucas's forecast, there were only four members there. But it was fairly early in the evening.

'That's Sir John Webster, the chairman,' said Carmichael, indicating a man reading *The Times*. 'I told him on Friday that he could be expecting you. And Captain Reilly is over there.' He waved a nonchalant hand towards a man on the other side of the room. 'I'll mention to him that you'll be speaking to him later on.'

'Sir John, I'm Divisional Detective Inspector Hardcastle of the Whitehall Division, and this is Detective Sergeant Marriott.'

Webster, surprisingly agile for a man of about seventy, dropped *The Times* on the floor as he rose to his feet. 'How d'you do?' he said, clasping Hardcastle's hand. 'Understand you want to talk to me about this fellow Briggs. Bad busi-

34

ness, Hardcastle, bad business.' He waved a hand at a couple of leather armchairs. 'Sit yourself down. You too, Sergeant.' He beckoned a steward. 'Get these gentlemen a drink, Barnes, and I'll have another brandy and soda while you're about it.'

'That's very kind of you, Sir John,' said Hardcastle. 'A whisky if I may.'

'Blended or malt, sir?' asked the steward.

'What is it that Major Carmichael drinks?' asked Hardcastle.

'That'll be the Glenlivet, sir. A very fine malt. Probably the best.'

'I'll have that, then, please.'

'And for me, too,' said Marriott.

'Trouble brewing in the Balkans, Inspector,' said Webster while they were waiting for the drinks. He waved a hand at the crumpled newspaper by his feet.

'So I gather, sir,' said Hardcastle. 'My sergeant here was telling me all about it this morning.'

'No good will come of it, you mark my words. Always a hotbed of unrest.' Webster uttered a brief word of thanks as the steward set down the drinks. 'Still, if it comes to anything, and it probably will, they'll have to do without me at my age. Did my bit with Kitchener in the Sudan, don't you know, and with "Bobs" in South Africa fighting the Boers. Charming man, "Bobs". Died last year. Great loss.' He took a sip of his brandy, and brushed his flowing white moustache. 'But you haven't come here to listen to my war stories, Hardcastle. What exactly is it you want?'

'I was told that you were in the club last Tuesday evening, sir.'

'Yes, I was.'

'And Briggs was the steward on duty?'

'Yes. He went off at eleven. Carmichael doesn't like keeping the staff on too late, so if we want anything after that, we send for the sergeant-porter. Mind you, if it's just drinks, we help ourselves and leave a chit at the desk.'

'The night porter, Hicks, tells me you left at about one o'clock, sir, along with Major Groves and Colonel Fitzpatrick.'

Webster gave a hollow laugh. 'Yes, *and* I regretted it. Took them back to my place at Albany and we had a few drinks. They'd both been in the Boer War, the second one, that is,

35

and fought it all over again. Had a sore head the next morning, Inspector, I can tell you.'

'And they left you at what time, sir?'

'About ten past two, I suppose. Had to throw the buggers out.'

'Thank you very much, Sir John. I don't think I need to bother you any further.'

'Look, Inspector, what's this about? Surely you don't think any of the members had anything to do with young Briggs's death.'

'Good heavens no,' said Hardcastle. 'I just need to verify that Briggs was actually here until eleven.'

'Well, I can assure you he was,' said Webster.

'I don't suppose you'd know whether he had any enemies among the staff, would you, sir?'

'No idea,' said Webster, 'but he was a bit of an oily fellow. Always sickeningly deferential, if you know what I mean. Never took to the fellow really. Wouldn't have trusted him an inch. I mean to say, courtesy's one thing, but toadying up like he did, well, quite unnecessary in my view.'

'Thank you, sir,' said Hardcastle as he and Marriott rose to their feet. 'And thank you for the whisky.'

Captain Reilly was a man of about fifty and possessed the bloodshot eyes of the habitually heavy drinker.

Refusing another drink, Hardcastle explained briefly why he and Marriott were asking questions of the members.

'Saw Briggs a couple of times, Inspector. We were playing cards through there.' Reilly waved a hand towards a door at the far end of the smoking room, which Hardcastle presumed was the card room. 'Geoffrey Hunt, Victor Dawson, "Horry" Davenport and I were playing pontoon for a couple of hours. Well, for an hour, I suppose, then it was down to three. Davenport lost heavily and reckoned he couldn't cover any more losses, so he went back to the smoking room. But the three of us carried on.'

'When you say he lost heavily, Captain Reilly, how much are you talking about?'

Reilly sat back in thought for a moment or two. 'I suppose he must have kissed goodbye to about twenty-five pounds altogether.'

'The night porter told me that you all
Hardcastle knew that Reilly had not left, but w
usual little game of pretending to be a trifle d

'Not me, Inspector. I live here. Widowed, y'
the other three could all have gone at the same
really no idea. I certainly left the card room witl
Hunt, but I went straight upstairs to bed.'

'I've just asked Sir John Webster if Briggs had any enemies
on the staff here, but he didn't know. I was wondering, as you
live here, if you were aware of anyone who might have wanted
him dead.'

'Quite a few, I imagine. Nasty piece of work was Briggs.
Could've done with a kick up the arse, if you ask me. And if
he'd been in my regiment, he'd've got one.' Reilly gave a
cynical grin. 'And I'd've been the one doing the kicking.'

Before leaving, Hardcastle stopped at Sir John Webster's
chair again. 'One other thing, Sir John. Did you notice Mr
Davenport come into the smoking room from the card room
at any time during the evening?'

'Seem to recall it, Inspector, yes,' said Webster, briefly
lowering his copy of *The Times* to answer, 'but I couldn't tell
you the time.'

'And was he still here when you left with Colonel Fitzpatrick
and Major Groves?'

'Damned if I know, Inspector. Didn't really notice, and we'd
all had a drop too much, if you know what I mean.'

Five

Gazing through a cloud of pipe smoke, Hardcastle studied
the crowbar that lay in the centre of his desk. 'If we could
find out where this jemmy came from, Marriott, we might be
halfway to finding out who hit Briggs on the head with it.'

'Could try the local ironmongers, I suppose, sir,' volunteered Marriott.

. what I was thinking. Get Catto in here.'

ondering, as usual, what he had done wrong, Catto entered ne DDI's office with a certain measure of apprehension. 'Er, you wanted me, sir?'

'This here jemmy, lad.' Hardcastle carefully wrapped the crowbar and pushed it towards the DC. 'Get yourself round a few ironmongers and show it to them. See if you can find out where it came from, and if they remember anyone buying it . . . or one like it. Got that?'

'Yes, sir.'

'Start with them nearest to Hatfield Street, then go round them close to Malacca Street and this here Kendall's in Pall Mall. And don't take all day.'

'Right, sir,' said Catto, relieved that he was not to be reprimanded for some peccadillo.

'And if anyone of 'em so much as lays a finger on it, I'll have you for breakfast, my lad.'

'What do we do now, sir?' asked Marriott, once Catto had departed.

Hardcastle pulled out his watch. 'If we take a growler, we've just got time to nip round to the back door of Kendall's and catch George Hicks, the night porter, on his way home. I think that there's more to learn about Joseph Briggs, and I've a feeling Hicks might know more than he's telling.'

On Hardcastle's instructions, the cab driver set him and Marriott down in Pall Mall, from where they walked round to St James's Square. As they approached the rear entrance to Kendall's, they were just in time to see George Hicks coming out.

'Remember me, Mr Hicks?'

This sudden confrontation with the two detectives clearly startled the night porter. 'Oh, good morning, sir,' he said nervously. 'I was just off home.'

'And where would that be?' asked Hardcastle.

'Broadway, sir. Me and Queenie has got rooms there, over a boot makers.'

'Is that a fact? And how d'you get there, eh? Catch a bus, do you?'

'No, I walk. It's not far across the park.'

'So you must cross the footbridge over the lake,' said Hardcastle thoughtfully. 'That'd be the most direct way, wouldn't it?'

'Yes, that's right,' said Hicks, but there was a certain reluctance in his admission.

'Well, I won't keep you long, Mr Hicks, because I know you'll want to get home to your missus.'

'Oh, she won't be there right now.'

'Really? Where's she gone then?' asked Hardcastle.

'She'll be at work. Starts at eight in the morning until six at night. But sometimes she'll do a few hours in the evening if they're short-handed like.'

'And where's work?'

'It's the Rising Sun in Hatfield Street. Jed Parsons is the guv'nor there.'

'Well, well, well,' said Hardcastle, in such a way that it further discomfited the already uncomfortable Hicks. 'That's where Joseph Briggs was living right up until he got topped a week ago.' And he remembered that Parsons had called one of the barmaids Queenie.

'Was it?' asked Hicks lamely.

'You know bloody well it was, my lad, because your missus would have told you,' said Hardcastle sternly. 'And what's more, coming to work the way you do, at the time you do, you must have been crossing the bridge in St James's Park round about a quarter to twelve on the night he was murdered. Right there on that very bridge. What did you see?'

'Nothing, sir. It was as quiet as the grave.'

'They ain't the words I'd've chosen in the circumstances,' said Hardcastle drily. 'So, nobody about, is that what you're saying?'

'No, nobody, sir.'

'Well, we'll see about that.' Some sixth sense told Hardcastle that Hicks was not telling the whole truth, and he decided that the Kendall's night porter needed a little gingering up. 'For a start, I'll have a look in that attaché-case you're holding behind your back, that you're very keen for me not to see.'

'There's nothing in it, guv'nor,' said Hicks, a note of despair creeping into his voice. 'Honest.'

'If there's nothing in it, what are you carting it about for?'

'I meant nothing important. It's only me razor, and a bit of soap and a towel.'

'Don't they have soap and towels at Kendall's then?' asked Hardcastle acidly, as he held out a hand. 'Let's have it.' Taking the small leather case from the unwilling Hicks, he handed it to his sergeant. 'Have a dekko in that, Marriott,' he said.

Balancing the case on one hand, Marriott opened it with the other. 'Good gracious, sir,' he said in parodied amazement, 'it's a bottle of your favourite.' And he turned the case so that Hardcastle could see the bottle of Glenlivet malt whisky that lay inside it.

'So, you've been thieving whisky from your employers, Hicks,' declared Hardcastle, fixing the unfortunate porter with a steely gaze.

'It's perks, sir,' said the anguished Hicks. 'We all do it at the club, and they know it goes on. They turns a blind eye, see.'

'So, if I has a word with Major Carmichael he'll tell me it's all right, will he?'

Hicks remained silent, knowing full well that he would be facing dismissal if this aggressive policeman did speak to the club secretary.

'Yes, I thought so,' mused Hardcastle, shaking his head. 'D'you know how long I've been a police officer, Hicks?'

'No, sir,' said Hicks, his gaze concentrated on the attaché-case that Marriott was still holding.

'Twenty-three years, Hicks, and I've nicked more tea-leaves than you've had hot dinners. So don't try coming the old madam with me.' Hardcastle leaned close to the night porter. 'Got that, have you?'

'Yes, sir,' said Hicks miserably.

'Right. Now then, I'm getting tired of standing here in the street, so we'll go and have a cup of tea.'

This sudden change in the attitude of the police disconcerted Hicks even more, but he sensed that whatever the inspector had in store for him, it would not be to his advantage.

When they reached a nearby café, Hardcastle commandeered a table in the corner, out of earshot of the few other customers there.

'Me and Sergeant Marriott here'll have tea, Mr Hicks, good and strong mind. And two sugars in mine.'

Further taken aback by this sudden geniality, Hicks did not demur, but went to the counter, to return moments later with three cups of tea.

'Now, you told me last Friday that you didn't know Briggs, but you do, don't you?'

'Well, sort of slightly.'

'Sort of slightly, eh?' Hardcastle repeated the words sarcastically. 'Don't take me for a fool, Hicks,' he said. 'Your missus works in the pub where Briggs had a room for the past year. She must have mentioned him before telling you about his murder, being as how he worked at the same place as you.'

Hicks took time stirring his tea before looking up. 'He was making a play for her affections, guv'nor.'

'Ah! Now we're getting to it. And you didn't much care for that, I suppose.'

'Course not.'

'What d'you mean by making a play for her affections?' Marriott asked.

Hicks switched his gaze to the sergeant. 'My Queenie is very easy on the eye,' he said, 'and being a barmaid she's friendly an' all. She reckoned Briggs thought she was giving him the come-on.'

'And was she?'

'No, she wouldn't do nothing like that,' said Hicks indignantly.

'So what were you worried about? It happens all the time in pubs. A pretty girl behind the bar's going to get all sorts of propositions put to her, but as a rule none of them's serious.'

'Yeah, but Queenie said Briggs kept badgering her to go up to his room with him.'

'And did she go?' Marriott continued to press the night porter.

A flash of anger crossed Hicks's face. 'No, she never. She's a respectable woman is my Queenie.'

'I heard that Briggs wasn't liked too well in the club, Hicks,' said Hardcastle, taking the questioning back from Marriott. 'Is that right?'

41

'I dunno about that, sir. Like I said the other day, I never saw him in the club. Different shifts, see.'

'But you must have heard any gossip that was going the rounds. After all, there's some staff that live in. Chambermaids and that sort, that he might have been chasing.'

'Yeah, but I never get to talk to them. They never come anywhere near the desk, see. There'd be hell to pay if the major caught 'em sneaking down there.'

'So you didn't hear anything about him, is that what you're saying?'

'No, well, except for the one time . . .'

'Go on.'

'When I come on duty one night, Jack Lucas told me that one of the members had complained about Joe Briggs. He reckoned there'd been a bit of a barney going on in the front hall between Mr Davenport and the major. Right by the porter's desk, Jack said.'

'What was that about?' Hardcastle asked.

'Seems that Mr Davenport was complaining that Briggs had spilt a drink over him and then hadn't never apologized.'

'Why didn't Briggs get the sack then? That's what usually happens, isn't it?'

'I dunno, guv'nor, but I did hear later that the major had spoken to some of the other members about it and they said as how Mr Davenport had been drunk at the time and it was him what had knocked the drink over, not Briggs.'

'And what else did Jack Lucas have to say about Briggs?'

'Nothing direct. But he said that Briggs wasn't generally liked by the members or the staff.'

'Give a reason, did he?'

'Not really. It was just a feeling.'

'And what did you think of Briggs, eh?' Hardcastle finished his tea and took out his pipe.

'Like I said the other day, I never met him.'

'Is that a fact? Here's a man who was making improper suggestions to your wife, but you never tackled him about it. Is that the up and down of it, Hicks?'

'Only the once.'

'And when was that?' Hardcastle finished filling his pipe, and started searching his pockets for matches.

'About a month ago, I s'pose. I'd gone into the Rising Sun to give Queenie some housekeeping money. It was Saturday night, see. And Briggs was there, leaning on the bar sort of mooning at her.'

'And what did you do about that?'

'I told him to lay off. I told him she was a married woman and wasn't interested in the likes of him.'

'And what did Briggs say to that?' Hardcastle finally got his pipe going and leaned back, a satisfied look on his face.

'He said she was old enough to make up her own mind. So I grabbed hold of him. I was so angry that I was going to knock him down.'

'And did you?' Hardcastle gazed at the night porter with an amused expression.

'No. Jed Parsons come round the bar and said that he wasn't going to have no roughhouse in his pub, and if we wanted to make a scrap of it to take it outside or he'd call the law.'

'And did you? Take it outside?'

'No, I didn't want to be late for work, so I left it.'

'But you got your own back, didn't you, Hicks? You waited by the bridge in St James's Park last Tuesday, when you was on your way to work. And when you met Briggs coming the other way, you hit him over the head and pushed him in the lake.'

Hicks leaped up so rapidly that his chair fell over with a clatter. 'No, I never, guv'nor, so help me. That'd be mad, that would. I know my Queenie would never have fallen for Briggs's charms, so really I had nothing to worry about. I wouldn't go so far as to get topped for doing him in.'

'Pick up your chair and sit down, Hicks,' said Hardcastle who, throughout Hicks's histrionic protestation of innocence, had remained impassively seated. 'You're making a spectacle of yourself.'

Hicks meekly resumed his seat. 'Well, I never done him,' he said, looking shamefaced at his outburst. 'I dunno who it was topped him, but it weren't me.'

'We'd better let you go home, then,' said Hardcastle.

'What about the whisky, sir?' asked Marriott, tapping the attaché-case that rested, now, on the table.

'Don't know anything about any whisky,' said Hardcastle

as he made for the door, followed by Marriott. 'Thanks for the tea, George,' he said over his shoulder. 'We'll let him think we're a bit soft, Marriott,' he added in an aside, 'and it might teach Carmichael to do his job instead of strutting about like a crow in a gutter.'

'What d'you make of him, sir?' asked Marriott later, as the two of them strode down Whitehall towards Cannon Row police station.

'All wind and piss, Marriott. You saw Briggs's body after they'd dragged him out of the lake. He's a big bugger. And there ain't enough of Hicks to fight his way out of a paper bag. It's humbug, Marriott.' With a wave of his hand, Hardcastle dismissed Hicks's claim to have been on the point of setting about Briggs in the Rising Sun.

'But he could have hit him with the jemmy we recovered, sir. Having an iron bar would have evened the score, so to speak.'

'Yes, that's more like it, Marriott. I reckon Hicks could get a bit spiteful if someone started making a play for his missus. If I recall, she's a pretty young lass.'

'Why didn't you nick him for thieving the whisky, then, sir? That'd be a start.'

Hardcastle tapped the side of his nose with a forefinger. 'Give him enough rope, Marriott, and he'll hang himself. But I'd rather have a bit more to front him with before we have him in.' And hailing a passing cab, he said, 'On second thoughts, we'll start right now with the landlord of the Rising Sun.'

'Mr Hardcastle!' said a surprised Jed Parsons. 'You're up and about bright and early this morning.' He pulled two pints without waiting for the DDI's order.

'George Hicks,' said Hardcastle, taking the head off the beer for which he had made no attempt to pay.

'What, Queenie's husband you mean?'

'That's him.'

'What about him?' asked Parsons.

'I've been talking to him this morning, and he told me that about a month ago he had a bit of a bull and cow in here with Joe Briggs, and threatened to knock him down.'

44

Parsons laughed. 'News to me, but if he did, I wasn't here to see it. George Hicks would have been taking a chance throwing a punch at Briggs. Wouldn't mind betting Joe'd done a bit of milling in his youth.'

'Hicks said you were here and got between them. He said you'd call the police if they didn't take their argument outside.'

'Load of claptrap, guv'nor. It never happened. Not as far as I know, anyhow.'

'That's no surprise,' said Hardcastle. 'Is Queenie Hicks in this morning?'

'Sure. She's out back washing up some glasses. D'you want a word with her?'

'It won't take long,' said Hardcastle.

'Hold on then, guv'nor. I'll give her a shout.'

Although they had caught a glimpse of Queenie on the first occasion they had called at the Rising Sun, the two detectives had not really taken note of her. But as she emerged from the back room of the saloon bar, it became apparent that she was a very attractive young woman. Rich auburn hair, piled high, and a white blouse and black skirt, she was dressed in similar fashion to Polly Francis. It crossed Hardcastle's mind that perhaps the late Joseph Briggs was drawn to women of like appearance.

'Jed says you want to talk to me,' said Queenie, regarding the two policemen with a measure of apprehension.

'You probably know that I'm investigating the murder of Joe Briggs, Mrs Hicks,' Hardcastle began.

'Yes, it's awful, ain't it?'

'This morning we spoke to your husband.'

'What you been talking to my George for?' A slightly worried look crossed Queenie's face.

'Quite simple really. Your husband worked at Kendall's, same as Joe Briggs. And we have to ask questions of all sorts of people.'

'Oh!' Queenie appeared relieved, but Hardcastle wondered if she had a deeper reason to be concerned that he had been questioning her husband.

'Get Mr Hardcastle and the sergeant another pint,' said Jed Parsons as he passed behind Queenie on his way to serve a customer. 'On the house.'

Queenie drew the beer with ease, demonstrating by the way

45

she pulled on the pump handles that there was strength in her slender arms.

'Your husband was telling me that you were having a bit of trouble with Joe Briggs on account of him making eyes at you, and pestering you to go up to his room. Is that true?'

Queenie burst out laughing and, placing her hands on her hips, said, 'There ain't nothing unusual in that, mister. It's why landlords employ pretty barmaids. Brings the customers in, don't it? Happens all the time.'

'But George seemed to think that Briggs was being more trouble than most.'

Queenie laughed again. 'Nah!' She leaned forward and folded her arms on the bar as if to impart a confidence. 'Between you, me and the gatepost, Mr Hardcastle, my George is a bit jealous. He seems to think that every man what comes in here takes a fancy to me.'

Hardcastle was not surprised at Hicks's suspicion, but kept his opinion to himself.

'So Joe Briggs wasn't a problem.'

'No, he wasn't. Course he invited me up to his room, and I knew what that was all about. I told him he'd stand a better chance of winning if he put a fiver on an outsider at the Derby.' Queenie paused for a moment. 'Come to think of it,' she said, 'he did.'

'Did what?'

'Put a fiver on Durbar the Second in the Derby this month, and it romped home. I said he ought to buy drinks all round, but he said he couldn't afford it.'

'Did he say why, Mrs Hicks? I mean if he'd just had a big win on the horses, he could have put his hand in his pocket, surely?'

'Be a first if he had,' said Queenie scornfully.

'Did he ever mention being blackmailed?' asked Marriott.

'Blackmailed?' Queenie scoffed at the idea. 'Anyone trying to put the black on Joe would be asking for it. He was a big fellow, and he told me once he'd done a bit of boxing a few years back. When he was in the fire brigade, I think he said.'

Seated behind his desk at Cannon Row police station, Hardcastle was in expansive mood.

'Well, m'boy, light up if you want,' he said, and waited until Marriott had lit a cigarette. 'Looks like we're learning a bit more about Briggs every second. So he was in the fire brigade, eh? And he couldn't afford to buy a round even after he'd had a win on the Derby. I reckon that note we found in his room at the Rising Sun was from the bloke what done him in.'

'But why should he do that, guv'nor?' Marriott, recognizing the relaxed tenor of their conversation, lapsed into the informal mode of addressing his chief.

'Blackmailers are funny people, m'boy. They get a bit cross if their victims don't pay up. And if they don't there's only one way to deal with it.' Hardcastle paused, thinking about what he had just said. 'If only to let anyone else he might be blacking know that he ain't playing games.'

'Or *her*, guv'nor,' said Marriott.

Hardcastle expelled smoke and gazed thoughtfully at his sergeant. 'You might just be right at that, m'boy,' he said. 'I've known blackmailing to be a woman's game before now.'

Six

Hardcastle decided that it was time, once again, to visit Major Carmichael at Kendall's, mainly to enquire into the matter of Briggs's altercation with Mr Horace Davenport. But first, he intended to make a call on the London Fire Brigade in the hope that he might discover something about the late Joseph Briggs's background.

Hardcastle and Marriott were first shown into the office of the Brigade Secretary at the headquarters in Southwark Bridge Road. But when Hardcastle announced who he was, and that he was enquiring into the murder of Joseph Briggs, a former member of the Brigade, the Secretary conducted him straight to the office of Lieutenant-Commander Sampson Sladen. 'The Chief Officer likes to deal with the police himself,' he said.

'I read about his murder in *The Times*,' said Sladen, thought-fully stroking his beard. 'Can't say I'm surprised, either.'

'Oh? Why's that?'

'Very handy with his fists was Briggs. There was one occasion when he set about another fireman up in the men's quarters and knocked him down.'

'What was that about, Commander?'

'I've no idea, and it wasn't really important.'

'What did you do? Sack him?'

'No,' said Sladen. 'The fireman he struck swore it never happened. Said it was an accident, and that he'd fallen over and hit his head on a chair. Load of tommy-rot if you ask me, but none of the others was prepared to say anything. But I keep my ear to the ground, Inspector, and I knew that the rest of Briggs's watch was scared of him, or so I heard. They were all big men, but he was bigger, if you take my meaning. Anyhow, I had Briggs in and told him that I knew what had happened, and that if he made just one more slip he'd be out.'

'Why *did* he leave then, Commander?' asked Hardcastle, under no illusion that the Chief was a man to be reckoned with.

'I sacked him,' said Sladen. 'The second time he broke the rules.'

'Caught fighting again, was he, sir?' asked Marriott.

'No, asleep on duty.'

'But aren't firemen allowed to sleep on duty, sir?' Marriott had always been somewhat mystified by the practices of a fire brigade that put men on continuous duty for three or four days at a time. 'You mentioned quarters just now.'

'Quite right, Sergeant, they are permitted to sleep on duty. But not on the fireground,' replied Sladen with a grim smile. 'Briggs was found sleeping on one of the engines while his colleagues were sweating their guts out dousing a big blaze at a Tooley Street warehouse. It was made worse by the fact that Tooley Street's always been an emotive place in the annals of the brigade. Ever since the fire there over fifty years ago.' The Chief Officer paused, his expression implying disappointment rather than anger. 'We only took him on because he'd been in the Royal Navy,' he said sadly. 'The brigade always likes to recruit from the navy.'

48

'Where did he go from here, Commander?' asked Hardcastle.

'Got a job with Simcock's Brewery as a drayman, I think. God knows how because I refused him a reference.'

'Have you any idea how long he'd been in the navy?'

'Seven years. Enlisted as a boy seaman. Discharged time-expired.'

Fortunately, the offices of Simcock's Brewery were also in the Southwark Bridge Road, and the two policemen walked there from the fire brigade headquarters.

After Hardcastle had explained the reason for his visit, he and Marriott were shown into the office of the managing clerk, a man named Partridge. And Hardcastle spelled out, once again, why he was interested in the brewery's former employee, the late Joseph Briggs.

After removing his celluloid cuff guards, the managing clerk crossed to a wooden cupboard in the corner of his cramped office. Eventually unearthing a file, he sat down behind his desk again. He studied the file closely for some minutes before taking off his pince-nez, and sitting back to gaze at Hardcastle.

'Dismissed,' he said.

'I'm not surprised,' said Hardcastle, who was slowly beginning to realize that the murder of Joseph Briggs might well have been something that the smoking-room steward had brought upon himself. 'Why?'

'Very simple, Inspector,' said the managing clerk. 'He was a thief.'

'And what was he stealing?'

'Beer, what else?' Partridge smiled. 'We have inspectors who do random checks on our draymen, Mr Hardcastle. And they very soon discovered that Briggs was occasionally dropping off a barrel to an unscrupulous licensee who was not a customer of ours, and splitting the proceeds with him. What he would do was deliver short to one of the bigger public houses, relying on the barrels not being counted in, or being counted in by a cellarman who was prepared to turn a blind eye for a bribe.'

'So why didn't you prosecute him, Mr Partridge?' asked Marriott.

'Too much trouble, Sergeant. Having people wasting their time going to court. All that sort of thing. It all costs money, you see, and we're in the business of making money, not wasting it. It was much easier just to sack the man.'

'But what about the corrupt licensee who received the barrels, Mr Partridge?' asked Hardcastle, the policeman in him resenting that a thief and his accomplice should escape the just deserts of their crimes.

The managing clerk shrugged. 'Not one of our customers, Inspector, and therefore not our problem.'

'Was the pub the Rising Sun in Hatfield Street, Westminster, by any chance?'

Partridge skimmed through the few sheets of paper that comprised the file in front of him. 'Yes, it was, as a matter of fact.' He glanced up. 'How did you know that? Are you investigating those thefts as well as Briggs's murder?'

'No, it was just a hunch,' said Hardcastle blithely. 'As a matter of interest, why did you take him on, when he'd just been dismissed by the London Fire Brigade?'

'It wasn't relevant, Inspector,' said Partridge. 'He told us he'd passed out from heat exhaustion at the scene of a fire – understandable, I suppose – but had been accused of sleeping on duty and dismissed. Well, even if it was true, there was no chance of his sleeping on duty as a drayman, I can assure you of that.' The managing clerk gave a dry chuckle. 'Anyway, he was obviously a strong man, and we were looking for people who could heave a tun barrel down a cellar chute. We were after men with brawn not brains, and the job of a drayman's not everyone's cup of tea.'

'Does the name Polly Francis mean anything to you, Mr Partridge?' Marriott asked suddenly.

'Yes, it does. Why d'you ask?'

'Just a name that's come up in our enquiries.'

'She worked here for a while.'

'Doing what?' asked Marriott.

'She was a clerk in the despatch dock,' said Partridge. 'She used to handle the paperwork for the deliveries, making out the dockets for the draymen and filing them when they came back.'

Hardcastle had not thought to pose that question, and was

secretly pleased that Marriott had done so. 'So she'd have had personal contact with the draymen,' he said.

'Of course,' said Partridge, thinking that this policeman was a little slow to grasp what he had just said.

'How long was she here?'

'I'll have to check that, Inspector.' Partridge returned to his cupboard for a ledger. 'Started on Monday the third of May 1913 and was dismissed on Tuesday the seventeenth of June the same year for unauthorized absence. Her pay was twelve shillings and sixpence a week.'

'Unusual, employing a female clerk, isn't it?'

'Much cheaper than hiring a man, Inspector,' said Partridge with an arch smile.

'This unauthorized absence. Did she give any reason?'

'No she didn't. She'd been warned several times about bad timekeeping, but that was the last straw. I sacked her on the spot.'

Hardcastle did not bother to mention that the day of Polly Francis's unauthorized absence was the day she had appeared at Great Marlborough Street police court to answer a charge of soliciting prostitution.

'Well, if that don't beat cock-fighting, Marriott,' said Hardcastle when they were back at the police station. He took off his shoes and began to massage his feet. 'How come Briggs gets a job at a prestigious gentlemen's club like Kendall's when he'd been given the old heave-ho from the London Fire Brigade and sacked by Simcock's for thieving?'

'And we haven't found out yet why he left the navy, sir.'

'That's this afternoon's job, Marriott,' said Hardcastle. 'In the meantime, Major Carmichael's due another visit. See if he can tell us how he was persuaded to take on a rogue with a record like Briggs's.' He put his shoes on again. 'And while we're at it, we'll see if we can't charm a drop more of that Glenlivet out of him, an' all.'

But, irritated by constant visits from the police, Carmichael did not offer them any malt whisky. At least, not to start with.

'But of course Briggs provided a reference, Inspector,' he said, raising his eyebrows. 'We wouldn't dream of taking on

51

a man without one, and if you care to come with me, I'll show it to you.' And without waiting for Hardcastle's assent, he marched off towards his office on the far side of the smoking room.

Major Carmichael spent a moment or two searching an oak filing cabinet before producing a slim docket. He extracted a sheet of paper and handed it to Hardcastle.

The DDI ran his eye down the glowing testimonial that claimed Briggs had been employed as butler, from 1909 to 1912, by one Sir George Howard at his country house in Shropshire.

'Very impressive, Major,' said Hardcastle, handing the reference back to Carmichael. 'And did you take it up?' he asked, well knowing that the major could not possibly have done.

'No, I didn't. It's obvious that Sir George Howard is a person of substance – you only have to look at the address – and he wouldn't have written that if it was untrue.'

'Pity,' said Hardcastle, 'because Sir George Howard – if he exists – didn't write it. That bit of paper is about as truthful as if I was to tell you I'd swum the Channel before coming to work this morning.'

'And what d'you mean by that, Inspector?' snapped Carmichael, riled by Hardcastle's flippancy.

'What I mean, Major, is that for the four years before coming here, Briggs worked as a drayman for Simcock's Brewery until he was sacked for thieving. And before that he was a fireman, but got slung out for what we in the police would call neglect of duty.'

Slack-jawed, Carmichael gazed at Hardcastle, a stunned expression on his face. 'I don't believe it,' he said, clearly appalled at this revelation of his own inadequacy.

'If you don't believe it, Major, you can go where Sergeant Marriott and me went earlier today. To the London Fire Brigade and Simcock's Brewery. They'll tell you what I just told you.'

'Good God, but this is terrible, Inspector. It's a crime, surely, falsifying a reference, is it not?'

Hardcastle laughed, which did nothing to comfort Carmichael. 'Yes, it is, Major,' he said, 'under the Servants' Characters Act of 1792, but you'll have a job prosecuting Joseph Briggs for it, won't you?'

'I think I need a drink.' Carmichael gave the impression of having been severely shaken by what Hardcastle had told him, casting, as it did, a justifiable aspersion on his efficiency as a club secretary. Placing his hands on his desk, he forced himself into an upright position. 'Whisky, Inspector? And you, Sergeant?'

Once the Glenlivet was poured, Hardcastle turned to the other matter that interested him. 'I understand that a Mr Davenport had occasion recently to complain to you about Briggs's behaviour, Major.'

'How did you know about that?' asked Carmichael sharply.

'I'm a detective,' said Hardcastle mildly. 'I'm paid to find things out.'

'It was all a mistake, as it happened.' Carmichael lowered his voice, even though the door to his office was firmly closed. 'Between you and me, Inspector, Horace Davenport was a little tipsy. He seemed to think that Briggs had spilled a glass of whisky over him. But after I made some enquiries, Mr Davenport admitted that he may have made a mistake and apologized.'

'Apologized to Briggs?'

'Good heavens, no. To me. One does not apologize to servants.'

'What sort of enquiries did you make?'

For a moment it appeared that Carmichael was not going to answer. But then he relented. 'I spoke to Major Groves, informally of course. Apparently he was in the smoking room at the time, but said that he hadn't seen Briggs misbehave in any way.' He waved a dismissive hand. 'All a storm in a teacup, really.'

'Or in a whisky tumbler,' said Hardcastle drily, as he drained his glass.

'How is it, Marriott,' asked Hardcastle, while he and his sergeant consumed a sandwich and a pint of beer in the Red Lion pub in Crown Passage, 'that Briggs is able to charm his way into one job after being sacked from his previous one? Not once but twice.'

'And was being blackmailed at the same time, sir,' said Marriott, 'if that letter we found was anything to go by.'

'No, Marriott, it don't add up,' said Hardcastle, knocking out his pipe in the bar ashtray.

Their meagre lunch concluded, the two detectives returned to Pall Mall where Hardcastle hailed a cab. 'Admiralty, cabbie,' he said, and in an aside to Marriott, added, 'Always believe in going to the top.'

'D'you think they'll be able to tell us anything, sir?' asked Marriott, as the cab passed Trafalgar Square and turned into Whitehall.

'Time will tell, Marriott. Time will tell,' said Hardcastle mysteriously.

Waiting until Marriott had paid the fare, Hardcastle swept in through the impressive entrance to the building in Whitehall whence the Lords Commissioners of Admiralty commanded the fleet. For a few moments, the doorkeeper studied Hardcastle, eventually concluding that he was not a naval officer. 'Can I help you, sir?' he enquired.

Hardcastle told the doorkeeper what he wanted and, after some delay, a messenger was found to escort the two detectives to a small room on the first floor where they were handed over to a lieutenant who introduced himself as Hugo de Courcy.

'And how may I be of service to you, gentlemen?' he asked.

Once again, Hardcastle recounted the reasons for his enquiry.

Nodding from time to time, the lieutenant made notes on a foolscap pad. Replacing the cap on his fountain pen, he put it down beside the pad. 'It will take a few moments to get the appropriate documents, Inspector,' he said. 'They're kept in the vaults, you see. But in the meantime, you'll not be averse to a dish of tea, I take it.'

'Most kind,' murmured Hardcastle, and settled himself down for what he imagined would be a long wait.

De Courcy struck a brass bell on his desk and a clerk appeared. 'Perhaps you'd order some tea for these two gentlemen, Rawlings. Oh, and a cup for me. When you've arranged that, go down to the records section and draw the service history of this man.' He handed the clerk a slip of paper upon which he had written Briggs's name and details.

To Hardcastle's surprise, the tea arrived within five minutes, and Briggs's record of service only moments later.

'Now then, let me see,' said de Courcy, stirring his tea with one hand while riffling through the file with the other. 'What exactly did you want to know, Inspector?' he asked, looking up.

'Whether he got into any trouble while he was in the navy, Lieutenant. You see, I've learned that Briggs was a bit handy with his dukes when he was in the fire brigade.'

'His dukes, Inspector?' De Courcy looked puzzled by the term.

'His fists, Lieutenant.'

'Ah, I see.' De Courcy examined the file again. 'After a fashion,' he said, smiling. 'He was heavyweight champion of his squadron at one time. And, according to this' – de Courcy tapped the file with an elegant forefinger – 'there were high hopes that he might even go on to become champion of the Royal Navy.'

'But he didn't?'

'No, he left the service.'

'Why was that?'

'He'd completed his engagement. He'd entered as a boy in 1899 and served seven years.'

'And left with a clean sheet?'

'Not quite. He did, as you surmised, get himself into a bit of trouble.'

'What sort of trouble?'

'He struck an officer in a pub in Portsmouth.'

'So why wasn't he court-martialled? That's a serious offence in the navy, isn't it?'

'Extremely so,' said de Courcy sternly, 'and he *was* court-martialled, but was found not guilty. At least of the assault. In the old days they wouldn't have worried too much about what he had to say, and he'd've been flogged round the fleet.' The lieutenant assumed an expression that seemed to imply regret that such punishments were no longer available to a ship's captain.

'How did he get away with it, then?'

De Courcy closed the file. 'The oldest defence of all, Inspector. He claimed that the officer had made homosexual advances to him, as a result of which Briggs knocked him down.'

'But surely it was Briggs's word against the officer's?'

'Unfortunately, Inspector, it seemed that the officer concerned had a reputation for that sort of thing, and Briggs's defending officer adduced it in evidence by calling witnesses. Consequently, it wasn't long after Briggs's court martial that the officer was himself cashiered. Some unsavoury business with a midshipman according to this.' And once again, de Courcy tapped the file.

'You said just now that he'd been cleared of the assault, Lieutenant. Does that mean he was convicted of something else?' asked Marriott.

De Courcy consulted the file once more. 'Yes, he was, Sergeant. Briggs was a petty officer at the time of the assault, but he was disrated to ordinary seaman, by the same court martial, for being drunk and disorderly. Three months later, his engagement expired and his captain refused him permission to extend his service.'

'I'm obliged to you, Lieutenant de Courcy,' said Hardcastle, rising to his feet. Pausing at the door, he asked, 'As a matter of interest, did you have an enquiry about Briggs from Lieutenant-Commander Sladen of the London Fire Brigade?'

'If we did, there's no record of it here, Inspector,' said de Courcy. 'My predecessor may know, but he's now flag-lieutenant to Admiral Beatty in HMS *Lion*, lucky fellow,' he added with a grin. 'I've only recently returned from sea duty myself, and quite frankly I'm fretting to get back again. There's no doubt that trouble's brewing up in the Balkans, you know. Austria-Hungary is doing a lot of sabre-rattling and there are rumours that the fleet may have to mobilize. Fortunately most of it's at Portland.'

Seven

'Come in and tell me how you got on with your crowbar enquiries, Catto,' said Hardcastle, standing in the doorway to the CID general office.

'I did the rounds, sir, like you told me,' said Catto, following the DDI into his office.

'I should hope so, and are you going to let me in on the results, or is it a secret?'

'Er, no, sir,' said Catto, who was never quite sure when Hardcastle was joking.

'Well, get on with it, lad.'

'Altogether, I tried about eight ironmongers in the area, sir, and they all said the same thing. They're a common make and there's hardly anything to distinguish one from the other.'

'So that's it, is it?' asked Hardcastle.

'No, sir,' said Catto, risking a smile.

'Well, don't stand there grinning like a Cheshire cat, lad. Out with it.'

'The owner of the ironmongers in Palmer Street told me he'd supplied one just like it to Kendall's, sir, about three weeks ago.'

'What did he do, this ironmonger of yours, deliver it, did he?'

'No, sir. He said a bloke called Bert something came in and bought it over the counter.'

'So how does he know that this Bert something works at Kendall's, eh, Catto?'

'The chap at the ironmongers said he'd been in several times before and what he gets goes on the Kendall's account, sir. Oh, and he said this Bert walks with a limp.'

'Shouldn't be too much of a problem finding him,' mused Hardcastle. 'Well done, lad,' he added as an afterthought.

'Thank you, sir,' said the delighted Catto. It was not often that a word of praise from the DDI came his way. Or, for that matter, anyone's way.

'Ask Sergeant Marriott to come in, will you.'

'Catto's tracked down a shop in Palmer Street that sold a crowbar like the one found in the lake, Marriott,' said Hardcastle when his sergeant had joined him. 'And it was sold to someone called Bert who works at Kendall's. Get hold of the one found in the lake and we'll have another trip up there.' He seized his bowler hat and umbrella. 'I'm getting fed up with traipsing up and down to that damned club, Marriott,' he muttered.

57

By now it was five o'clock in the afternoon of what had been a busy but revealing day.

'I'm afraid Major Carmichael's gone home, sir,' said Sergeant-porter Lucas, as the two detectives strode into the foyer of Kendall's. 'Anything I can do?'

'As a matter of fact, it was you I wanted to see, Mr Lucas, seeing as how you're the senior member of staff.' Hardcastle paused. 'And you are, aren't you?'

'Indeed I am, sir. So how can I help you?'

'You've got someone on your staff called Bert. Walks with a limp,' said Hardcastle.

'That'd be Bert Walker, sir, sort of handyman. Does all the odd jobs. He was with Nosey's Bodyguard in the Sudan with Kitchener, but copped a bullet in his knee. Been here ever since.'

'Nosey's Bodyguard!' exclaimed Hardcastle. 'What sort of regiment is called Nosey's Bodyguard?' He had never served in the army and found its traditions and language completely beyond his comprehension.

'Northumberland Fusiliers, sir,' said Lucas. 'It's their nick-name, see.'

'I see. Well, if Mr Walker's here, I'd like a word with him.'

Lucas sucked through his teeth. 'Bit awkward that, sir. He'll be downstairs somewhere, but I can't bring him up here to the front hall. Against the rules, see. If one of the members—'

'In that case, I'll see him downstairs.' Hardcastle was beginning to find the ludicrously antiquated customs of Kendall's extremely irritating, if not downright obstructive. 'Perhaps you'd get someone to show me and Sergeant Marriott the way.'

'If you're sure, sir,' said Lucas doubtfully. But what concerned him more was the possibility that Major Carmichael might discover that the sergeant-porter had allowed these two policemen to roam about the club's premises.

'Let's not waste any more time, Mr Lucas,' said Hardcastle impatiently.

Following the liveried page-boy whom Lucas had summoned to show the detectives the way, Hardcastle and Marriott descended to the basement of the old clubhouse. At the foot of the stairs, they turned into a corridor – its ceiling almost completely obscured by pipework – that ran the length of the building. A man was approaching them from the opposite direction. Walking with a limp, his left leg stiff, he was wearing a green and yellow striped waistcoat and a green baize apron.

'That's him, sir,' said the youthful page in a piping voice. 'These gents is from the police, Mr Walker,' he announced as they came face to face.

'Oh aye,' said Walker, carefully surveying Hardcastle and Marriott. 'And what can I be doing for you?'

'Is there somewhere we can talk?' asked Hardcastle.

'Better come in the staff room,' said Walker, opening a door. 'Fancy a cup of tea, guv'nor?'

Hardcastle glanced at the collection of stained cups grouped on a table covered in American cloth and declined Walker's offer. 'I understand from one of my officers that about three weeks ago you bought a crowbar from the ironmongers in Palmer Street.'

'What of it?'

'Was that the one?' asked Hardcastle, once Marriott had unwrapped the jemmy recovered from the lake.

Walker peered closely at the crowbar. 'Could've been,' he said.

'But you're not sure?'

'One crowbar looks much like another, guv'nor, don't it?'

And with that proposition, Hardcastle was forced to agree.

'Why did Kendall's suddenly decide they wanted another crowbar, Mr Walker?' Marriott asked.

'They didn't, I did.'

'Why?'

'Because someone'd nicked the last one, that's why.' Walker wiped his nose on his sleeve and sniffed loudly. 'And before you ask, no, I don't know who nicked it.'

'When did you discover that the last one had gone missing?' Marriott was finding it difficult to extract information from this old soldier.

'Just before I bought the new one.'

'Have you still got the new one, Mr Walker?'

'S'pose so, unless someone's nicked that an' all. Wanna see it?'

'Yes, please.'

Tutting irritably, Walker limped from the room, to return moments later carrying a crowbar similar in every particular to the one the police had found. 'There y'are,' he said, dropping it on the table with a loud crash, an action that implied impatience with what he thought were footling questions. 'Anyway, what's all this about people nicking bleedin' crowbars? Someone found out they're made of gold all of a sudden?' he asked, cackling.

'That jemmy,' said Hardcastle, pointing to the one Marriott was guarding, 'was the one used to kill Joseph Briggs.'

'Is that a fact?' said Walker, peering more closely at what the police referred to as 'an exhibit'. 'Well, bless my soul.'

'You don't seem surprised,' said Hardcastle.

'Well, it stands to reason that if Briggs was topped, he had to be topped with something, don't it.'

Hardcastle was now certain that the murder weapon had been stolen from Kendall's and the one Walker had purchased some three weeks ago had been bought to replace it.

But that in itself posed a number of questions. It was unlikely that Briggs would have stolen the very crowbar that had been used to kill him – unless it had, in turn, been stolen from him – and it was equally unlikely that anyone unfamiliar with the 'below stairs' area of the club would have risked being seen there.

'The jemmy that went missing, Mr Walker,' said Hardcastle. 'When did you last see it?'

'About a couple of days before I went and got the new one, I s'pose.' Walker sat down on a kitchen chair, pushing his stiff leg out straight in front of him.

'And where would that have been, that you last saw it?'

Twitching at his straggly moustache, Walker pondered the question for a moment or two. 'Yes, I remember now,' he said. 'I was up in Captain Leighton's room. Just back from India on pension. Madras Light Infantry, he is, or was. Good lot, that, the old Madras, allowing they're Indian Army, mind you, but not bad in the line. I did a bit in India, you know. That was before I remustered. Anyhow, what was I saying? Oh yes, what with having nowhere to live yet, Captain Leighton put up here.'

'What's any of that got to do with the crowbar?' asked

60

Marriott, becoming increasingly frustrated at the ease with which Walker digressed.

'I was coming to that, guv'nor. A couple of days after the captain come here, his kit turned up from India – well, Southampton, I s'pose – and I had to go up to his room and open it up. Bleedin' great wooden crate it were.'

'And you used the crowbar to open it.'

'Course I did,' said Walker with a throaty laugh. 'Can't open a crate like that with your fingers.'

'And the crowbar . . .?'

'Yeah, well that's the thing, ain't it? I forgot it, see. Next morning I went to open a case of tumblers – the major's always ordering new tumblers, Gawd knows why, we've got hundreds – and I couldn't find me crowbar. Then I remembered I'd left it in Captain Leighton's room. So up I goes, but it weren't there. I had a word with Doris, her what does, and she said as how she ain't seen it. And I never saw it again.'

'So it's possible that this is the one,' said Marriott, gesturing at the jemmy he had brought with him.

'Yeah, could be. Here, I tell you what, there was a sort of little bump on the other side, like when it was made.'

Using the paper in which it had been wrapped, Marriott carefully turned the crowbar. There on the other side was a small protrusion, a defect in the manufacture.

'That's it. That's my jemmy,' said Walker, leaning forward to take hold of it.

'Don't touch it,' said Marriott sharply.

'Why not? It belongs to the club.'

'So it might,' said Hardcastle, 'but right now it's evidence. It's the weapon that killed Briggs.'

'Well, I'm buggered,' said Walker.

Returning once more to the entrance hall, Hardcastle asked Lucas where he could find Doris.

'What, Doris the chambermaid, sir?'

'I imagine so,' said Hardcastle. 'I'm told by your man Walker that she cleans Captain Leighton's room.'

'She'll likely be upstairs somewhere, sir,' said Lucas.

'Then perhaps you'd get her down here. I want to talk to her.'

'It's a bit difficult, sir. You see, if one of the members happens to catch a sight of her—'

'Mr Lucas, I don't give a fig what the members think, if they're capable of thinking at all, that is, but I'm investigating a murder. I don't have time to tramp about all over this bloody mausoleum you call a club. And if Major Carmichael don't like it, I'll happily tell him that myself.'

'Oh, no offence, sir,' said the chastened Lucas, 'but it's just that I have to do what I'm told.'

'Well, right now I'm doing the telling,' said Hardcastle, 'so be so good as to get hold of this Doris person.'

Without further ado, Lucas despatched his page-boy to find her. Within minutes the chambermaid appeared, looking even more apprehensive at being in the entrance hall than Lucas did for allowing her to be there.

'Doris, I'm Divisional Detective Inspector Hardcastle, and I'm investigating the murder of Joseph Briggs.'

'Ooh!' said Doris, blushing to the roots of her hair. She was a young girl, probably no older than sixteen or seventeen, and seemingly overawed by the presence of the two policemen.

'I think you may be able to help me,' Hardcastle continued in a kindly way that was alien to the officers under his command. 'Do you recall Mr Walker, the handyman, asking you if you'd found a jemmy in Captain Leighton's room? This would be about three weeks ago.'

'Yes, sir,' said Doris. 'Mr Walker said he'd been opening a case for the captain – him what'd just got back from India – but had left his jemmy up there after he'd finished. But it weren't there. That was the following morning. The captain had gone downstairs and I had a good look round, but there was no sign of it.'

'Did you ask Captain Leighton if he'd seen it?'

'Ooh no, sir. I wouldn't never do that. If any of the members is in their rooms, we have to say sorry for interrupting and go back when they ain't there.'

Hardcastle decided that Doris was too innocent to be involved in the theft of a crowbar, thanked her and turned back to the sergeant-porter. 'I don't think Doris can assist me any further, Mr Lucas,' he said.

Lucas dismissed the chambermaid with a wave of his hand, and the young girl fled, clearly relieved to escape from what, to her, had been an ordeal.

'Where will I find this Captain Leighton, Mr Lucas?'

'I do believe he's in the smoking room, Inspector. Bear with me for a moment and I'll find out.' And with that the page-boy was despatched yet again.

Seconds later he was back. 'Yes, sir,' said the boy to Lucas. 'He's in the corner by the window.'

'Good, I'll speak to him there,' said the DDI.

'But, sir—'

'Thank you, Mr Lucas,' said Hardcastle. 'Come, Marriott.'

Captain Leighton was probably in his mid-forties, but looked quite a few years older. Doubtless, thought Hardcastle, a result of long service in India and an excess of gin and tonic, a tumbler of which stood on an occasional table near Leighton's right hand. He was reading a copy of the *Morning Post*.

'Captain Leighton?'

The man stood up, dropping his newspaper to the floor and allowing his monocle to fall to the extent of its black ribbon. 'Yes, I'm Valentine Leighton,' he said. 'Have we met?' There was a questioning look on his face.

'I shouldn't think so. I'm Divisional Detective Inspector Hardcastle of the Whitehall Division.'

'Oh, I see.' Leighton rapidly withdrew the hand that he was about to offer. The expression on his face implied that if Kendall's had resorted to admitting policemen to its member-ship, it had clearly gone downhill since he last visited. 'Hardcastle, you say? Mmm!'

'I'm investigating a murder, Captain Leighton.' Hardcastle was impervious to the man's superior attitude, if for no better reason than that it was not unique in his experience. 'The murder of one of the club's servants, a man named Joseph Briggs.'

'And how does that affect me, may I ask?' Leighton sat down and waved a hand towards the vacant chairs near his table. 'You'd better sit down, Inspector and you, er . . .?'

'This is Detective Sergeant Marriott,' said Hardcastle, and was secretly delighted at the pained expression that piece of information brought to Leighton's face.

'How can I help you?' drawled Leighton, although the way he posed the question led Hardcastle to believe that the retired Indian Army officer would not go too far out of his way to do so.

'About three weeks ago, your belongings arrived from India via Southampton, I believe.'

'Yes.'

'And Walker, the club's handyman, came to your room here in the club, and opened a wooden crate for you.'

'Yes. What of it?'

'He tells me that he left his crowbar in your room, but that when he sent a chambermaid to look for it the following morning it was no longer there.'

'I hope this Walker person is not holding me responsible for the loss of his crowbar,' said Leighton, screwing his monocle into his right eye and staring at Hardcastle.

'No. All I wish to know is whether you saw it.'

'Yes, I did. But once the damned man started to open the crate, I got so sick of the noise he was making that I came down here and had a drink. When I returned to my room, an hour or so later, he'd cleared away the crate and put all my things into the wardrobe and the drawers of the chest.'

'So, apart from when he started unpacking, you didn't see the crowbar. It was not in your room on your return?'

'Yes, it was, and I chucked the bloody thing into the corridor. Dammit, man, don't tell me you've nothing better to do than investigate some petty pilfering. Anyway, what's so damned important about a bloody crowbar?'

'It was the crowbar that was used to murder Briggs.'

Leighton's monocle dropped from his eye. 'Christ! If you imagine that I had anything to do with the murder of – what's the man's name? – Briggs, then I suggest you're not very good at your job, Hardcastle.'

'We shall see, *Leighton*,' said Hardcastle as he and Marriott stood up.

'Since we're in the mood for getting up people's noses, Marriott,' said Hardcastle, as he hailed a cab, 'we'll see if we can't upset Jed Parsons at the Rising Sun in Hatfield Street.'

'Evenin', gents.' Parsons greeted the two policemen as if

they were old friends, and promptly placed two pints of bitter on the bar.

Hardcastle took a draught of his beer. 'You stopped selling Simcock's ale, then?' he asked casually.

There was a moment's hesitation before Parsons said, 'We've never sold Simcock's, Mr Hardcastle.'

'Not what I've heard.'

'Well, you must have been told wrong,' said Parsons, but it was obvious from the expression on his face that he was somewhat concerned about Hardcastle's comments.

'As a matter of fact, Mr Parsons, it was Simcock's themselves that told me. You see, Sergeant Marriott and me had to go there this morning to see if we could find out a bit about Joe Briggs.'

'Oh, I see,' said Parsons. 'I believe he used to work there.'

'Yes, he did. Got the sack though.'

'Really? I didn't know that. I thought he'd just got a better position at Kendall's. But then you'd know that of course.'

'You didn't ask why he got the sack,' said Hardcastle, playing the landlord along.

'Well, it don't really matter now, do it?' Parsons wiped the top of the already clean bar.

'I s'pose not,' said Hardcastle, 'but it was for nicking barrels of beer and selling them to landlords who didn't enquire too deeply into where they come from.' He put his empty glass on the bar. 'Me and Sergeant Marriott'll have another two pints, if you don't mind.'

'There's a lot of that goes on in the trade,' said Parsons, quickly drawing more beer.

'I know. But the man at Simcock's said that this was one of the pubs that was involved.'

Parsons looked thoughtful. 'Now you come to mention it, Mr Hardcastle, I did have a barrel once, but the drayman said it was on offer, see. He said the brewery – Simcock's that is – was trying to bump up trade a bit. And they was offering these barrels at knock-down prices. But it was just the once.'

'And would this generous drayman have been called Briggs, by any chance?'

Parsons seemed to give the question great thought. 'D'you

know, Mr Hardcastle, I do believe it was, now you come to mention it.'

'Yes, I believe it was too,' said Hardcastle. 'Still, I don't have time for that now, but I might have to look into it once the murder of Joe Briggs is out of the way. It all depends how much help I get.'

'If there's anything I can do, just say the word,' Parsons said, a little too hurriedly.

'You can have a look at this here for a start.'

Marriott displayed the crowbar. 'Ever seen that before, Mr Parsons?' he asked.

'Was that what poor Joe was done with?' asked the landlord, examining the jemmy closely.

'Yes, that's it.'

Parsons shook his head. 'No, never seen it before.'

'Not in Joe's room?'

'No.'

Hardcastle glanced along the bar. 'Mrs Hicks, just come here a minute, would you?'

'Yes, what is it?' asked Queenie Hicks.

'Have a look at this, Mrs Hicks, and tell me if you ever saw it before.'

Queenie looked at the crowbar and shook her head. 'No, I haven't. It's a bit like the one we keep here, but that's still under the counter.' She shot a glance in Parsons' direction and he nodded.

'And you didn't see it in Joe Briggs's room ever?'

'No, never,' said Queenie, and then blushed scarlet as she realized the involuntary admission she had just made.

Eight

'All we really found out yesterday, Marriott, is that things is more complicated than I thought.' Hardcastle took out his pipe and scraped at the bowl with a penknife. 'Our friend

Briggs managed to get himself busted down from petty officer in the navy. Then he gets chucked out of the fire brigade, sacked from Simcock's, and somehow works himself into a job at Kendall's on a false reference.' Slowly, he began to fill his pipe with St Bruno. 'If you or me had tried that, we'd've fallen at the first fence.'

'And you caught Queenie Hicks on the hop with that question about whether she'd seen the crowbar in Briggs's room, sir.'

Hardcastle laughed. 'Yes, you're right there, Marriott,' he said, expelling a plume of smoke and sitting back with a satisfied expression on his face. 'I reckon she was up the stairs for a bit of nookie with Briggs on more than one occasion.'

'That could make George Hicks a suspect, I suppose, sir. After all, he was pretty sure his missus was playing fast and loose with Briggs. Supposing he found out for certain she was messing around and decided to teach Briggs a lesson with the crowbar.'

'Hicks was certainly in the right place that night, Marriott, but I'm not sure he's got it in him. Then there's Polly Francis who's folded her tent and disappeared into the night. If she found out that Briggs and Queenie Hicks was up to a bit of hanky-panky, she might have taken it into her pretty head to sort him out. I seem to remember some poem we had at school about a woman scorned.'

'What about Captain Leighton, sir?'

Hardcastle scoffed. 'Well, I ain't exactly crossed him off the list, Marriott, but I reckon he's all wind and piss. All right when it comes to kicking a few sepoys up the arse, but he'd be no great shakes at working out how to murder someone and get away with it. Not unless he had a havildar to tell him how to do it.'

'A havildar, sir?'

'It's an Indian sergeant, Marriott. Mrs Hardcastle's old man was in the Gunners in India. Knew all the lingo.'

'One way or another, I reckon Briggs must have collected a few enemies over the years, sir,' continued Marriott thoughtfully. 'And Hicks did tell us he was going to chin Briggs for making eyes at his missus.'

'Not according to Jed Parsons he wasn't, Marriott,' said Hardcastle. 'Mind you, I'm not too happy about Parsons, neither. Apart from being in this racket with Briggs, nicking barrels of Simcock's beer, I wouldn't be surprised if he hadn't dipped his wick with the fair Queenie. Or with Polly Francis for that matter.'

'I suppose it comes down to who nicked the crowbar from outside Leighton's room, sir.'

'Maybe, Marriott. There again, maybe not. But even if it was, it could've been anyone.' Hardcastle struck another match and relit his pipe. 'Mind you, there's only one man in that club who's free to roam wherever he likes – upstairs and downstairs – without anyone asking questions.'

'D'you mean Major Carmichael, sir?'

'Exactly, Marriott.'

'But why would the major want to murder Briggs, sir? If he's taken a dislike to him, all he's got to do is sack him.'

'Might not be that easy,' said Hardcastle. 'I think we'll do a bit of digging into the major. See what he's made of.'

'But how are we going to do that, sir?'

'Hicks,' said Hardcastle.

'Hicks, sir?' Marriott was frequently confused by the mercurial changes in his chief's thought processes.

'Kill two birds with one stone, my lad. We'll catch him coming off duty again like we did last time. Tomorrow morning. He'll be off his guard after a nine-hour stretch of night duty. And he still don't know whether I'm going to do him for nicking whisky from the club.'

'Right, sir.'

'But before that, we'll go and see his missus, Queenie, before she leaves for work. If we knock on her door at about half past seven, we can have a word with her. Be better than speaking to her at the Rising Sun with that Jed Parsons earwigging all the time.'

'Right, sir,' said Marriott again, but with less enthusiasm than before.

'No good you sitting there with a sour face, neither, Marriott. We've a murder to solve. Anyway you're only a stride from Broadway, being as how you're in quarters at Regency Street. I've got to come from Kennington. Mind you,' he added thoughtfully, 'I reckon the Commissioner can stand me a cab, seeing as how the weather might just be inclement.'

68

'D'you think Hicks will know anything about Carmichael, sir?'

'Don't know till we ask, Marriott, but we'll start by having a quiet little chat with Carmichael himself.'

'But if Briggs's topping's down to him, he won't tell us anything, sir.'

'Not directly, Marriott, not directly,' said Hardcastle, tapping the side of his nose with a forefinger. 'I'll ask him about Leighton. You'd be surprised what people will tell you about themselves when you're asking about someone else.'

'Evening, sir.'

'Evening, Mr Lucas.'

'Bless me, sir, we're seeing more of you and the sergeant here, than we see of some of the members.'

'And you haven't seen the last of us either, Mr Lucas, not by a long chalk,' said Hardcastle.

'I suppose you'll be wanting the major, sir.'

'Yes, I will, but I want a word with you first.' Hardcastle put his elbow on the sergeant-porter's counter and leaned forward confidentially. 'What time did the major leave here the night that Briggs was murdered?'

Lucas looked startled by the question. 'Here, you don't think he had anything to do with it, do you, sir?'

'What, an upright officer and gentleman like him, Mr Lucas? Don't be daft, now. No, I just wondered if he was likely to know anything on account of I don't want to waste his time, nor mine, asking him questions what he wouldn't know the answer to.'

'Oh, I see. I don't know for sure, but I don't think he was here late that night. He doesn't live in the club, you see, sir. He's got a place in Clarges Street, number twenty-seven. Usually I calls a cab for him, but he'll sometimes walk if it's a fine night.'

'Clarges Street, eh?' mused Hardcastle. 'He must have a fair bit of brass.'

'Between you and me, Inspector,' said Lucas, lowering his voice, 'the major ain't short of a bob or two.'

'Them times the major walks home to Clarges Street, does he go out of the back door?' That Carmichael had claimed to have left *after* Briggs went home interested Hardcastle.

69

Lucas gave a derisory snort. 'The major go out of the back door? Not on your life! He ain't a back-door sort of man.'

Hardcastle laughed. 'I reckoned that might be the case,' he said. 'Anyhow, I need to have a word with him.'

'Boy!' Lucas shouted to the page. 'Go and see if the major's in his office. If he is, tell him Inspector Hardcastle and Sergeant Marriott are here, wanting a word. Hurry now.'

Moments later, the youth returned. 'Major Carmichael asked if you'd be so good as to come with me, sir, please,' he said to Hardcastle.

Carmichael was clearly in an affable mood. 'Inspector,' he said, 'come in, come in. Let me get you a drink. You too, Sergeant.' And he promptly stood up and dispensed liberal measures of Glenlivet.

'Your good health, Major,' said Hardcastle, raising his glass.

'Yours too,' said Carmichael. 'Now then, what can I do for you?'

'I hope I can speak confidentially, Major,' Hardcastle began, 'because this is a rather delicate matter.'

'Of course, of course.'

'About Captain Leighton . . .'

'Ah, Captain Leighton, yes. Madras Light Infantry, you know. Or was. Just retired and returned to England. Don't think he's too happy about it either. A lifetime of soldiering in the sub-continent doesn't exactly fit one for civilian life in the Old Country, don't you know. Anyway, what about him?'

Hardcastle recounted the saga of the missing crowbar in detail.

'And you've spoken to Walker, have you . . . and Doris?' A slight frown settled on Carmichael's face at this apparent affront to his authority over the staff. 'And you say this fellow Walker went off and bought a new crowbar?'

'Yes, according to the officer who made the enquiry, and Walker agreed.'

'He shouldn't have done that, Inspector,' said Carmichael, the frown becoming even more pronounced. 'I can't have the staff going off spending the club's money without authority.'

'Yes, well, be that as it may, Major, I'm more interested in Captain Leighton. Is he married, d'you know?'

Sitting beside Hardcastle, Marriott was wondering where

70

his chief's line of questioning was leading. After all, the DDI had already said that he thought Leighton's involvement in the matter of the missing crowbar was irrelevant.

'Married? Yes, I believe so. I seem to recall his saying something about his wife staying with her sister in Berkshire while he found a house in London somewhere. But surely, Inspector, you can't suspect him of having anything to do with Briggs's death.'

'Good heavens, not at all,' said Hardcastle, waving a hand of dismissal. 'But it's in a policeman's nature to investigate every lead.'

'Yes, of course. I suppose so. Very much the same with the army. You wouldn't believe the amount of paper that's generated by a court martial. And I've been involved with a few over the years.'

'I suppose it's quite difficult to find a suitable property in London these days,' said Hardcastle, as though he were an expert in such matters.

'So I've heard, Inspector.' Carmichael rose to his feet. 'Another drop of malt?' he asked. 'I suppose I was lucky finding my place in Clarges Street when I came out of the army.'

'Oh, I imagined that you'd've lived in the club, Major.'

Carmichael gave a short laugh. 'I don't think my wife would have taken too kindly to that, Mr Hardcastle,' he said, placing refilled tumblers in front of the two detectives. 'I've been out of the service now for, what, ten years. Very fortunate to find this billet at Kendall's. Most chaps seem to finish up as secretaries of golf clubs. Well, that's all right if you like the game, but personally I think it's a good walk spoiled, as Bernard Shaw is supposed to have said.'

'What regiment were you in, Major?' Hardcastle asked. He was not really interested, but he wanted to learn as much of Carmichael's past as he could.

'The Northamptonshire Regiment, Fifty-Seventh of Foot,' said Carmichael with obvious pride. 'Everywhere there was fighting the Steelbacks were there.' His eyes took on a glazed appearance. 'Badajos, the Crimea, the Relief of Ladysmith.' He glanced at Hardcastle. 'I was there, you know . . . at Ladysmith. You should have seen the Steelbacks sweeping in to relieve the Natal Field Force. Ah, wonderful days, Inspector, wonderful days.' The major took a sip of his whisky. 'Mind you, it's all about to happen again.'

'Really?' said Hardcastle.

'You mark my words, Inspector. This business in the Balkans is going to lead to trouble. One or two of the members here are still serving, some of them at the War House. The Germans are a bloodthirsty lot. Any excuse for war and they'll be in it, believe me.'

'But that won't affect us, Major, surely?'

'I wouldn't be too sure of that,' said Carmichael. 'Between you and me, I've heard that plans are being drawn up,' he added mysteriously.

'Well, we didn't learn too much about Major Carmichael, sir,' said Marriott, as he and Hardcastle walked back to Cannon Row police station.

'Don't you be too sure about that, Marriott. We now know where he lives – twenty-seven Clarges Street – and that he was in the Northamptonshire Regiment at the Relief of Ladysmith. For what that's worth. And although he's got a wife, he spends most of his time in the club. Now, what does that tell you?'

'That he don't get on with his missus, I suppose, sir.'

'Exactly, Marriott. I think we'll set a couple of the lads on doing a little observation on the major. See what that throws up.'

When Detective Constables Catto and Wilmot appeared in his office, Hardcastle stared at them for a moment or two. 'I've got a special job for you two, and I don't want it buggered up. Understood?'

The two DCs chorused assent. 'Yes, sir,' they said.

'Right then. Clarges Street. Know where that is?'

'No, sir,' said Catto unwisely.

'No?' echoed Hardcastle. 'You disappoint me, Catto. It's on Vine Street's patch. And if you can't find it, ask a policeman. Major Clive Carmichael, the secretary of Kendall's, lives at number twenty-seven, and I want him watched, see?'

'What are we looking for, sir?' asked Wilmot, the senior of the two.

'Anything, Wilmot. Anything and everything. I've got a

feeling that the bold major ain't all he's cracked up to be, and I want to know what he gets up to. But discreet, mind. If he spots you that'll likely put paid to my chances of getting any more of his Glenlivet out of him.'

Catto glanced at Wilmot, wondering what malt whisky had to do with their assignment.

'Take it turn and turn about,' continued Hardcastle. 'Fix it up between yourselves. And I don't want you following him into the club.'

'Very good, sir,' said Wilmot, who had already worked out for himself that such a course of action would be unwise if they were to remain discreet.

'Right, off you go.'

Once the two men had left his office, Hardcastle took out his hunter, flicked open the cover and stared at it for a moment. 'See you in Broadway at about five and twenty past seven tomorrow morning, Marriott.'

Hardcastle was there first and glanced ostentatiously at his watch as Marriott joined him. 'Ah, good, you're here at last.'

'But it's only just twenty-five past now, sir,' complained Marriott.

'Always parade early, Marriott, that's the golden rule. Right, now I've had a gander up and down the street and there's only one boot makers, a bit along from the Feathers pub. So the flat over it should be where the Hickses live.' And with that, he strode off.

Queenie Hicks was obviously far from ready for work when she answered the door. She wore a full-length satin peignoir with a rather revealing neckline, and her auburn hair tumbled loose around her shoulders.

'Oh my God!' Queenie's greeting as she recognized the detectives was anguished, and her hand went to her mouth. 'Whatever is it? Has something happened to my George?'

'Not that I know of, Mrs Hicks,' said Hardcastle, 'but Sergeant Marriott and me would like a few words with you.'

'What time is it?'

'Half past seven,' Marriott volunteered.

'I'm getting ready for work,' said Queenie. 'Got to be at the Rising Sun by eight.'

73

'I don't s'pose Jed Parsons'll be too vexed if you was a few minutes late,' said Hardcastle. 'Now then, are you going to let us in, or d'you want to stand here in the street half dressed while we have a talk?'

By way of a reply, Queenie Hicks turned and mounted the stairs. 'Now what's this all about?' she asked when the three of them were seated in the tiny sitting room at the front of the flat.

'I don't think you've been quite honest with me, Mrs Hicks,' Hardcastle began.

Queenie coloured slightly. 'I don't know what you mean,' she said, tossing her head, but her protestation was less than convincing.

'When we had a chat with you, the day before yesterday, I asked you if you'd ever seen a crowbar in Joe Briggs's room at the Rising Sun.'

'Yes, and I told you I'd never.'

'So you did,' mused Hardcastle before turning to his sergeant. 'What was it that Mrs Hicks said when we spoke to her last Tuesday, Marriott, about never going up to Briggs's room?'

Marriott pulled out his pocket book. 'Mrs Hicks said: "I told him he'd stand a better chance of winning if he put a fiver on an outsider at the Derby", sir.'

'Yes, a fiver on an outsider at the Derby.' Hardcastle nodded as he savoured the words aloud. 'But you did go up to his room, didn't you, Mrs Hicks? Because the next day, when I asked you if you'd seen the crowbar in Joe Briggs's room, you said no. Now then, my girl, if you'd never been up there – which is what you claimed – I'd've expected you to say just that.' He paused, staring at the girl. 'So what was going on between you and Briggs, eh?'

Queenie began to cry. 'Oh Lord! I don't know what I'll do if George ever finds out. It was only a couple of times, when I was working late. I usually only do eight in the morning to six at night, but when Jed's short-handed, I sometimes do a late shift an' all. We need the money, you see, and George don't get paid all that much.'

'Are you telling me that Briggs paid you for cuddling up to him in his bed?'

'No, he never.' Queenie's tears stopped as abruptly as they had begun. 'What sort of girl d'you think I am?' she demanded.

'I think you're the sort of lass who cheats on her husband, Mrs Hicks. But I'm also thinking that Joe Briggs was a bit too persistent for your liking and he had to be got rid of.'

The look of astonishment that crossed Queenie Hicks's face was undoubtedly genuine. 'You don't mean you think I done for Joe, do you, mister?'

'Well, did you?'

'Of course I never. I swear it.'

'What about your husband George? He told me once that he was going to have a go at Joe. Threatened to punch him . . . in the Rising Sun.'

'What?' Queenie laughed. 'He's all mouth and trousers is my George. He couldn't fight his way out of a paper bag, George couldn't.'

Which was exactly the view that Hardcastle had expressed to Marriott about George Hicks. 'He must have heard something, Mrs Hicks.' The DDI continued to press the girl. 'You didn't think you could keep your goings-on with Joe Briggs a secret for ever, did you? In a crowded pub, suddenly you disappear for half an hour, just after Joe Briggs has come in from the late shift. Or in the afternoon when he was off earlies.'

Once more Queenie dissolved into tears. 'It was only a couple of times,' she said again.

'Did Jed Parsons know what you were up to?' asked Marriott.

Switching her attention to the sergeant, Queenie shook her head. 'No, of course not,' she said, dropping her gaze coyly in a vain attempt to convince the good-looking Marriott.

'How did you get away with it then?' persisted Marriott.

'It's too busy in the pub for Jed to notice me missing. Anyway I have to go out the back from time to time. Cutting a few sandwiches, and washing up and that.'

'We'd better let you get ready for work, Mrs Hicks,' said Hardcastle, standing up. 'Don't want you getting into trouble with Jed Parsons, do we.' But he was more concerned about being too late to catch George Hicks than he was about causing his wife to be late for work.

As the trio reached the front door, Queenie Hicks said,

75

'Here, you won't go telling anyone what I said about me and Joe, will you?'

Hardcastle and Marriott strode along Queen Anne's Gate and into St James's Park on their way to Pall Mall. Crossing the very bridge from which Joseph Briggs had probably been pushed nine days ago, Hardcastle said, 'This bloody enquiry gets worse, Marriott. How the blue blazes did Queenie Hicks get upstairs and into Briggs's bed without Parsons noticing she'd gone?'

'Maybe he did notice, sir, but said nothing.'

'Why should he do that, eh?' Hardcastle stopped and turned to face his sergeant.

'Because Queenie was free with her favours in his direction as well, sir? Or maybe he was copping a few quid from Briggs for his bit of fun with her.'

'You could be right at that, Marriott,' said Hardcastle mildly. 'Running a bloody brothel.' But inwardly he was furious that the possibility had not immediately occurred to him. 'Well, if that Jed Parsons thinks he can pull the wool over my eyes, he's got another think coming.' And, as they crossed The Mall towards Marlborough Road, he barked at the policeman on the traffic point. 'Put your bloody chinstrap down, lad. What'll the King think if he drives down here?'

Nine

'I've got a feeling that there's more to George Hicks than meets the eye,' said Hardcastle, as he and Marriott turned into Pall Mall. 'And I think he might just run when he catches sight of us.' He paused, formulating a plan. 'Now then, last time we met him on his way home, he turned right when he came out of the back of the club, and he'll likely do so again this morning. Man of set habits, see. So I want you to hang about at the east end of St James's Square, Marriott, and I'll go in the west end so's I come up behind him. But keep out of sight.'

Unsure what Hardcastle had in mind, or what Hicks's 'running' would prove, Marriott did as the DDI had ordered.

At two minutes past nine, Hicks emerged from the back entrance to Kendall's and turned right, as the DDI had anticipated.

'Good morning, Mr Hicks,' said Hardcastle in a loud voice as he came up behind the night porter.

Hicks, encumbered with his attaché-case, glanced over his shoulder, recognized the DDI and started running. But as he reached the south-east corner of the square he was confronted by Marriott who was almost as surprised as Hicks that Hardcastle's prediction had been realized.

'If you're in training for the Olympics, my lad,' said Hardcastle as he strolled up to where Hicks was being held in a firm grip by Marriott, 'they ain't for another two years. So why was you running, eh?'

'I was in a hurry, guv'nor,' said the breathless Hicks.

'He was in a hurry, Marriott,' echoed Hardcastle sarcastically before returning his attention to Hicks. 'And why was you in such a hurry, eh, George? Have something to do with what you've got in that smart attaché-case of yours, would it?'

'I was hoping to catch Queenie before she went to work,' said Hicks lamely, attempting to deflect Hardcastle's interest in what he was carrying.

'She starts work at eight o'clock, as you well know,' said Hardcastle, 'because you told me so. And I know she went off as usual this morning, because Sergeant Marriott and me was speaking to her just before she left.'

'What about?' Hicks tried to sound indignant, but he was clearly worried.

Hardcastle ignored the question. 'Let's have a dekko in that,' he said, reaching for the attaché-case that Hicks was still holding tightly.

With a sigh, Hicks handed it over.

'Well, would you have a gander at that, Marriott,' said Hardcastle, as he opened the case to reveal a bottle of Courvoisier cognac. 'Only the best for our Mr Hicks.' He closed the case and handed it to Marriott. 'George Hicks, I'm arresting you for stealing that bottle of brandy.' He paused. 'And for trying to come it over me, a divisional detective inspector with twenty-three years' experience of nicking villains.'

'But it'll mean the boot, guv'nor,' whined the ashen-faced Hicks.

'You should've thought of that, my lad. I gave you the benefit once, but I ain't doing it twice. You're just a thieving little sod, and you're about to get done for it.'

At the police station there were more surprises. Detective Sergeant Wood was despatched to make urgent enquiries of the Criminal Records Office across the road at New Scotland Yard. Half an hour later, he returned clutching a file.

'Got something interesting there, Wood?' asked the DDI.

'Not the first time he's been knocked off, sir,' said Wood with a grin.

'Let's have it then.'

'Born in Bermondsey in 1886, sir, and has three previous convictions. In 1906, aged twenty, he got done for nicking an overcoat from Gamages in High Holborn. Got a carpet. Er, I mean three months, sir.'

'I do know a carpet's three months, Wood,' said Hardcastle impatiently. 'Still, three months for an overcoat is cheap at half the price,' he mused, 'or would have been if he'd got away with it. Yes, go on.'

'In 1907 he was nicked for being a suspected person loitering with intent to steal purses in Kingston market, and got another carpet.'

'He gets around, does our Mr Hicks,' said Hardcastle, lighting his pipe. 'And the third?'

'That was in 1910, sir.' Wood glanced up. 'Done for living off the immoral earnings of one Queenie Attwood on Vine Street's toby. Six months that time.'

'Well, well,' said Hardcastle. 'I wonder if Queenie Attwood has become Queenie Hicks. If they're properly wed and churched, that is.'

'Want me to get one of the lads to check at Somerset House, sir?'

'No, don't worry about that, Wood. I'll sweat the truth out of the carney little bugger if I have to.'

'Looks like he's gone straight since he came out of the nick in 1910, sir,' suggested Wood.

'Gone straight my arse,' exclaimed Hardcastle. 'Just means he ain't been caught. Get him up here. And tell Sergeant Marriott to come in.'

George Hicks carved a sorrowful figure as Marriott conducted him into Hardcastle's office. Deprived of his braces, necktie and bootlaces, he was able only to shuffle in, holding up his trousers.

His pathetic appearance did not, however, prevent him from making a protest. 'It was perks, guv'nor,' he began. 'Like I said the other day, everyone knows it happens.'

'So you'll be calling Major Carmichael to tell the court it was all above board, will you, Hicks?'

Hicks let that suggestion pass. 'If you're doing me for it, why aren't you nicking all the others? The head steward, Charlie Wilson, and Barnes, the other smoking-room steward. They're all at it. And Jack Lucas an' all.'

'Proper little thieves' kitchen that Kendall's, ain't it, Hicks?' Hardcastle leaned forward in his chair, linking his hands loosely on his desk. 'Who's Queenie Attwood?' he asked suddenly.

The question obviously took Hicks aback. 'Er, I, er, I don't know no Queenie Attwood,' he said.

'You've got a short memory, Hicks.' Hardcastle drew the night porter's criminal record towards him. 'It says here you got a half a stretch in 1910 for living off of her immoral earnings.'

'That's all in the past,' said Hicks churlishly. 'Anyway I've got nothing to say.'

Hardcastle rose threateningly from behind his desk. 'Don't you come the old monkey with me, Hicks, because right now I've half a mind to put you on the sheet for the murder of Joseph Briggs.'

'I never murdered no one, guv'nor, that's the God's honest truth,' pleaded Hicks. 'I mean, nicking the odd bottle's one thing, but topping's not my game.'

'Nicking the odd bottle, eh?' Hardcastle sat down again. 'Read his form, Marriott,' he said. 'Just in case he's forgot.'

Taking Hicks's record from the DDI, Marriott read out his other two convictions: 'Done for nicking an overcoat from Gamages, and for sus in Kingston market.'

'What was you doing down Kingston, Hicks?' asked Hardcastle.

'Went there for a day by the river,' said Hicks miserably. 'I was having a look round the market when this bluebottle nicked me. But I wasn't doing nothing wrong.'

'They all say that. So, is this Queenie Attwood now Mrs Queenie Hicks?'

There was a long pause before Hicks eventually nodded. 'Yes,' he said quietly.

'And she's still getting on her back for a few quid, is she? With you copping the fee.'

'No, she ain't,' said Hicks angrily. 'She's turned respectable now. That's why she's working at the Rising Sun, pulling pints.'

'Well, once you've been up before the beak this morning, Hicks, I reckon she'll have to go back on the game to make ends meet. If she ain't on it already. And I've a mind she is.'

'Look, about this brandy, guv'nor . . .' Hicks pointed at the bottle now standing on Hardcastle's desk.

'What about it?'

'I mean if I was to tell you what was going on, could you sort of—?'

Hardcastle hit the top of the desk with the flat of his hand so violently that not only did Hicks jump, but so did Marriott. 'If you think you can trade with me, my lad, you're mistaken. I know what's going on. You and Jed Parsons had a nice little thing running there. Any one of the customers at the Rising Sun who fancied a bit of jig-jig was taken in hand, so to speak, by your missus. Her or Polly Francis,' he added, making a wild guess.

'How did you know about her?'

'I'm not a detective for nothing, lad,' said Hardcastle, 'but what I'm more interested in now is knowing where she's gone.'

'I dunno, guv'nor, honest. I ain't seen her for about a fort-night. But if I do see her, I'll let you know,' said Hicks in a vain attempt at appeasing this aggressive policeman.

Hardcastle laughed. 'You won't be seeing her where you're going, Hicks. Not for a few months. And that's if the beak's in a good mood this morning, which I doubt.'

It was gone half past eleven by the time Marriott returned from Bow Street police court.

'Well?' said Hardcastle.

'Three months hard, sir.'

'Only a carpet? I think the beak at Bow Street's getting soft in his old age.' Hardcastle stood up. 'And now, Marriott, we'll go and break the sad news to Major Carmichael that he'll be parading one man short for night duty.'

When the two detectives arrived at Kendall's just after midday, they found the club secretary in the entrance hall, talking to Sergeant-porter Lucas.

'Good afternoon, gentlemen,' Carmichael said wearily. He was obviously getting tired of frequent visits by the police.

'I'm afraid we have some bad news for you, Major,' said Hardcastle.

Carmichael cast a quick glance at Lucas and then said, 'You'd better come through then.'

The major cast a listless hand at the armchairs in his office. 'Take a seat,' he said. 'Now, what's this bad news?'

'I'm afraid you're short of a night porter, Major,' said Hardcastle.

'Hicks, you mean? Why's that?'

'I arrested him this morning, just as he was leaving the club. He had in his possession a bottle of Courvoisier cognac which he freely admitted was the property of Kendall's.'

'I don't believe it,' said Carmichael, shifting forward in his chair and staring at the DDI.

'Well, the magistrate at Bow Street believed it. Gave him three months hard labour.'

Carmichael fell back, his face a picture of a man betrayed. 'But I always regarded him as an honest servant of the club. Always punctual, and an impeccable sick record. In fact, he had no sick record at all. Three months hard labour seems a trifle harsh for a first offence, but I suppose you'd know more about that than me, Inspector.'

'Oh, it wasn't a first offence, Major,' said Hardcastle, and went on to tell Carmichael that Hicks had three previous convictions. 'And, as a matter of interest, he told me that he wasn't the only one stealing spirits from the club. He said that

81

Wilson and Barnes were at it. Lucas, too. But maybe he was just being spiteful.'

'Oh my God,' said Carmichael, 'this is terrible.'

'Did Hicks provide you with a reference, Major?'

'Of course.' The secretary crossed to his filing cabinet and took out a slim file. 'It's here,' he said, taking out a sheet of paper and handing it to the DDI.

'So he worked as a footman at Lord Wilmslow's place in Rutland in 1910, did he?' Hardcastle glanced up. 'That must have been the half of 1910 when he wasn't doing six months in Wormwood Scrubs for living off of the immoral earnings of a woman he now calls his wife, Major. And as far as I can see, he's still living on her earnings as a prostitute.'

'But this is disgraceful,' said Carmichael with a suitable display of outrage. But the news that Hicks had been living on the earnings of his wife appeared to disconcert him less than Hardcastle's suggestion of widespread thefts from the club.

'D'you have a copy of *Burke's Peerage* here anywhere, Major?'

'Of course.' Carmichael's terse reply implied that a club like Kendall's could not possibly survive without such a publication.

'In that case, I'll take a little wager with you that if you look up Lord Wilmslow, you won't find him. Because I reckon he don't exist. Just like Sir George Howard never existed.'

'This is terrible,' said Carmichael once again. 'I could lose my job over this, you know.'

'D'you mind if I have another look at that bogus reference Briggs gave you, Major? The one from that Sir George Howard who don't exist.'

Carmichael returned to his filing cabinet and handed over the forgery.

'Mmm!' Hardcastle placed the two sheets of paper side by side on Carmichael's desk. 'You don't have to be a handwriting expert to see they was written by the same hand, Major,' he said, further discomfiting the secretary. 'And I'd've thought that a knight, to say nothing of a peer of the realm, would have used headed notepaper, wouldn't you?' He looked up.

But Major Carmichael had his eyes closed.

*   *   *

'I reckon that took the wind out of the major's sails, eh, Marriott?' Hardcastle had taken off his shoes and was massaging his feet. 'Heard anything from Wilmot or Catto, have we?'

'Catto's in the office now, sir. He did the late shift yesterday.'

'Fetch him in, then.'

Minutes later, Catto appeared, hovering in the doorway of Hardcastle's office.

'Well, don't stand there like a wet weekend, Catto. Anything to report?'

'Yes, sir. Major Carmichael left Kendall's at about nine o'clock last night—'

'What d'you mean, *about* nine o'clock?'

Catto glanced down at his pocket book. 'Two minutes past nine, sir,' he said.

'You know I don't like sloppy reporting, Catto. All right, get on with it.'

'He took a cab to twenty-seven Clarges Street, sir, and at nine thirty-two a young woman arrived, also in a cab. She knocked at number twenty-seven and was admitted by the major.' Catto glanced up. 'She left again at ten minutes to twelve . . . exactly . . . sir.'

'Description?' snapped Hardcastle.

Again Catto consulted his notes. 'Five foot seven or eight, sir, slim build, green eyes and auburn hair. She was dressed in—'

'Never mind what she was dressed in, Catto. How did you get near enough to see the colour of her eyes? Or are you just guessing because she's got auburn hair?'

'Oh, no, sir,' protested Catto. 'I sort of collided with her.'

'Oh, I see. You sort of collided with her, did you? And how did that happen?'

'I wanted to get close enough to get a good description, so I sort of arranged to bump into her.'

'And did you have a conversation with her . . . when you bumped into her?'

'Not as such, sir, no. I said I was sorry and so did she. She said something like "Ever so sorry, love". And she had a cockney accent, sir.'

'And where did she go? Follow her, did you?'

'I was going to, sir, but she saw a cab, hopped in it and off she went. There wasn't no other cab in the street. Sorry, sir.'

'Get the plate number?'

'Yes, sir.'

'Good. Have a word with Public Carriage Branch and find the cabbie. See where she went. But I've got a bloody good idea where she was making for.' Hardcastle turned to Marriott. 'What d'you think?'

'Sounds very much like Queenie Hicks, sir.'

'Yes, it does. And if it was her, it would explain why she looked worn out when we saw her this morning. And why she could afford a satin housecoat that wouldn't have given her much change out of four guineas.' Hardcastle searched his pockets for matches. 'I wondered why the major went a bit white when I told him Hicks had been living off of his wife's earnings from prostitution, Marriott. But it's obvious now, ain't it?'

'To say nothing of racing around in a cab, sir,' said Marriott. 'I'd've thought the tram was more her style.'

'More to the point, Marriott, where was the major's wife while all this was going on? On the other hand, perhaps he was lying when he told us he was wed. There's something a bit fishy going on here. He takes on two servants at the club, both of 'em with snide references which'd be obvious to a blind man. Then one of these upstanding employees gets knocked on the head and dumped in His Majesty's lake.'

A frown crossed Marriott's face. '*His Majesty's* lake, sir?'

'St James's is a royal park, Marriott. Course it's His Majesty's,' said Hardcastle with a twinkling eye. Becoming serious again, he turned back to Catto. 'You and Wilmot can forget about following Carmichael for the time being, Catto—'

'Very good, sir.'

'And don't look so pleased about it. You're not off the job that quick. You and Wilmot concentrate on twenty-seven Clarges Street for the next few evenings, and if any more young ladies of the night happen to turn up you're to follow 'em when they leave. Including the one you saw last night. Got it?'

'Yes, sir.' The disappointed Catto had thought that his boring assignment had come to an end.

'And don't let any of 'em see you, specially the major.'

'An interesting turn, sir,' said Marriott, once Catto had left to impart the bad news of their continuing observation to Wilmot.

Hardcastle leaned down to replace his shoes and spats. 'Could explain a lot, Marriott, the major enjoying a screw with Queenie Hicks. I wonder how often that happens, and if there's any others. Like Polly Francis, for instance.'

'If Polly's at it, sir, it would explain why she hasn't been nicked recently. Still on the game, but by special arrangement, as you might say. You going to talk to the major . . . or Queenie Hicks, yet, sir?'

Hardcastle gave a throaty chuckle. 'No, not yet, Marriott. I've a feeling that there's more to learn about Major Carmichael. Supposing Briggs found out what he was up to – the major, I mean – and tried putting it across him for a few sovereigns. Good motive for topping Briggs, wouldn't you think? And from what I know of ex-army officers, they don't usually have two ha'pennies to rub together.'

'But it was Briggs who was being blackmailed, sir, if that note we found in his room was anything to go by.'

'Marriott,' said Hardcastle, shaking his head, 'so far in this murder nothing is what it seems.' Standing up, he pulled out his watch, glanced at it, wound it and dropped it back into his waistcoat pocket. 'I think we'll wander round to the Rising Sun. I fancy a wet and it's well past time we gave that Jed Parsons a bit of a shaking-up.'

Queenie Hicks looked quite alarmed to see Hardcastle and Marriott walk into the saloon bar. 'Here, what d'you want?' she whispered furtively, after looking left and right. 'I hope you ain't been blabbing about me and Joe.'

'No, Queenie. We haven't been blabbing, but we have been giving evidence. Leastways, Sergeant Marriott here has. Your George got himself three months hard labour at Bow Street this morning.' But before Hardcastle had the chance to tell her what he had been convicted of, she fainted.

Another barmaid rushed to her aid. 'Here, what you been saying to her?' she demanded, affording Hardcastle a brief, malevolent glance.

'I was just telling her that her husband got himself sent

down for a carpet this morning,' replied Hardcastle, having almost convinced himself that Queenie Hicks was putting on an act. 'Where's Jed Parsons?'

'He's in the back room doing the books,' said the barmaid as she sloshed cold water over Queenie's face.

'Doing 'em, or cooking 'em?' asked Hardcastle as he raised the flap in the bar and walked through.

''Ere, where d'you think you're going?' The barmaid stood up, defiant.

'It's all right, Babs,' said Queenie, as she staggered to her feet, 'they're the law.'

Ten

From the expression on his face, Jed Parsons was not at all happy to see the local DDI and his sergeant.

'Oh, it's you, Mr Hardcastle,' he said, turning in his chair. 'Busy?'

'Very. In fact Sergeant Marriott here's spent half the morning at Bow Street getting your Queenie's husband locked up for three months.'

'*What?*' Parsons leaped from his chair. 'What for?'

'Thieving bottles of spirits from Kendall's, where he works. Or should I say where he used to work, because I doubt they'll want him back again after he's done his bird-lime.'

'Oh my Godfathers! Does Queenie know?'

'Yes, I told her just now. She threw a fit of the vapours and collapsed on the floor, but only for a few seconds. Barbara, your other barmaid, chucked a bucket of water over her. She seems all right now.'

'Nicking spirits, you say?'

'That's right, Mr Parsons. Bit odd really because I got the impression that George Hicks don't drink much. So I asked him what he did with all these bottles he was nicking.'

'What did he say?' asked Parsons nervously.

'He told me he sold 'em,' said Hardcastle, making up the story as he went along.

'And I always thought he was a straight sort of bloke.' Parsons shook his head in contrived wonderment. 'Did he say who he sold 'em to?' he asked, endeavouring to make it sound like an offhand question, the answer to which did not really interest him.

'Not yet,' said Hardcastle, 'but he will, *and* before you can say Jack the Ripper. When Sergeant Marriott and me takes a trip down to the nick he's locked up in, he'll peach, don't you worry about that.'

'You look as though you could do with a wet, Mr Hardcastle,' said Parsons, in an attempt to divert the course of this worrying conversation. 'A pint of best, is it?'

'I was wondering if you'd got a drop of Glenlivet,' said Hardcastle. 'I've become quite partial to the malt of late.'

'Of course. And you too, Sergeant?'

'Very kind,' murmured Marriott.

'Won't keep you a moment,' said Parsons and headed for the bar.

'Our Mr Parsons seems all of a quiver this evening, Marriott,' said Hardcastle with a sly smile. 'Bit of a guilty conscience there, I wouldn't mind betting.'

'D'you think he's been buying these bottles from Hicks, sir?'

'Racing certainty, Marriott, racing certainty.'

'Going to nick him for it, sir?'

'Not yet, no,' said Hardcastle. 'I think we'll play him along a bit. We've got bigger fish to fry, like who done for Briggs. And I think that Jed Parsons might know more than he's telling.'

'Here we are, gents.' Parsons returned with a full bottle of Glenlivet and three tumblers, and proceeded to pour a substantial measure into each. 'Good health!'

'Interesting fingerprint there, Marriott. D'you see that?' Hardcastle peered closely at the bottle as if he had made a startling discovery.

'Oh yes, so there is.' Marriott could not see any marks, but followed the DDI's lead in his campaign of harassing Parsons.

'All sorts of people handle the bottles in a pub, Inspector,' said Parsons hurriedly, unaware that it was virtually impossible to identify the owner of a fingerprint with the naked eye. And in the absence of another with which to compare it.

'Yes, I suppose they do,' said Hardcastle, leaning back and taking a sip of his whisky. 'Funny thing,' he continued conversationally, 'it was a bottle of Glenlivet we caught Hicks with.' He thought it unnecessary to mention that it was the theft of a bottle of brandy for which Hicks had been convicted. 'By the way, how much is Queenie paid for getting on her back for your customers, Mr Parsons?'

'Do what?' The question, coming out of context, clearly unnerved Parsons, and he put his tumbler back on the table more forcefully than usual. 'I don't know what you're talking about, Inspector.'

'I'm talking about Queenie Hicks selling her favours to those what's prepared to pay. And while she's here in your pub.'

'Who told you them lies, Mr Hardcastle?'

'A little bird,' said Hardcastle enigmatically.

'Well, I don't know nothing about that,' said Parsons, but his denial was unconvincing. 'She always works hard when she's here. D'you think I wouldn't notice if she scarpered off for a quick tumble?'

'Have you seen Polly lately?' asked Marriott.

'Polly? Polly who?' It was obvious that Parsons was becoming rattled by the detectives' probing enquiries, and was playing for time.

'You must remember Polly,' continued Marriott. 'Polly Francis, Joe Briggs's fiancée, or so she reckoned.'

'Oh, that Polly,' said Parsons lamely. 'No, Mr Marriott, I ain't seen her in here for a few weeks. As a matter of fact, I think she only come in the once. That time I told you about.'

Hardcastle drained his glass and stood up. 'Thanks for the Scotch, Mr Parsons. No doubt we'll be seeing each other again.'

'Any time, Inspector. You're always welcome at the Rising Sun.' But it was said without any sincerity.

'Goodbye, Queenie,' Hardcastle called out as he and Marriott walked through the saloon bar and into the street.

When the two policemen were well clear of the pub, Parsons beckoned to Queenie. 'For Gawd's sake come in the back for a minute, love. Quick,' he said.

'Whatever's wrong?' asked Queenie, once the door of the office was firmly closed.

'What have you been saying to them coppers?' demanded Parsons menacingly.

'Nothing, Jed. Why?'

'I reckon they're on to us. That bloody Inspector Hardcastle was asking whether you was on the game. Somehow he's found out about you, Barbara and Polly turning tricks. We'd better knock it on the head for a bit, my girl. I don't want to finish up in clink for running a whore-house.'

'But I've got to keep on with it, Jed,' whined Queenie. 'I need the money now George is in the nick.'

'Yeah, well we'll have to think of something,' said Parsons, pouring another two fingers of Glenlivet into his glass and downing it in a single swallow.

'I fancy we upset one or two people yesterday, Marriott,' said Hardcastle the next morning, as he slowly filled his pipe.

'But are we any nearer finding out who killed Briggs, sir?' asked Marriott.

'No,' said Hardcastle cheerfully, 'I don't think we are, Marriott, but like Mr Micawber I'm hoping for something to turn up. And it will, you mark my words.'

'By the way, Catto found the cabbie, sir.'

'What cabbie are you talking about, Marriott?'

'The one who took that doxy home from the major's place in Clarges Street.'

Hardcastle leaned forward, his interest aroused. 'And?'

'You were right, sir. He dropped her off at the boot makers in Broadway where Queenie Hicks lives.'

'I knew it,' said Hardcastle, banging the top of his desk with a clenched fist. 'Where's Catto now?'

'In the office, sir.'

'Fetch him in.'

'You wanted me, sir?' asked Henry Catto, approaching the DDI's desk in his usual state of anxiety.

'What happened last night, Catto?'

Bearing in mind Hardcastle's previous admonition about sloppy reporting, Catto referred to his pocket book before answering. 'Major Carmichael arrived home at twenty-seven Clarges Street at six o'clock precisely, sir. On foot. And he looked a bit flustered.' He glanced up from his notes. 'Like he was in a muck-sweat about something, sir.'

The whisper of a smile crossed Hardcastle's face. 'Sounds as though someone'd rattled him off, don't it, Marriott?' he said.

'Then at seven sixteen, a woman arrived and was admitted to number twenty-seven by the major hisself, sir. She left again at twenty minutes past eleven.'

'Description?'

'About twenty-three years of age, sir, five foot six or seven, auburn hair and green eyes. A pretty young thing, she was, sir.'

'That's the same as the description you give me of the woman who called there the night before last, who we now know is Queenie Hicks. Are you sure it wasn't the same woman, Catto?'

'Quite sure, sir. It was definitely a different woman.'

'Seems to me, Marriott, that the major's taken a fancy to copper-nobs.'

'I'm wondering if it might've been Polly Francis, sir,' said Marriott. 'She's got auburn hair.'

'I know. That's why I said it,' muttered Hardcastle. 'And did you follow her when she left, Catto?'

'Yes, sir. It was a bit of luck that there was another cab going by just as she got into hers. I managed to hail him and he stopped just—'

'Oh, for pity's sake, Catto, don't keep me in suspense with all that fiddle-faddle. Where did she go?'

'A pub called the Rising Sun in Hatfield Street, sir.'

'Gordon bloody Bennett!' exclaimed Hardcastle. 'That bugger Parsons is running a knocking-shop under our very noses, and it looks like he's harbouring Polly Francis an' all. I wouldn't mind betting she was upstairs with her legs spread even while we was partaking of his stolen whisky last evening.'

'But would it be a brothel if Queenie and Polly were going to some other place to do business with their clients, sir, like to Major Carmichael's?' Marriott asked. 'The Rising Sun wouldn't be a brothel if these doxies weren't giving pleasure on the premises.'

'I don't give a fig where they're doing it, Marriott,' said Hardcastle crossly. 'We either do him for keeping a bawdy house, living on immoral earnings or harbouring prostitutes on licensed premises.' He turned to glare at his unfortunate constable. 'And what section's that, Catto?'

'I, er, well, sir, I think—'

'You don't bloody know, do you, Catto? Well, I'll tell you. Licensing Act 1910, section seventy-six. You need to bone up on your law if you're ever going to be as clever as Sergeant Marriott here. Now bugger off and see if you can spot any more redheads going into Major Carmichael's place.' But then Hardcastle called him back. 'No, on second thoughts, you and Wilmot keep an eye on the Rising Sun. If you see any obvious street-women leaving there, follow 'em and see where they go.'

'What are you going to do about it, sir?' asked Marriott, once Catto had fled the wrath of his DDI.

'Nothing, Marriott,' said Hardcastle, who by now was beginning to recover from the news of Parsons's duplicity. 'Not at present, anyway. I don't want to upset the apple cart, because I'm bloody sure we'll find the answer to Briggs's murder somewhere in the Rising Sun.'

'Supposing the Uniform Branch find out and do Parsons in the meantime, sir?'

'Fat chance of that, Marriott, but I'll have a word with the sub-divisional inspector at Rochester Row, just in case he gets up early one morning and takes it into his head to stir things up.'

Determining that there was nothing he could do the following day, a Sunday, Hardcastle spent it with his family at home in Kennington. Alice Hardcastle prepared the usual roast beef and Yorkshire pudding without which, Hardcastle often declared, Sunday would not be Sunday.

After lunch, the headstrong Kitty went for a walk with her current beau, while the younger Maud stayed in to help her mother with the washing up. The Hardcastles' son Walter, however, was bubbling over with news of the crisis now gripping the whole of Europe.

'And what are you getting all intelligent about, Wally?' asked his father, lowering his *News of the World* to gaze in disbelief at the unusual spectacle of his fourteen-year-old son with his head buried in an atlas.

'I'm trying to work out what's going to happen when the war starts, Dad.'

'War, lad, what war? What in the name of Hades are you talking about? There ain't going to be a war.'

'My pal Charlie Pender's father is a sergeant in the Grenadiers. And he reckons his dad says there's going to be one. He says that there's plans being made at Wellington Barracks and next week they're going down to Salisbury Plain to practise, which they don't usually do at this time of the year.'

'Well, if your pal Charlie Pender's old man was a colonel, I might have a mind to believe it,' said Hardcastle. 'But he's pulling your leg, my son. If someone takes it into his head to bump off some archduke in a place we've never heard of, I don't see what that's got to do with us.' And with that dismissal of the war clouds that were, at that very moment, gathering over Austria-Hungary and Serbia, he resumed reading about a vicar who had been unfrocked for an indiscretion with a church-warden's wife.

The scene in the Marriotts' police quarters in Regency Street, less than a mile from Cannon Row police station, was not unlike that in the Hardcastles' household. The Marriotts, however, enjoyed lamb rather than beef, and after lunch Charles Marriott spent twenty minutes or so scanning *The People*. He did not much care for that particular Sunday newspaper, but his wife Lorna enjoyed reading it and so he yielded to her wishes.

The Marriotts' daughter Doreen – at three, rapidly developing into a tomboy – played happily with a black-faced doll, a recent birthday present from a favourite aunt. Doreen's older brother James was lost in a world of his own, playing with a wooden model of a Dreadnought, accurately crafted by Fred Wilmot whose hobby, when he had time to spare from his police duty, was carpentry.

Lorna came into the room with a tray of tea and set it down on a table near the armchair where she habitually sat. Glancing down at James, still absorbed in make-believe, she said, 'Charlie, do you really think there's going to be a war?'

'No, love. If Ernie Hardcastle says there isn't, that's good enough for me.'

Lorna made a sour face. 'I sometimes think you rely too much on him,' she said.

'He's a good detective,' said Marriott, as ever quick to defend his chief.

'So he might be,' said the perceptive Lorna, 'but he's not a soldier, is he?'

It was on the Monday morning that Hardcastle's Micawberish hope that something would turn up came to fruition. A man, an obvious labourer of some sort, presented himself at the front door of Cannon Row police station.

'And what can we do for you?' asked the constable stationed there.

'I want to see whoever's in charge of this murder,' said the man.

'And which murder might that be?' The constable stood four-square across the entrance to the station, his thumbs tucked under the buttons of his tunic pockets. He was accustomed to people arriving at Cannon Row under the impression that they were calling at New Scotland Yard itself.

'Joe Briggs.'

'Ah, in that case, culley, you'd better wait here.'

The PC entered the station and spoke to the sergeant on duty. Minutes later the man was ushered into Hardcastle's office.

'This man claims to have information about the Briggs murder, sir,' said the station officer.

'Does he indeed?' Hardcastle surveyed the man critically. About forty years of age, he was clutching a brown derby in his hand, and wore a waistcoat and a leather apron. 'Who are you?'

'Jess Woodhall, sir.'

'You'd better sit down and tell me what you know about Briggs's murder, then.' Hardcastle spoke sceptically. In his experience members of the public claiming to have important information about a murder rarely had.

'I don't know if it'll be of any help, sir,' Woodhall began, 'but I work at Simcock's brewery in Southwark Bridge Road.'

Hardcastle cast a fresh eye over Woodhall, taking in his clothing. 'As a drayman?'

'Yes, sir.'

'Go on.'

'Well, I got to know Joe Briggs when he was working there. We worked the same dray, and he told me one day as how he'd been in the navy before getting chucked out of the fire brigade for kipping on duty. Anyhow, it weren't long after that he got the boot from Simcock's. Some tale about him nicking the odd barrel and knocking it out, see.'

'What's the point of this, Mr Woodhall?' asked Hardcastle.

'Well, about a week after he left, I saw him when I was delivering up west. So we had a wet together that evening, just for old times' sake, and he told me he wasn't having any luck finding a position.'

'But he got a job eventually,' said Hardcastle.

'Yes, guv'nor, and I think I give him a bit of an 'elping hand there.'

'How?'

'I told him to go to Kendall's. That's a gents' club in Pall Mall—'

'I know where Kendall's is,' said Hardcastle wearily. 'Are you going to tell what you know about the murder of Briggs, or do I have to guess?'

'No, I'm coming to that, sir. I told Briggsy that he'd best not mention being chucked out of Simcock's, nor the fire brigade, but just to mention he'd been in the navy. Major Carmichael's a bit disposed to them that's been in the army and the navy, see. Mind you, he'd rather have army.'

Hardcastle's eyes narrowed and he leaned forward. 'And how come you know this Major Carmichael, then?'

'I was in the same lot as him, sir. The Army Service Corps. Lance-sergeant farrier, I was,' said Woodhall proudly. 'Done me seven with the colours and packed it in after we'd sorted out the Boers.'

'So you were at the Relief of Ladysmith with the major, were you?' Hardcastle forbore from mentioning that Carmichael had claimed to be in the Northamptonshire Regiment.

Woodhall laughed. 'I was, but he weren't, sir. Depot man was the major. Never went out of England to my knowledge, and he got the push just after the war was over. Well, sort of.'

'I think you'd better explain that, Mr Woodhall,' said Hardcastle, his interest now thoroughly aroused.

'It was after I got back from South Africa that word was

94

going round the depot. Major Carmichael was a quartermaster officer, see. Not a proper gent, if you take my meaning.'

'No, I don't.'

'It means he come up through the ranks. When he was a regimental quartermaster sergeant – that's warrant officer rank – he was commissioned as what they calls a lieutenant QM officer. But by the time he was made captain, he was in charge of a base supply depot. Them's what supplies food to the army, among other things. Anyhow, one day they done a check and found a lot of food had gone missing. Sides of bacon, joints of meat, all that sort of stuff. They had a court of inquiry but couldn't prove Carmichael had pinched it, but he was ordered to resign his commission. Neglect of duty, they called it.'

'So he wasn't a major at all?'

'Nah, guv'nor, but that's what he calls hisself now. Who cares, anyway?'

'Did you tell Briggs about this, Mr Woodhall, before he got the job?'

'Yeah, I did sort of mention it.'

After the departure of ex-Lance-sergeant Woodhall of the Army Service Corps, Hardcastle sent for Marriott and recounted what he had just heard from the Simcock's drayman.

'Looks to me like Briggs squeezed Carmichael into taking him on, Marriott, or he'd blab the story about his military past to whoever runs Kendall's.'

'That'd be why Carmichael never took up the reference, sir. He must have known it wasn't kosher.'

'So what about Hicks? He had a phoney reference an' all.'

'I think Queenie Hicks might know the answer to that, sir,' said Marriott.

'Yes, I think you might be right,' said Hardcastle. 'And I think it's time we had her in the nick and give her a good talking to. That young hussy ain't coming across.'

But as Hardcastle stood up and seized his hat and umbrella, Catto appeared in the office.

'Saturday night, sir.'

'Don't come rushing in here saying things like "Saturday night", Catto. What about Saturday night?'

'I was keeping observation outside the Rising Sun in Hatfield

Street as directed, sir, and I saw the first auburn-haired woman . . .' Catto paused and looked up from his notes. 'I think you said she was called Queenie Hicks, sir.'

'Yes, yes, get on with it,' muttered Hardcastle.

'And at seven fifteen, she proceeded to Buckingham Palace—'

'*What?*' exclaimed Hardcastle.

'Where she met a man, sir, outside the south-centre gate.' Catto afforded himself a brief smile. 'They then walked to a hotel in Buckingham Gate where they stayed for approximately two hours.'

'What happened then?' demanded Hardcastle.

'They came out of the hotel and the gent hailed a cab. They both got in and I followed in another cab.'

Hardcastle raised his eyes to the ceiling. 'I don't give a fig if you was on a bicycle, Catto.'

'No, sir. The cab took them as far as Broad Street, near the junction with Lexington Street. The gent got out and left the woman to carry on in the cab alone. As you was aware of the identity of the doxy, sir, I deemed it proper to follow the gent, and he went into number seventeen Broad Street.'

'What did he look like, Catto?'

'Bit of a toff at first glance, sir, but I did notice that his shoes was a bit down at heel.'

Eleven

'On second thoughts, Marriott,' said Hardcastle, once Catto had left the office with instructions discreetly to discover the identity of the occupant of 17 Broad Street, 'I'll send Wood round the Rising Sun. Fetch him in if he's here.'

Moments later, Detective Sergeant Wood, pleased to have a few minutes' respite from struggling with a complicated report, entered the DDI's office. 'Yes, sir?'

'D'you know the Rising Sun in Hatfield Street?'

'Yes, sir. Run by Jed Parsons.'

'Good. Go round there and bring in Queenie Hicks. She's a barmaid there. And if you get any old madam from Parsons, you can nick him an' all. I'm getting fed up with the lot of them.'

Three-quarters of an hour later, Wood reappeared in Hardcastle's office. 'She's downstairs in the interview room, sir, but she's kicking up a bit of a fuss.'

Hardcastle chuckled. 'I'll bet she is,' he said. 'Be a touch of the jitters, that will.'

When the DDI and Marriott entered the interview room at the front of the police station, Queenie Hicks leaped to her feet. 'What the bleedin' hell's this all about?' she demanded. 'I'm pulling pints round the Rising Sun when one of your rozzers comes in and nicks me without so much as a by-your-leave.' The demure character of the woman they had inter-viewed three days earlier had all but vanished.

'You weren't arrested, Queenie,' said Hardcastle mildly. 'I just wanted to have a chat with you.'

'You could have done that round the pub,' said Queenie angrily. 'You never had to have me dragged all the way round here. Anyway, if it's about Joe Briggs getting done in, I don't know nothing.'

'Who was the man you met last Saturday night, Queenie?' asked Hardcastle, as he sat down opposite the girl.

'Don't know what you're on about,' said Queenie defiantly.

'I've had you watched, my girl, and I know what your game is. And I know you've been popping round to Clarges Street to give the galloping major a ride.'

'What of it? T'ain't agin the law, is it? Not as if I was whoring on the street. What him and me does indoors ain't none of your business. He's took a fancy to me and that's that.'

'And what does his missus think about it?' asked Hardcastle. 'Or your poor husband who's working his fingers to the bone sewing mailbags, eh?'

Queenie scoffed. 'The major ain't got a missus, and as for George Hicks, well he can rot for all I care. Anyhow, George knew what I was doing.'

'That's a bit of a different tale from the one you told the

last time I spoke to you. There was you pleading not to tell anyone you'd been spreading your legs for Joe Briggs, and all the time you've been making a business out of it with the major.'

'So what?' said the still defiant Queenie.

'And four years ago your George went down for half a stretch for living off of your immoral earnings, didn't he?'

'How d'you know about that?'

'Because I'm paid to know about things like that, Queenie. Now then, how did your George get a job with Kendall's, him having been in the nick three times before?'

'Joe fixed it,' mumbled Queenie. 'He reckoned as how he could square it with the major to take him on.'

'So long as you went round to Clarges Street whenever he wanted you to pleasure him, eh?'

'What of it?'

'So, this is the set-up, is it? You turned a trick or two for Joe Briggs so's he'd put in a word with Carmichael for your George, but to clinch the deal, you had to get on your back for the major an' all, whenever he flicked his fingers.'

'Jobs is hard to come by these days,' said Queenie miserably, 'and money's bleedin' tight.'

'So how much does the major pay you?'

'Quid a tumble,' said Queenie.

'Daylight robbery,' said Hardcastle, 'but let's get back to last Saturday night. Who was the toff you met outside Buckingham Palace, eh?'

Queenie shifted uncomfortably in her chair. 'I dunno his name. He's someone what used to come in the pub. I s'pose he took a liking to me 'cos he asked me out for supper. So we went to a hotel in Buckingham Gate and he bought me a slap-up meal. A real gent, he is.'

'Just supper, was it?'

'Course it was,' protested Queenie unconvincingly. 'Watcha take me for?'

'So this nice gent meets you right outside the Palace and takes you for supper, but he never told you his name. Don't take me for a fool, Queenie. Who was he?'

Queenie looked down and picked a tiny piece of fluff from her skirt. 'He was called Fred Hopkins,' she mumbled.

'Was he indeed?' said Hardcastle, not believing a word of it. 'And where does he live?'

'I dunno.'

'You don't know? Even though you went with him in a cab and he got out in Broad Street before sending you back to the Rising Sun?'

Despite being alarmed at how much Hardcastle knew of her activities, Queenie still managed to respond spiritedly. 'I tell you, mister, I don't know where he lives. He told me he had to meet someone up west and that he was going to walk the rest of the way from Broad Street.'

Hardcastle thought that that might well be the story the mysterious stranger had told Queenie, but thanks to Catto he knew differently.

'How about Polly Francis, Queenie?' Marriott asked. 'Is she still living at the Rising Sun?'

'Never heard of her,' snapped Queenie.

'Really? Oh, I think you have.' Marriott regarded Queenie with an amused smile.

'Looks like we'll have to get a warrant to search the Rising Sun, don't it, Marriott?' said Hardcastle.

'Want me to slide up to Bow Street and get one now, sir?' asked Marriott, well knowing that his chief had no intention of searching Parsons's pub. At least not yet. 'I could catch the beak when he rises for lunch, and we could turn over Jed's boozer this afternoon.'

'Be a shame that,' said Hardcastle, running a hand round his chin. 'It'd mean that when Jed Parsons asked how we knew where to find Polly, we'd have to tell him who told us.' Not that he ever disclosed his sources of information. Unless it suited him to do so. 'And we'd have to tell Polly an' all.' He picked up his pipe and began to tease the dead ash with a letter opener. 'On the other hand, if Queenie here tipped us the wink, we wouldn't have to say anything about where the information came from. Of course, if she didn't, I'd still say she did.' Glancing at the girl, he added, 'So you might as well tell me, my girl.'

'She was there, but she ain't now,' said Queenie, realizing she was damned either way.

'Oh? And when she did leave?'

'Last Friday night.'

'That'd be just after Sergeant Marriott and me had a chat with Jed Parsons, I suppose.'

Queenie nodded. 'But for Gawd's sake don't say I told you, mister. She's a savage bitch is that Polly Francis, and I can do without having me nose busted, thank you very much.'

'Where did she go from the Rising Sun, Queenie?'

There was a moment's pause before Queenie replied. 'Back to her place at Malacca Street,' she said eventually.

Hardcastle took out his watch and glanced at it. 'I s'pose you'd better be getting back to work, Queenie,' he said, 'but I shouldn't say anything about our little chat to Jed Parsons. If he asks what it was all about, you can tell him I wanted to talk to you about your husband George.'

'Don't you worry about that, mister,' said Queenie earnestly. 'I ain't saying nothing to nobody. As for that Jed Parsons, I'll tell him to mind his own.'

'Thanks for coming in,' said Hardcastle with a smile.

'Sod you, mister,' said Queenie as she swept from the room.

Once the girl had departed, Hardcastle leaned back in his chair and lit his pipe. 'Seems to me, Marriott,' he said, 'is all we've done so far is uncover a little ring of prostitutes working from the Rising Sun. That's all very interesting but, apart from doing the Uniforms' job for 'em, it don't get us any nearer coming up with who topped Briggs.'

'D'you reckon her story about Polly Francis going back to Malacca Street is kosher, sir?' asked Marriott. 'I wouldn't've reckoned on that Mrs Winston welcoming her with open arms.'

'There's one way of finding out,' said Hardcastle. 'Take Catto and Wilmot off the observation they're doing on the Rising Sun, and put them on Malacca Street. If Catto spots the second girl he saw coming out of Carmichael's place the other night, then we'll know it was Polly Francis as well as Queenie what's been on her back for him. Seems to be doing all right for himself, does the major.'

It was an hour later that Henry Catto returned from making his enquiries in the West End of London.

'Found him, sir.'

'Found who, Catto?' asked Hardcastle.

'The man who lives at seventeen Broad Street, sir. Him what took Queenie Hicks to the hotel in Buckingham Gate last Saturday evening.'

'So who is he?'

'He's called Horace Davenport, sir, and he lives there with his missus Rose.'

Instructing Catto to keep observation on Mrs Winston's house in Malacca Street, Hardcastle dismissed him with a wave of the hand.

'Wasn't Horace Davenport one of them who was playing cards at Kendall's the night that Briggs got done in, Marriott?'

Marriott flicked open his pocket book and studied it briefly. 'That he was, sir, along with Dawson, Hunt and Captain Reilly.'

'Interesting,' mused Hardcastle. 'I wonder how many other members of that select gentlemen's club is enjoying a screw with the whores of Hatfield Street. I think we might be getting somewhere at last,' he continued. 'You see, Marriott, the one link between Kendall's and the Rising Sun knocking-shop is the late Joseph Briggs.'

'And George Hicks, sir,' said Marriott, 'who obviously knew that his missus Queenie was on the game. After all, he got done for living on her earnings four years ago.'

'As you say, Marriott, and George Hicks. But Briggs is the one who's dead. I wonder why he should have got himself topped. Whatever the reason, I'm bloody sure he was pimping for Queenie and Polly Francis, and maybe a few others what we don't know about.'

'Don't forget the letter we found in his room, sir, that seemed to point to him being blackmailed.'

'Yes, but what was the point of that, Marriott? Like I said before, it don't add up.'

'Could've been one of the girls, sir.'

'I doubt it,' said Hardcastle. 'They ain't exactly making a secret of what they're up to. But it might have been another whore who we've yet to track down. One who had something to hide.'

'What about Carmichael, sir? He definitely said he was married, and Lucas said so as well.'

'Probably a tale he told the chairman. What's his name?'

'Sir John Webster, sir.'

'Yes, that's him. He probably told him the tale so's he could escape from the club, legitimate like, to have it up with Queenie Hicks and Polly Francis.'

'D'you reckon he might have done for Briggs, sir?' asked Marriott.

'I must say it's beginning to look like a possibility,' said Hardcastle, slowly tapping his teeth with the stem of his pipe. 'And I think we're going to have a little chat with him.'

Marriott glanced at his watch. 'Now, sir?'

'No, not now,' said Hardcastle, putting his pipe in the ashtray. 'We'll catch him at home, away from that damned club of his. Get him off his guard. Come to think of it, I might even nick him. In the meantime, we'll make a few enquiries about him. See if what ex-Sergeant Woodhall had to say is the true version.'

'Where do we do that, sir?'

'At the War Office, Marriott. Where else?'

Colonel the Honourable Alistair Todhunter assumed a bemused expression when Hardcastle explained the reason for his enquiry.

'*Major* Carmichael, you say? But he was an officer, man. Are you really suggesting that he may be mixed up in a murder?' The tone of Todhunter's voice implied that such a possibility was beyond belief.

'I don't know, Colonel, but I'm obliged to make thorough enquiries into such a matter.' Hardcastle had avoided mentioning what Woodhall had told him: that Carmichael had only been a captain.

'And you say he's the secretary of this Kendall's, eh what?'

'Yes, he is.'

Todhunter wrinkled his nose. 'Not in the top league, of course. I'm a member of the "In-and-Out" myself.' And seeing Hardcastle's quizzical expression, he added, 'The Naval and Military in Piccadilly. Although I happen to know that General Lord Slade's a member of Kendall's.' He shook his head, as though unable to grasp such poor taste in a man who was both a peer of the realm and a general.

'Is there any possibility that you can tell me something

about this man Carmichael, Colonel?' asked Hardcastle, already tiring of Todhunter's condescending prattle.

'Shouldn't take a moment to dispel your suspicions, Inspector.' Todhunter crossed the room to a communicating door, and addressed someone in the next office. 'See if you can find any record of a Major Clive Carmichael, Sarn't Williams, will you?' He glanced over his shoulder. 'What regiment did you say, Inspector?'

'He said he was in the Northamptonshire Regiment, Colonel,' said Hardcastle, choosing not to mention Woodhall's claim that Carmichael had been in the Army Service Corps.

Todhunter sniffed and repeated the information to the unseen Williams.

After Hardcastle and Marriott had endured a ten-minute monologue from Todhunter on the possibility of war, Sergeant Williams came into the office. 'We only have a record of a *Captain* Clive Carmichael, sir,' he said, 'and he was in the ASC,' he added, placing a thick file in front of the colonel.

'Good God!' said Todhunter, and spent a few minutes going through the file before looking up, a pained expression on his face. 'It seems he's not all he claims to be, Inspector. Calls himself a major, does he? Not surprised really. He was a ranker, you know.'

'A ranker, Colonel? But I thought he—'

'Ranker is a term we use for those commissioned from the ranks, Inspector.' Todhunter could not have been more scathing if he had said 'a *derogatory* term'.

'Like General Robertson, you mean?' In the Metropolitan Police everyone rose from the bottom, and Hardcastle wondered why the army should look down its collective noses at a soldier who had done so.

'Not quite,' said Todhunter. 'This fellow was a quartermaster, and in an artisan corps at that.' And he went on to outline Carmichael's service history, the details of which were more or less as Woodhall had recounted. 'But it appears that he got into hot water over some missing stores. Quite a lot of missing stores actually.' The colonel thumbed through a few more pages of the docket before glancing up. 'You must understand that this is all in the strictest confidence, Inspector, but it was strongly suspected that he had sold some foodstuffs from the store he was in charge of and pocketed the proceeds. However, although a court of inquiry found no proof, he was required to resign his commission for not doing his job properly. How on earth he got a job as secretary of Kendall's is a complete mystery.'

'And to me, Colonel, but I shall ask him.'

'Good God, man, you can't do that,' said the appalled Todhunter. 'This is all highly confidential,' he added, tapping the docket to emphasize his point.

'You needn't worry about that, Colonel,' said Hardcastle as he and Marriott stood up. 'You've merely confirmed what I heard from another source.'

'What source was that?' demanded Todhunter, frowning.

'I'm afraid that's highly confidential, Colonel,' said Hardcastle with a smile. 'Good day to you, and thank you for your assistance.'

'Bit snotty, that colonel, sir,' said Marriott as he and Hardcastle left the War Office and turned towards the police station.

'Bloody snob more like,' muttered Hardcastle.

Hardcastle waited until six o'clock before summoning Marriott.

'What's the name of that new detective that's been inflicted on us, Marriott?'

'Kimber, sir. Ted Kimber.'

'Any good, is he?'

'Showed up well when he was out on winter patrol, sir.' Among his other duties, Marriott was responsible for overseeing the young Uniform Branch constables who patrolled in plain clothes before being selected for the CID. 'Good arrest record.'

Hardcastle grunted. 'Fetch him in here then.'

'Sir?' Kimber appeared promptly in the DDI's office.

'You reckon you're a good detective, Kimber?'

'I hope so, sir.'

'So do I, or you won't last long, lad. Now then, I've got a special job for you.'

'Yes, sir.'

'Don't keep saying "Yes, sir", just listen.'

104

Kimber only just prevented himself from saying 'Yes, sir' again.

'Know where Clarges Street is, lad?'

'Turning off Piccadilly between Bolton Street and Half Moon Street, sir,' replied Kimber without hesitation.

'How d'you know that?' Hardcastle asked. 'At Vine Street, were you?'

'No, sir, but I've made it my business to get to know central London.'

Hardcastle gazed at the youngster suspiciously. He did not much care for over-confident detectives. 'Well, you won't get lost then, will you? Now, take a cab to the bottom end of Clarges Street and walk up to number twenty-seven. Knock on the door and if someone answers, make up a name and say you're looking for them, and does the occupant of number twenty-seven know where they lives. Then get another cab and get back here as fast as you can and report. Got that?'

'Yes, sir.' Kimber was completely mystified by this instruction, but knew better than to question his DDI.

'And whatever name you say you're looking for, don't say Carmichael,' said Hardcastle as the young DC hastened from the office.

Half an hour later, the enthusiastic Kimber returned.

'I called at twenty-seven Clarges Street, as directed, sir, and the door was answered by a man probably about fifty years of age. He had iron-grey hair, brushed flat, and a guardee moustache. I asked him if he knew where a Mr Fowler lived, but he said he'd never heard of him, sir.'

'Just what I wanted to hear, Kimber,' said Hardcastle. 'Right, carry on.'

'Good bit of work, sir,' said Marriott when the young detective had left the office.

'He's got the makings has that young lad,' said Hardcastle. 'But there's no need to tell him so. Not yet anyway.'

'Are we going to see the major then, sir?'

'Captain,' said Hardcastle, a stickler for accuracy, 'but I don't know why these people bother. Carmichael's not in the army any more. I mean, coppers don't go around calling themselves "Inspector" or whatever they were, not once they're out of the force, do they? But yes, we are going to see him, Marriott. Should be an interesting little chat.'

105

Twelve

'I reckon this place is worth a bob or two, Marriott,' said Hardcastle as he strode across the pavement to Carmichael's house, and hammered on the front door.

There was a considerable delay before Carmichael opened the door, and to describe his reaction to the arrival of the two detectives as one of surprise would be an understatement.

'Inspector, what on earth—?'

But Hardcastle was equally surprised to see that Carmichael was wearing a full-length silk dressing gown and a pair of extraordinary leather slippers with turned-up, pointed toes.

'We'd like a word with you, Major,' said Hardcastle.

'Er, well, it's not a very opportune moment—'

'It's important . . . and urgent,' said Hardcastle, who had no intention of being balked by some fallacious excuse on Carmichael's part.

'You'd better come in then.' With evident reluctance, Carmichael led the two officers into the sitting room and closed the door. 'Take a seat, gentlemen, and tell me what is so urgent that it can't wait until tomorrow morning.'

'I'm not too happy about you, Major, or should it be "Captain"?' Hardcastle began, having decided to dispense with the niceties that had, hitherto, been a feature of their conversations.

'What the hell d'you mean by that remark, Inspector?' Carmichael demanded fiercely.

'Exactly what I say. You weren't a major at all. You were a captain and, from what I gather, lucky to have got away with not being cashiered.'

'Now look here—'

'It's too late for blustering, Captain Carmichael,' said Hardcastle. 'And I for one don't like being made a monkey

106

of. Ladysmith be damned. The nearest you got to Ladysmith was probably Ladywell in south-east London. I know all about your capers with the food at the supply depot of your old regiment which, I understand, was the Army Service Corps, and not the Steelbacks as you was so fond of calling them.' He paused to glance around the ornately furnished room. 'And I daresay your thieving paid for a lot of this.'

'I shall sue you for slander,' Carmichael said in a low, menacing voice. 'The police aren't exempt from such actions, you know.'

Hardcastle was beginning to enjoy himself. 'To be a slander it's got to be published to a third party,' he said quietly, 'and Marriott here's as deaf as a post when it suits him, aren't you, Marriott?'

'Pardon, sir?' said Marriott.

'That business with the army was all a misunderstanding, Inspector.' Realizing that Hardcastle knew all about him, Carmichael adopted a more conciliatory tone. 'But that's the penalty of command. If one is in charge of something that goes wrong, one has to pay the price. I'm sure that you, as an inspector, fully understand that.'

'And presumably Sir John Webster knows all about your history, does he?'

But before Carmichael could answer, the door opened to reveal a naked Queenie Hicks on the threshold. 'Cuddles darling, what are you—?' But as she moved further into the room and caught sight of the two detectives, she let out a loud scream. 'Oh my Gawd!' she cried, and fled from the room.

'Sorry to have interrupted your little soirée, Captain,' said Hardcastle with just the trace of a smile.

'Now look here,' said Carmichael angrily, 'I don't know what you want, Inspector, but what I do in my own home is my business and nothing to do with you.'

'Quite right,' agreed Hardcastle. 'If your wife don't mind, I certainly don't.'

'I don't have a wife,' said Carmichael curtly.

Ignoring that confirmation of what he already believed, Hardcastle said, 'But it's what you do in that club of yours that interests me. And what you do in St James's Park.'

'And what d'you mean by that?' Carmichael demanded.

'Joseph Briggs found out about your military past, didn't he? And that's why you gave him a job as smoking-room steward. Because if you hadn't, he'd've blown the gaff to Sir John, and you'd've been out on your ear. And by the same token, he worked George Hicks into the club as night porter.'

'They had references from—'

'Come off it, Captain. Those references were as bent as a hairpin, and you knew they were. But you had to hang on to your post as secretary because you knew that you'd never get another job if you was to get tossed out of there. And you would if Briggs had blabbed.'

Carmichael lifted his head to stare wearily at Hardcastle. 'It's true, Inspector, but what did you mean just now when you mentioned St James's Park?'

'Seems to me that if Briggs had put the gas on you once too often, that might be a good reason to top him.'

'Top him? I don't—'

'Don't come it, Carmichael. You came up through the ranks of the army. You know what I'm talking about. Your dandifying might pull the wool over the eyes of them in your precious club, but it don't fool me.'

'I had nothing to do with Briggs's death, Inspector, I assure you.'

'Well, I ain't necessarily satisfied with that, and I shall have to make more enquiries at Kendall's. And I don't want you getting in my way neither.' Hardcastle paused. 'Of course, Captain, anything you might hear about the death of Briggs, you'll pass on to me, won't you?'

'I know nothing about it, Inspector.' Carmichael, disconcerted by Hardcastle's blatant revelations, was now seriously worried that his inglorious military past was about to be revealed to the chairman of Kendall's.

'We'll see about that,' said Hardcastle ominously. 'And now, Captain, we'll leave you to enjoy the rest of your evening.'

Standing on the kerb of Clarges Street, his eye searching for a cab, Hardcastle said, 'Well, Marriott, we certainly pricked his balloon for him, but we didn't learn a great deal.'

'Except that Queenie Hicks is even more of a handsome woman than I first thought, sir.'

Hardcastle smiled. 'Yes, you're right about that, Marriott,' he said.

It was at about a quarter past eleven the following morning that the early-turn station officer entered Hardcastle's office.

'We've just had a telephone call from Kendall's, sir,' said the station-sergeant. 'From someone who calls himself the sergeant-porter. Lucas is his name.'

'What's he want?' asked Hardcastle as he lit his pipe and expelled a plume of smoke.

'Seems that a Major Carmichael's shot hisself in the club, sir, according to this here Lucas.'

'Really?' said Hardcastle mildly. 'Dead, is he?'

'Yes, sir.'

'That'll be guilty knowledge, most likely.'

'I've sent a message for the PC on seven beat to take up post there, sir.'

'Fat lot of good he'll do,' muttered Hardcastle. He stood up and took his bowler hat and umbrella from the hatstand. 'Better go and have a look, I suppose.' And stepping into the corridor, he called for Marriott.

On their arrival at Kendall's, Hardcastle and Marriott were met by a scene of confusion. Several members were gathered in the entrance hall, quietly conversing with each other, and the policeman who had been posted there was talking to Sergeant-porter Lucas.

As the policeman saw Hardcastle, he turned and saluted. 'All correct, sir.'

'Glad you think so,' said Hardcastle, who was always cynical about the requirement that officers should thus report, even when things were manifestly not all correct.

Sir John Webster, the club chairman, detached himself from one little group of members and approached Hardcastle.

'A terrible business, Inspector,' he said.

'Where's the body, Sir John?' Hardcastle asked.

'In his office, Inspector,' said Webster.

Following the chairman through the now familiar smoking room, where more members were whispering to each

109

other, Hardcastle and Marriott stopped on the threshold of the secretary's office.

The body of Carmichael was slumped at its desk, its head on the leather-edged blotter across which a dark pool of blood was spreading. In the secretary's right hand was a revolver.

Moving further into the office, Hardcastle studied the wound on Carmichael's right temple.

'Looks like he put the revolver to his head and pulled the trigger, Marriott,' said Hardcastle.

'Yes, sir.' There were times when Marriott wondered why his DDI so often stated the obvious.

'When was the body discovered, Sir John?' asked Hardcastle.

'It must have been about half an hour ago, Inspector.'

'And who found him?'

'I did.'

'And did anyone hear the shot?'

'Yes, me.'

'Perhaps you'd better start at the beginning, Sir John.'

'It was at about a quarter to eleven, I suppose . . .' Webster broke off. 'Would you care to take a seat, gentlemen,' he said.

'Yes, but not here, Sir John.' Hardcastle turned to Marriott. 'Get that PC in here and tell him to guard the door. Should've been doing that already,' he muttered, half to himself. 'Don't want any nosey parkers popping in here for a cheap thrill.'

The chairman and the two policemen adjourned to another room that Webster said was his own office, and sat down in the comfortable leather armchairs with which it was furnished.

'You were saying, Sir John?'

'I went into Carmichael's office at about a quarter to eleven to speak to him, and he seemed perfectly all right.'

'What did you want to talk to him about, sir?'

'I suppose you know that Austria-Hungary declared war on Serbia today, Inspector . . .'

'No, I didn't know,' said Hardcastle, wondering what that had to do with Carmichael's apparent suicide.

'It almost certainly means there will be a war.'

'I'm sorry, Sir John, I don't quite follow what that has to do—'

'There's a fear in government circles that Germany will

become involved – it's all a matter of treaties, you see – and if that happens the Huns will almost certainly go through Belgium to attack the soft underbelly of France.' Webster ran a hand over his knee. 'And if that happens we will be obliged to go to Belgium's aid.'

'Does all that have something to do with Carmichael's death, Sir John?' asked Hardcastle, weary of this oft-repeated dissertation on the possibility of war.

'Only indirectly, Inspector. You see, many of the members of Kendall's are either serving officers or are on the reserve. If the army is mobilized, they will almost certainly have to join their regiments. The one or two sailors, too. The committee held an emergency meeting last evening, and it was decided that any officer who was required to go to war should have his annual subscription waived for the duration of hostilities, and that's what I wanted to speak to Carmichael about. He has to liaise with the treasurer over such matters. Consequently, I told him that I had something important to discuss with him in my office, sooner rather than later.'

'And what happened then, Sir John?'

'I closed his office door and couldn't have gone more than halfway across the smoking room when I heard the sound of a gunshot coming from his office. I went back and found him exactly as you saw just now. I really have no idea why the poor fellow should have done such a thing.'

'I think I have,' said Hardcastle.

'Oh?'

'Yes, Sir John. You see, Carmichael wasn't all he claimed to be.'

'I hope you're going to elaborate on that, Inspector.'

'The first information about his army service came from an ex-lance-sergeant,' Hardcastle began.

'A lance-sergeant?' exclaimed Webster, 'but surely to God, you don't think that—'

'If you'll let me finish, Sir John . . .' And Hardcastle went on to tell the chairman what he had learned about Carmichael.

'Good grief!' was all that Webster managed to say when the DDI had finished. 'I find that almost impossible to believe.'

'If you need confirmation, Sir John, Colonel Todhunter at the War Office will, I'm sure, provide it,' said Hardcastle, unworried by that snobbish soldier's caveat of confidentiality. 'I presume you didn't take up references?'

'References? Good God, man, one doesn't take up references for an officer. I spoke to a fellow who'd been in the Northamptonshires.'

'And did he know Carmichael?'

'No, as a matter of fact, he didn't. Said something about him probably having been in another battalion, or on detached duty. Something of the sort. But why should that have had anything to do with Carmichael blowing his brains out, what?'

'Sergeant Marriott and me saw Captain Carmichael last evening, Sir John,' said Hardcastle. 'I wanted to know if he was being blackmailed by Briggs who, I found out, knew about his being nearly court-martialled. That's why he took Briggs on, despite him having been chucked out of the fire brigade and dismissed from a brewery for thieving. He was being threatened, see. And he took on Hicks, the night porter, for the same reason.'

'What was wrong with Hicks, for goodness' sake?'

'Ah! Captain Carmichael didn't tell you then. I arrested Hicks last Friday and he's doing three months for stealing spirits from the club. Mind you, Sir John, he'll settle in all right. He's been in prison three times before, once for living off his wife's prostitution.'

'I don't believe it,' said Webster wearily, but he obviously did.

'And all of that would have been a good reason for Carmichael to murder Briggs, you see.'

'Heavens above!' Webster was obviously finding it very difficult to take in all that Hardcastle was telling him. 'One takes on an ex-officer in all good faith, only to discover that the fellow's an out and out rogue.' He shook his head slowly, presumably at his own gullibility in trusting the wily former quartermaster. 'Standards are slipping, Inspector. There's no doubt of that.' He pinched the bridge of his nose. 'D'you really think Carmichael was mixed up in this business with Briggs?'

'It's a possibility I'm still considering, sir. In the meantime, I'll arrange for an officer to take Carmichael's fingerprints.'

'What on earth for?' Webster stared at Hardcastle.

'We recovered the crowbar that was used to kill Briggs, Sir John, and it came from here. There was a fingerprint on it what I have high hopes of matching. If it's Carmichael's, then my case is solved, I reckon.' But even as he said it, Hardcastle was unsure whether that would result in him discovering the murderer of Joseph Briggs.

'But I still don't see why Carmichael should have chosen this morning to kill himself, Inspector.'

'I suppose he thought I'd told you what I'd learned about him, sir, and when you said you wanted to see him urgently, he obviously thought the game was up.'

'Inspector, you've depressed me immeasurably,' said Webster, shaking his head again. 'The secretary, a smoking-room steward and the night porter all turning out to be rogues. Goddammit, are there no principles any more?'

Hardcastle stood up. 'Well, I'd better get on, Sir John,' he said. 'I'll arrange to have the body moved as soon as possible.'

'I suppose there's no way that this can be kept out of the newspapers, is there, Inspector?'

'My job is to keep the King's Peace, Sir John,' said Hardcastle smugly, 'not to control what Fleet Street gets up to. But if what you say about a war turns out to be true, it's likely they won't have much time for the suicide of a tuppenny-ha'penny swindler.'

But that remark did little to comfort Webster. 'I suppose I'll have to start looking for a new secretary now,' he said with a sigh.

'Well, I'd be sure and take up references next time, if I was you, Sir John.'

Detective Inspector Charles Collins, head of the Yard's finger-print bureau, came to Kendall's himself.

'Thought I'd better have a look at this one in person, Ernie, seeing as it's you,' he said.

Hardcastle explained why he had suspicions about Carmichael. 'If you can make a match between his finger-prints and the thumbprint on the crowbar, Charlie, I reckon I might have my man.'

Collins chuckled. 'I'll do my best, Ernie, but if it's not his on the jemmy, I reckon you're up a gum tree.'

Hardcastle nodded. 'I've been up there for quite a time, Charlie, but do your best.'

At four o'clock that afternoon, DI Collins crossed the narrow roadway between New Scotland Yard and Cannon Row police station to tell Hardcastle that his best had not been good enough.

'Sorry to disappoint you, Ernie,' he said, 'but the thumbprint on the crowbar is nothing like your man Carmichael's. There's a composite right in the centre of Carmichael's thumb that definitely rules him out.'

'Thanks anyway, Charlie,' said Hardcastle. 'I'll just have to keep looking, I suppose.'

'Of course, if this war that everyone's talking about gets under way, you might find your murderer will join up just to get away from you.'

'A right bloody Job's comforter you are, Charlie,' said Hardcastle.

When Collins had left, Hardcastle went into the CID office on the other side of the corridor from his own office. 'Anyone seen Catto?' he asked.

Marriott stood up from behind his desk. 'He's still out on observation at Malacca Street, sir. Him and Wilmot.'

'Has he seen anything of Polly Francis yet?'

'Nothing yet, sir, but he has seen one or two men entering and leaving the premises.'

Hardcastle walked over to Marriott's desk and perched himself on the edge. 'One or two men?'

'Yes, sir.' Marriott leaned over and plucked a sheet of paper from a pile. 'About four different men entered – at different times – stayed for about half an hour and then left, sir,' he said, handing the report to Hardcastle.

'I don't believe it, Marriott,' said Hardcastle. 'Don't tell me that Mrs Winston's running a bleedin' knocking-shop an' all.'

'There might be an innocent explanation, sir,' said Marriott.

'Well, I can't think of one. Not if Polly Francis is back there again. However, it's time we had another chat with Queenie Hicks. She's been in Carmichael's house and I'd like to know what she saw when she was in there. Something we might not have seen.'

Thirteen

'What's that new man called, Marriott?'

'D'you mean Kimber, sir?'

'That's him. Where is he?'

'In the office, sir, doing the figures for last month's knock-offs and stops in the street.'

'What, on the twenty-eighth of July? Bit bloody late, but you mark my words, Marriott, the Metropolitan Police will eventually drive itself mad worrying about bloody figures. Anyway, that can wait. Get this Kimber in here.'

At twenty-two, Ted Kimber regarded himself as very fortunate to have been made a detective with less than three years' service. It was even more remarkable that he had done so while serving on A Division, an area not noted for a high incidence of crime.

'You wanted me, sir?'

'D'you know the Rising Sun in Hatfield Street, son?' asked Hardcastle.

'No, sir, but I'll find it.'

'Good,' said Hardcastle. 'Get round there and sit in the saloon bar. I'm sending you because you're new to plain-clothes work and Jed Parsons, the guv'nor, won't know you.'

Kimber appeared somewhat perplexed by this instruction. 'What d'you want me to do when I get there, sir?'

'Nothing, Kimber,' said the DDI. 'Just park your arse in a corner and have a drink. But don't get elephants.'

'*Elephants*, sir?' Kimber raised his eyebrows and began to wonder whether the CID was really all that he had imagined it to be.

'Good God!' exclaimed Hardcastle in mock desperation. 'You'll have to take him in hand, Marriott. It's rhyming slang,

Kimber. Elephant's trunk: drunk. How d'you expect to get on in the Department if you can't speak the lingo?'

'Oh, I see, sir.'

'Now then, there's a pretty young barmaid working there called Queenie Hicks. You won't have no bother identifying her because she's a good-looking doxy with auburn hair. That's right, ain't it, Marriott?'

'Very good-looking, sir,' said Marriott with a grin.

'But mightn't there be more than one girl who looks like her, sir?' asked Kimber, concerned that he should not slip up on this assignment.

'Well, like as not, everyone'll call her Queenie, so you shouldn't have a problem, should you?'

'I suppose not, sir,' said Kimber, who was, in fact, far from clear precisely what he was supposed to do, but thought it unwise at this stage to say so.

'Sergeant Marriott and me want to have a chat with Queenie, see, but not in the boozer. She usually knocks off about six o'clock and goes back to her place in Broadway. Got a flat over the boot makers there. Follow her, discreetly mind, and if that's where she fetches up, I want you to leg it back here and tell me or Sergeant Marriott. And if she don't go there, I want to know where she has gone.'

'Very good, sir.'

'Right then, hop it. And don't get taking a fancy to our Queenie, because she's on the game and she'd have you for breakfast, lad.'

Still mystified by this latest task, Kimber left the office. Far from pursuing dangerous criminals, it seemed to him that all he had done so far, in his short detective career, was to make discreet enquiries regarding the whereabouts of people he presumed were suspects of some sort.

'She might have an appointment with a client some other place, sir,' said Marriott.

'Kimber'll find out if she has, Marriott,' said Hardcastle, 'but it won't be with the late Captain Carmichael, that's a racing certainty.'

At twenty minutes to seven, a breathless DC Kimber returned.

'She's there, sir,' he said.

116

'Who's where, Kimber?' Hardcastle knew exactly who the DC was talking about, but was giving him a sharp reminder that he would not tolerate sloppy reporting.

'Er, Queenie Hicks, sir,' said Kimber, surprised that the DDI did not seem to know what he was talking about.

'Well, say so, lad. You can't expect me to remember what every one of my detectives is doing. I'm in charge of the CID for the whole of A Division. That's a square mile, same as the City police but they've got hundreds more detectives than I have, all kicking their heels up at Old Jewry waiting for a burglar to give himself up.'

'Sorry, sir.'

'And Queenie never caught sight of you tailing her, I hope.'

'Oh no, sir. Definitely not.'

'I hope so.' Not that Hardcastle really cared whether Queenie had spotted Kimber or not, but he was always conscious of the need to train his young officers properly. 'We shall pay her a visit, Marriott,' he said, seizing his hat and umbrella.

Although she had been naked on the last occasion she had met the two detectives, Queenie was far from embarrassed at seeing them again. In fact, she was her usual belligerent self.

'What the bleedin' hell d'you want now?' she asked. But relenting a little, she added, 'I s'pose you'd better come up, then.' And leaving Marriott to close the door, mounted the stairs.

The small sitting room was in no less disarray than it had been the last time Hardcastle and Marriott had called at the Broadway address. Queenie spent a few minutes clearing old newspapers and magazines from the worn chairs, and then took some dirty glasses out to the kitchen.

'What d'you want now, eh?' she demanded again, when eventually she sat down. 'I s'pose because you saw me in the altogether last time, you've come round here in the hopes of getting another glim.'

'We went to Kendall's this morning, Queenie,' said Hardcastle, ignoring the girl's coarse badinage.

'What, again? They'll be making you members soon.'

'How did you know we'd been so often?'

117

'The major told me you was always up there pestering him.'

'What else did he tell you?' Hardcastle hoped that Carmichael had shared other confidences with Queenie in the confines of his bedroom, confidences that might yet lead the police to the killer of Joseph Briggs.

'It's private,' said Queenie demurely.

'Well, you won't be having any more fun and games with the major,' said Hardcastle.

'Watcha mean by that?'

'He's dead.'

'*What?*' Queenie's shoulders slumped and she fell back in her chair, white-faced. 'He can't be.'

'I can assure you he is,' said Hardcastle. 'He blew his brains out in his office at the club. This morning.'

'Whatever did he do a daft thing like that for?' Queenie was clearly having trouble taking in the news of Carmichael's suicide.

'I was hoping you might tell me.' Hardcastle was certain that Carmichael had preferred to take his own life rather than face the consequences of his duplicity. Nevertheless, he still wondered whether there was anything else in the club secretary's past that might point to him being Briggs's killer.

'All I know is that after you come to Clarges Street last night, he weren't the same,' said Queenie. 'Poor old bugger couldn't even get a hard-on. I give it half an hour then I put me duds on and cleared off home.' She let out a deep sigh, presumably at the loss of a generous client. 'I think I could do with a drop of gin,' she said. 'Fancy one, do you?'

'No thanks,' said Hardcastle. 'Did the major' – he saw no point in complicating matters by using Carmichael's correct rank at this stage – 'ever say anything about his time in the army?'

'Nah! Mentioned it once or twice, but he never said anything much.'

'What else did he have to say? Ever mention a wife, did he?'

Queenie looked over her shoulder while she half filled a glass with neat gin. 'What is all this, mister? What him and me talked about is private, like I said.'

'I don't care how long you spent in Carmichael's bed,

Queenie. I'm not interested, and I'm not thinking of doing you for tomming, neither. Not so long as you help me. I'm only interested in who topped Briggs.'

'I told you before, mister, I don't know nothing about what happened to Joe. And I don't see what the major's got to do with it neither.' Queenie sat down and took a mouthful of her gin. 'Cor! That's better,' she said and rested her glass on the arm of her chair.

'I can see I'm going to have to square with you, Queenie, but I don't want you running to Jed Parsons and telling him. What we talk about here is between you, me and Sergeant Marriott. All right?'

Queenie wrinkled her brow, but nodded. 'Yeah, OK.'

'Your major wasn't all he made out to be,' said Hardcastle. 'For a start he was a captain, not a major.'

'They're all the same in the bed,' said Queenie, displaying an earthy wisdom. 'So what?'

'And I think he might have had something to do with Joe Briggs's murder.'

Queenie shot forward in her chair, nearly knocking over her gin. 'I hope you're bloody joking, mister,' she said, alarmed that she might have been sleeping with a murderer.

'It's possible.' But Hardcastle was less convinced of that possibility since receiving DI Collins's report about the thumbprint on the crowbar. He had decided, however, that Queenie Hicks needed to be shocked into imparting confidences.

'Seems like the men you sleep with have a habit of getting killed, Queenie, doesn't it?' said Marriott while the girl was making up her mind.

'That ain't funny,' snapped Queenie, and lapsed into silence again.

'Did he ever mention his wife?' Marriott asked.

'He never had no wife. Leastways, not any more. He said she'd died of the cholera. In India, years ago.'

Hardcastle decided against mentioning that according to the army, Carmichael had never served in India. 'Did he say where all his money came from? That's a handsome house in Clarges Street. Expensively furnished, too.'

'Yeah, it's a smashing place, ain't it,' said Queenie. 'S'matter of fact, he told me once it was family money. He reckoned

119

he'd been left it. He always said as how his old man was a lord, but his ma was a servant girl in some big house in Wiltshire. And this lord had put her in the family way.'

It seemed to Hardcastle that there was no end to Carmichael's fantasizing. 'Did he ever mention Briggs or, for that matter, your husband?'

'Only after Joe got done in. But it was the bother of having to get a new steward what was really vexing him. I suggested George for the job and he said he'd think about it.'

Hardcastle was beginning to believe that Carmichael had not shared any confidences of value with his attractive whore, and decided on another tack. 'This man you met outside Buckingham Palace, Queenie. What did you say his name was?' The DDI pretended not to recall that Queenie had told him he was called Fred Hopkins, a man he now knew to be Horace Davenport.

'I, er, I can't remember now.'

'It was only last Saturday, and you can't remember the name of this man. A man who often came into the Rising Sun and fancied you so much that he took you to a hotel and treated you to a slap-up dinner,' said Hardcastle mockingly.

'All right, so he was called Horry Davenport,' said Queenie, realizing that Hardcastle probably knew anyway, 'and he does live in Broad Street. But he's married, see, and that's why he took me to that posh doss-house in Buckingham Gate.'

'And did he buy you a slap-up dinner?'

'Nah, course not. We went there so's he could have his way with me. He took a room and we done the business.'

'How much did he pay you?'

At first, it looked as though Queenie was not going to tell Hardcastle, but then she said, 'A quid, bleedin' skinflint. Except that he never give me nothing, the tight bastard. He reckoned he'd come out without his wallet, but he said he'd square with me the next time I turned a trick for him, but there won't be no next time, not till he stumps up what he owes. An' I even finished up paying for the bleedin' cab. That's why he give me a lift, I s'pose, so's he could scarper when we got to Broad Street and leave me to pick up the tab.'

'Tell me, Queenie, how did you *really* come to meet this

Davenport? He'd never have set foot in the Rising Sun, not a toff like that, would he?'

'No, course not. Joe Briggs told me that there was a gent at the club who fancied a bit of under, and that I had to meet him outside of Buckingham Palace.'

'And Briggs took a share of what you made, did he?'

'Yeah. Five bob.'

'And the major?'

'Yeah, he fixed me up with him an' all. I never knew he worked at Kendall's though. Not first off. But the old major was a real toff. Always give me a couple of sovereigns, he did. One time he even give me a fiver. Not that I ever told Briggsy. He got his five bob and that was that.'

'And what did your George think about this set-up?' asked Hardcastle.

Queenie scoffed. 'George never give a fig who was poking me.'

'So you're not too bothered about him being locked up.'

'Nah! Far as I'm concerned, he can take a running jump at the moon. He's only interested in knocking out the stuff he thieved from Kendall's.'

'And who did he sell it to?' asked Marriott.

'Anyone as would have it,' said Queenie. 'Jed Parsons took most of it off him though. But for Gawd's sake don't tell him I told you. I'm in enough bleedin' trouble with him as it is.'

'What sort of trouble?' asked Hardcastle.

''Ere, this is between us, ain't it?'

'Of course.'

'Well, it was Jed that fixed me up first of all. Any time one of the customers wanted a bit of jig-jig, he set it up. He's got a room upstairs in the pub that he keeps special. He'd charge 'em a guinea and I'd get fifteen bob. But after you come round and started asking questions, he said we'd have to pack it in. But I told him I needed the money. We had a bit of a barney about it, but in the end he said we'd got to knock it on the head. And now the major's gone I'll be in right straits.'

'Who else was in on this, Queenie?'

'Barbara Burrows, she's the other barmaid, and Polly Francis.'

'So Joe Briggs was pimping for the three of you, was he?' With a sense of gloom, Hardcastle suddenly realized that, as an active procurer, Briggs could have made many enemies. A situation that would widen the field of suspects quite considerably. And the foremost of those could well be Jed Parsons, who had been deprived of his lucrative sideline.

'Yeah,' said Queenie, 'that's how I got fixed up with the major and Horry. But Polly never lived in the pub, not then anyhow. She'd just sit around in the saloon drinking sherry and lemonade, and purring like a tabby. Fancies herself does that one. Any takers she got, she'd cart 'em off to Malacca Street. And make 'em pay for the bleedin' cab, an' all.'

'And what did her landlady think about that?'

Queenie gave a derisive laugh. 'What, Flo Winston? She's been runnin' a whore shop there for ages.'

'And now?'

'Watcha mean, and now?'

'Is she still at it?' Hardcastle was inwardly furious that he had twice visited the house in Malacca Street and had been gulled by the apparently upright Mrs Winston, who now turned out to be a 'madam'. But at least it confirmed what Catto had said about numerous men calling at the house.

'Course she is. I'd've thought you'd have known that, seeing as how you're the big cheese around here.'

From Broadway, Hardcastle and Marriott walked through Caxton Street to the Royal Hotel in Buckingham Gate where, according to Queenie, she and Davenport had indulged in what the girl called 'a bit of jig-jig'.

'I'm interested in a Mr Davenport who took a room here last Saturday evening,' said Hardcastle, once he had introduced himself to the manager, a man named Donaldson.

'May I ask why?' The manager raised his chin slightly, looked down his nose and fingered the lapels of his morning coat.

'I'm investigating a murder,' said Hardcastle, in no mood to be balked by a petty jack-in-office.

'This Mr Davenport's murder?' Donaldson raised his eyebrows.

'No,' said Hardcastle.

'Well then . . .'

Hardcastle took a step closer to the manager. 'I know that

Davenport booked a room here last Saturday, Mr Donaldson, for the sole purpose of entertaining a prostitute. Now in my book that comes precious close to this hotel being a brothel.'

The manager's supercilious attitude vanished instantly. 'Perhaps it would be better if you came into my office, Inspector,' he said hurriedly, as he glanced around the crowded foyer.

'Might be for the best,' said Hardcastle.

'Now then, how can I help?' asked Donaldson, once he was settled behind the barricade of his desk.

'For a start, did a Mr Davenport book a room here last Saturday night?'

The manager rose from his chair and crossed the room. 'We start a new register every month,' he said, as he selected a slim volume from among the many on a bookshelf. Settling himself once more, he thumbed through the book. 'Oh!' he said, when he had found the page that recorded Saturday's bookings.

'Yes or no?' asked Hardcastle.

'It would appear not, Inspector. But there was a man who made a reservation here that evening. Gave the name of Carmichael. Er, unfortunately, he didn't pay his bill.' The manager looked up, frowning at the fact he had been duped.

The trace of a smile lit Hardcastle's face. 'Oh dear, very unfortunate,' he said. 'Run, did he, this Carmichael?'

'It would appear so. He'd booked the room for the night, and the chambermaid reported that the bed had been slept in, but I suppose he just walked out and the clerk didn't notice. If he left on the Saturday evening, it's very busy, what with the theatre crowd coming in for dinner and so forth.' Donaldson closed the register and placed a hand on top of it. 'Is that what you came about, Inspector? I mean it's tantamount to stealing, isn't it?' The manager looked hopeful that Hardcastle might recover his money for him.

'Probably an offence under the Debtors Act of 1869, but only if you can prove he had no *intention* of paying. But if you ever got him to court, he'd probably say he forgot.' From what Queenie Hicks had told him, however, Hardcastle was under no illusion that Davenport had never intended to pay, a fact borne out by his use of Carmichael's name. If it *was* Davenport. But if it was not, then Queenie had been lying and

123

Catto had got it wrong. 'But if you want my advice, Mr Donaldson, I'd put it down to experience. If you go seeking your civil remedy, as we call it in the police, you'll finish up paying more to the lawyers than this welsher owes you. And even then you might not get your cash.'

'I'm not sure that the board of directors would be prepared to accept that course of action, Inspector. It's a matter of principle, d'you see.' Donaldson gazed hopefully at the DDI. 'Do you happen to know where this Carmichael person lives?'

'No, I don't.' Hardcastle had no intention of revealing the true identity of the man who had called himself Carmichael, or of allowing process-servers and bailiffs to get in the way of his enquiries. At least, not until he had delved further into the activities of Mr Horace Davenport, gambler and confidence trickster.

Fourteen

Wednesday started badly for Hardcastle.

'Excuse me, sir.' The station-sergeant was carrying the charge book under his arm as he entered the DDI's office: an ominous sign.

'What is it, Skip?'

'It's Mr Syme, sir.'

'Oh no, not again. What's he been up to this time?'

'Chucked a brick through the window of Number Ten, sir. But there's a memo in the front office that says it's got to be reported to you.'

'Yes, I know,' said Hardcastle wearily.

Ex-Inspector John Syme, having first been reduced to the rank of station-sergeant, had been dismissed from the Metropolitan Police in 1910 for repeated insubordination. But Syme was not the sort of man to take such punishment without demur. Convinced that he had been unfairly treated, he petitioned the Commissioner, his Member of Parliament, the

Home Secretary and the King. And anyone else he could think of. When his intemperate letters brought no result, he began a campaign of malicious damage and, to quote one A Division policeman, 'was rarely seen outside Buckingham Palace without a brick in his hand'. But when he threatened to kill one of his former senior officers, the authorities decided to take action and he was imprisoned for six months.

Undeterred, Syme had carried on, and his arrest this morning was obviously the latest episode in what would prove to be a vain crusade and ultimately result in his confinement in Broadmoor criminal lunatic asylum. However, because of government interest, notably that of the Home Secretary, the Commissioner had ruled that whenever Syme was arrested a report must be sent to him by the DDI of the division concerned. Unfortunately for Hardcastle, that division was usually A Division.

'Let's have the details then.' Hardcastle examined the nib of his pen and dipped it in the inkwell before turning to a blank page in his day book.

The station-sergeant opened the charge book and glanced down at it. 'Sir, on Wednesday the twenty-ninth of July 1914 at eight fifty a.m. at Downing Street, Westminster,' he began, as though giving evidence, 'Syme was seen by the PC on Number Two post. The PC did not immediately recognize Syme, but when Syme drew level with Number Ten he took a brick from his right-hand coat pocket and threw it through the window. The window broke—'

'It would have done if the brick was thrown through it,' said Hardcastle drily, 'unless the window was open.'

'No, sir, the window was closed.' That Hardcastle was being facetious escaped the station-sergeant. 'Damage is estimated at three pounds ten shillings, sir.' He looked up. 'Apparently the brick also hit a table and chipped it, sir.'

Hardcastle sighed and threw down his pen. 'I don't know what he's hoping to achieve, Skip,' he said. 'But all he's doing at the moment is to make frequent appearances at Bow Street.' He looked up. 'I presume he'll be up there this morning.'

'On his way now, sir.'

'Good. Let me know the result.'

'Very good, sir.' The station-sergeant paused. 'Been quite a morning already, sir. A suffragette chained herself to the

125

Palace railings and another one tossed a brick through a Home Office window.'

'Never rains but it pours,' commented Hardcastle and, drawing an official form towards him, dipped his pen in the ink again. In his fastidious copperplate handwriting, he began: '*Commissioner (thro' Divisional Supt A, Chief Constable 1 & Asst Commissioner A Dept). Sir, I have the honour to report that . . .*'

It was nearly eleven o'clock by the time Hardcastle had finished the report for Sir Edward Henry, and he was determined to vent his wrath on somebody. And that somebody happened to be Jed Parsons, licensee of the Rising Sun.

Pocketing the search warrant that Detective Sergeant Wood had earlier obtained from Bow Street police court, Hardcastle summoned Marriott, and the three of them set off for Hatfield Street.

'Ah, Mr Hardcastle.' Jed Parsons glanced nervously at the trio of detectives and sensed immediately that they were not paying a social visit. It was a perception borne out by the DDI's next utterance.

'Jethro Parsons, also known as Jed Parsons, I have a warrant to search these premises,' Hardcastle announced in a loud voice, and was amused to see that the saloon bar emptied with what can only be described as indecent haste.

'What for?' asked the distressed Parsons.

'On suspicion of finding stolen property, harbouring prostitutes and permitting these premises to be used as a brothel.'

'I don't know who's been telling you these lies, Mr Hardcastle.' But Parsons had a very good idea who had informed on him, and was determined that he would have a sharp word with Queenie Hicks. Sooner rather than later.

As if reading the landlord's mind, Hardcastle asked, 'Is Queenie here?'

'No, she sent a boy with a message to say she was sick this morning.'

Hardcastle nodded slowly, thinking what a wise woman Queenie was. After her conversation with the detectives last evening, she must have known that Hardcastle would act on the information she had given him.

'Now then, Mr Parsons,' the DDI continued, gazing at the laden shelf at the back of the bar, 'I'm sure you'll be able to produce invoices to cover your purchase of all that alcohol. But to make it easy, let's start with the Glenlivet. I see you've got a couple of bottles of it there.'

Parsons forced a laugh. 'Well, if that was nicked, Mr Hardcastle,' he said, 'you'll have been drinking some of it, last time you was here.' It was a lame attempt to compromise Hardcastle, but the licensee had seriously underestimated the cunning detective.

'I don't remember drinking any Glenlivet,' said Hardcastle. 'Do you, Marriott?'

'No, sir, definitely not.'

Hardcastle leaned across the bar and seized Parsons by his waistcoat. 'Now you listen very carefully, culley. Last week there was a burglary at an off-licence not far from here, the owner of which was assaulted and a quantity of his alcohol taken. And if I run you in for it, the beak at Rochester Row court is going to believe every word I say. And faster than you can say Jack the Ripper, he'll send you up the road to the Old Bailey where you'll likely cop fourteen years.'

'Here, hold on, guv'nor,' squealed the terrified Parsons. 'I never had nothing to do with that, and you know I never.'

'Do I?' asked Hardcastle, determined to play Parsons along. 'Did you hear that, Marriott? He says he had nothing to do with it.'

'Amazing, sir,' said Marriott.

'All right, so I bought a few bottles from George Hicks, but I never knew it was bent,' said Parsons.

'Right, my lad, you can start by putting all your stolen property on the bar. *Now!*' Hardcastle turned to DS Wood. 'You can list it, Wood, and arrange for it to be taken back to the nick. Then we can have the pleasure of restoring it to Kendall's. That is where it came from, I presume, Parsons?'

'Yes, guv'nor.' The miserable licensee, deciding that honesty was the best policy, began to transfer a few bottles from the shelf to the bar.

'Is that all?' asked Hardcastle, once Parsons had completed his task. 'Just half a dozen?' He gazed sceptically at the six assorted bottles of whisky, brandy and gin. 'If you're trying to come it over Ernie Hardcastle, my lad,' he said, 'you'll live to regret it.'

'That's the lot, guv'nor, I swear,' said Parsons.

'Right. You stay here and guard that little lot, Wood, and Sergeant Marriott and me will take a look round upstairs.'

Followed by Marriott and Parsons, Hardcastle mounted the stairs to the first floor. 'Which is the room your girls use to entertain their clients, Parsons?'

'I don't know what you're talking about, so help me,' said the anguished landlord. 'There's nothing like that goes on here.' He paused. 'All right, it did happen once or twice, but I never knew nothing about it. When I found out, I knocked it on the head a bit sharp. I told the girls I could lose me licence.'

'I think you'll find it's a bit late for that,' said Hardcastle ominously. 'The licensing justices ain't too keen on pubs being used as knocking-shops.'

After a cursory glance at the rooms on the first and second floors, Hardcastle led the other two back to the ground floor, and into the office behind the bar.

'Now then, this is the score,' said the DDI, when all three were seated. 'Joe Briggs was pimping for Queenie Hicks, Barbara Burrows and Polly Francis. And very likely a few more.'

'I never knew that,' said Parsons.

'Just shut up and listen,' said Hardcastle. 'In the process of fixing 'em up with the likes of Carmichael and Davenport from the club, and God knows how many others, he knocked your little trade on the head, didn't he? And the girls were up for it, too. They'd rather go to a decent drum in Clarges Street, or be taken to a posh hotel, than have to put up with a sweaty ten minutes in one of your garrets. Specially when you took a quid off of the customers and gave the girls fifteen bob.'

'This is all lies, Mr Hardcastle.' Parsons was still trying to talk his way out of any responsibility for the activities of his two barmaids and Polly Francis.

'And you didn't like that, did you?' Hardcastle continued to press Parsons. 'So I suggest that you met up with Briggs a fortnight ago in St James's Park and killed him.'

As the enormity of Hardcastle's allegation sank in, rivulets of sweat began to course down Parsons's chalk-white face. 'I never, Mr Hardcastle. I might get up to a few capers, but I don't go in for no topping.'

'And the irony of it is that Briggs was probably the one who gave you the crowbar that did for him. How much did he charge you for it, eh?' But even as he said it, Hardcastle was doubtful that Briggs had stolen the jemmy from Kendall's. And it was even less likely, had he done so, that he would have given it to Parsons. But there was one thing that would decide it. 'I'm taking you to Cannon Row police station now,' said the DDI, 'where your fingerprints will be taken.'

'I don't know nothing about any crowbar, Mr Hardcastle.' In a vain attempt to stop his trembling, Parsons had intertwined his fingers so tightly that the knuckles showed white. 'And that's the God's honest truth. I don't know why you think I done for Joe. All right, he took the girls away, but that ain't worth getting hanged for. So why d'you want me prints?'

'Because I'm charging you with receiving stolen property,' said Hardcastle archly. 'And for allowing licensed premises to be used as a brothel, which you've just admitted. You're nicked.'

It was five o'clock by the time Parsons had been fingerprinted and charged with the two offences for which he had been arrested, and he was bailed to appear at Rochester Row police court the following morning.

'Tell Wood he can take that case to court tomorrow, Marriott,' said Hardcastle dismissively. He had lost interest in the fate of the Rising Sun's licensee after Detective Inspector Collins of the Fingerprint Bureau had told him that the impression of a thumb on the crowbar did not match that which he had taken from Parsons.

First thing on Thursday morning, Hardcastle, accompanied by Marriott, swept into the office of Harry Marsh, the sub-divisional inspector in charge of the area covered by Rochester Row police station.

'You're up bright and early this morning, Ernie,' said Marsh, and acknowledged Marriott with a nod. 'What's eating you?'

'Did you know you'd got a whore-house on your manor,

Harry?' asked Hardcastle. Such information was always passed to the senior officer of the station. It was not unknown for a venal beat constable to tip off brothel-keepers of any sudden police interest in their activities, usually in exchange for a free 'ride', or even a bribe.

'You're not talking about the one in Tachbrook Street, are you?'

'I do know my own bailiwick, Harry. Tachbrook Street's on Gerald Road's ground. No, I'm talking about Malacca Street. But you don't have to worry about the one at the Rising Sun in Hatfield Street. I nicked Jed Parsons last night for receiving, and for running a brothel there.'

'The Rising Sun?' Marsh was furious that the CID had arrested Parsons for an offence that should have been dealt with by his own men.

'I reckon he was thumbing his nose at you, Harry,' said Hardcastle, an amused smile on his face.

'And what's going on in Malacca Street, then?' demanded Marsh crossly. He was extremely irritated that a CID officer had discovered something that he should have found out himself.

Hardcastle outlined what he had learned from Queenie Hicks about Polly Francis's activities. 'Seems that one Mrs Florence Winston is the "abbess" there, Harry.'

'Thank you for letting me know,' said Marsh huffily. 'As you well know, Ernie, the investigation of brothels and prostitution is the responsibility of the Uniform Branch, and what we usually do is keep observation for a week or so to gather evidence.' He sensed that the divisional detective inspector was attempting to rush him into making a decision that he would rather delay.

'I've done that,' said Hardcastle. 'One of my officers – DC Catto, a very capable detective, I may say – has been watching the place. And he's seen various men going in and out at different times of the day. What's more, Harry, the Polly Francis I mentioned just now is someone I need to have an urgent chat with. I think she might be able to shed a bit of light on the murder of Joe Briggs.'

'If that's the case, why don't you just go and nick her?' asked Marsh irritably.

'Because I don't want to spoil anything you might be running.'

'Very kind, I'm sure,' said Marsh, only thinly veiling his sarcasm. 'So what d'you want of me?'

'Me and Marriott's going in there this morning anyway, Harry, and I wondered if you wanted to send some of your lads along with me, otherwise the evidence might disappear, particularly as we've been there twice before. Flo Winston struck me as a shrewd woman, and she might begin to smell a rat. And it ain't often the CID hands you a job on a plate, is it?'

The outcome of Hardcastle's somewhat strained conversation with Sub-Divisional Inspector Marsh was that Marsh had reluctantly sent an inspector, a sergeant and two constables to accompany the DDI and Marriott to Malacca Street.

It was obvious from the expression on her face that Florence Winston was expecting someone other than the police.

'Oh, er, I . . .' she said before lapsing into flustered silence. She glanced over Hardcastle's shoulder at the four uniformed policemen standing behind him.

The Rochester Row inspector, whose name was Glover, stepped forward and flourished an official form. 'I have a warrant to search these premises, madam, issued under the provisions of the Criminal Law Amendment Act of 1885.'

'What on earth does that mean?' asked Florence Winston, folding her arms and adopting an air of bewilderment.

'It means that you are suspected of running a brothel, madam,' said Inspector Glover, tucking the warrant into his tunic pocket. 'Carry on,' he added, turning to his sergeant.

'This is outrageous,' wailed Florence as the first of the uniformed policemen pushed past her.

Hardcastle was not much interested in whether Flo Winston was running a brothel or not. As far as he was concerned such establishments provided a service for those who wanted it, and he saw little harm in it. Unfortunately, as he knew well, brothels and prostitution often attracted other, more serious crimes.

Leaving the Uniforms to get on with the job that was their preserve, as Marsh had somewhat forcefully pointed out to him, Hardcastle turned his attention to Florence Winston. 'Where's Polly Francis, Mrs Winston?'

'She left. I told you that the last time you were here.' Florence tossed her head and primped her hair.

'But she came back, didn't she? So where is she?'

'I don't have the faintest, Inspector. She did come back, but only to pay me what she owed. And she didn't say where she was going after that. I think the poor dear was quite distraught about her fiancé being murdered like that.'

Hardcastle did not think any such thing. From having met the girl, and from what he had heard from Queenie, he was sure that Polly Francis was a conniving little vixen whose only interest in life was her own welfare. And it was always possible that the uniformed men, whose boots could be heard tramping about upstairs, might yet find her in bed with someone. But in that he was disappointed.

Inspector Glover had remained on the ground floor of the house while his men conducted their search. Ten minutes later, his sergeant and the two constables came down the stairs. One of the PCs was holding the arm of a scantily attired young woman, while the other had a firm grip on a man clad in singlet and trousers who was carrying the rest of his clothing over his free arm.

'These two were at it, sir,' said the sergeant to his inspector.

'Got their names, have you?'

'Yes, sir.'

'Are they the only ones you found?' asked Hardcastle. 'No one called Polly Francis?'

'No, sir, these was the only two,' said the sergeant.

'Is there any way my name can be kept out of this, Superintendent?' asked the man, addressing his question to the uniformed inspector.

'I'm an inspector not a superintendent,' said Glover, accustomed to such profitless flattery, 'and whether you are named in court will be a matter for the Rochester Row magistrate.'

Hardcastle stepped closer to the girl. 'What's this one's name, Skipper?' he asked of the Rochester Row sergeant.

'Rose Clarke, sir, with an "E",' said the sergeant.

'Where's Polly Francis, Rose?' Hardcastle asked.

'Dunno,' said the girl. 'Ain't seen her in ages.'

'How long ago is ages?'

'Must be all of three months, I s'pose,' lied Rose. 'But if you want a screw, mister, I'm up for it,' she added cheekily. 'And seeing as how you're a copper, you can have it on the house.'

'That's enough of that, Clarke,' said the PC who was still holding the girl's arm, and steered her towards the front door. But as he opened it, he was confronted by a man standing on the doorstep. The man took one look at the constable, turned and ran as fast as he could.

Thoroughly frustrated by his failure to locate Polly Francis, Hardcastle was not even cheered at Flo Winston's arrest, and he and Marriott adjourned to the Red Lion in Derby Gate for beer and sandwiches.

But worse was to come. When the two detectives returned to Cannon Row, Detective Sergeant Wood was waiting to speak to Hardcastle.

'What is it, Wood? You look as though you've lost a tanner and found a farthing.'

'It's Jed Parsons, sir.'

'What about him?' asked Hardcastle, his eyes narrowing.

'Skipped bail, sir. Never turned up at court this morning. The magistrate's issued a bench warrant for his arrest.'

'Did he have a surety, Wood?'

'Bailed in his own recognizance, sir, in the sum of five pounds.'

'Right, make sure it's put in the *Police Gazette tout de suite*, Wood.' Hardcastle turned to Marriott. 'The bugger's run,' he said, 'and he's risking losing five quid.'

'Must have known he was going to lose his licence, sir,' Marriott observed.

'Licence be buggered. There's more to this than meets the eye, Marriott. Despite what Charlie Collins said about the thumbprint on the jemmy not tallying with the one he took from Parsons, I reckon Parsons is tied up in Briggs's topping somehow.'

'Looks like it, sir,' said Marriott.

'By the way, sir, have you heard the news?' asked DS Wood.

'Don't tell me there's worse to come, Wood.'

'Russia mobilized today, sir. They reckon there's going to be a war.'

'I hope it keeps fine for 'em, Wood,' said Hardcastle caustically, 'but it's nothing to do with us.'

Fifteen

It had been Hardcastle's intention to restore the stolen liquor to Kendall's on Thursday evening, but that could not be done without an order of the court. And as Parsons had failed to answer his bail, the bottles of whisky, brandy and gin would have to remain in the property store at Cannon Row police station until such time as he was arrested and his case heard.

Nevertheless, Hardcastle decided that he would visit the club anyway, if for no better reason than to see if it yet had a new secretary. But, that apart, he was convinced that the answer to Briggs's murder lay somewhere within the walls of Kendall's.

'Good evening, sir.' Sergeant-porter Lucas was in his usual place behind the counter in the entrance hall.

'Is there a new man in Carmichael's office yet, Mr Lucas?' asked Hardcastle.

'Yes indeed, sir. Started the day before yesterday. A very nice gentleman. Well, he would be, seeing as how he's a Jolly.'

'A jolly what?' asked Hardcastle.

'A boot-neck, a Royal Marine, sir, same as what I was.'

'I see,' said Hardcastle, unimpressed by the naval and military argot that the staff of Kendall's were so fond of using.

'Captain Bradford, he's called, sir. I'll get the boy to take you through.'

Robert Bradford, a tall, slender man of about forty, sporting a monocle and a trim moustache, was standing up when the two policemen were shown into his office. Skirting his desk, he held out a hand. 'You must be Inspector Hardcastle,' he said. 'Sit down, my dear fellow, sit down. You too, Sergeant.'

'I've come to see you about the alcohol, Captain Bradford,' Hardcastle began, as he and Marriott took their seats in the familiar leather armchairs.

'Damn good idea, Inspector,' said Bradford, a twinkle in his eye. He struck a brass bell that had not been in evidence on the last occasion Hardcastle had been in the secretary's office. 'Don't keep a dog and bark yourself, eh what?'

Within seconds, Wilson, the head smoking-room steward, appeared in the doorway. 'Yes, sir?'

'Glenlivet for these gentlemen, large ones mind, and the usual brandy and ginger ale for me.'

'Very good, sir,' said Wilson.

'I know what you chaps drink, you see,' said Bradford. 'Made it my business to find out what's what around here, the minute I arrived. Not that I expect to be here for very long.'

'Is it a temporary appointment then?' Hardcastle asked.

'Probably,' said Bradford. 'Looks as though I retired from the Royals at just the wrong moment. There's going to be a war, you see. I'm certain of it. And if there is, their Lordships of Admiralty will have me back in uniform in a trice.'

'D'you think there really will be a war, Captain?'

'Yes, I do. And so do half the old codgers in there.' Bradford waved a disparaging hand in the direction of the smoking room. 'Not that it'll affect them much. Too damned old.'

Wilson returned, bearing the drinks on a silver salver.

'Your good health, Inspector.' Once the steward had departed, Bradford raised his glass. 'Yours too, Sergeant.'

'And yours.' Hardcastle had been quite taken aback by Bradford's affable approach, and was certain that if the ex-Royal Marine captain learned anything about Briggs's murder he would be sure to tell him.

'Now then, Inspector, you mentioned something about alcohol just now,' Bradford said, becoming serious. He opened a silver cigarette box emblazoned with the crest of the Royal Marines and offered it to Hardcastle.

'No thanks, I'm a pipe man.'

'Splendid! Carry on.' Bradford pushed the cigarette box in Marriott's direction. 'You were saying, Inspector,' he said as he lit a cigarette.

'Yesterday, I arrested a man called Jed Parsons, the licensee of the Rising Sun public house in Hatfield Street, for receiving stolen property.' Hardcastle began filling his pipe as he spoke.

'Good for you, old man,' said Bradford.

'And I took possession of six bottles of spirits. Two of Glenlivet, two of Courvoisier cognac and two of Gordon's gin. Parsons admitted that it all came from Kendall's, and he also admitted receiving it from the former night porter here, a man named Hicks, who's now doing three months hard labour for stealing some of it.'

'Ah yes, I heard all about that,' said Bradford. 'It was only allowed to happen because that scoundrel Carmichael wasn't keeping a close eye on things, but now we know why. The trouble was that no one else was too concerned with what he was up to either. I had a longish chat with the chairman and persuaded him to have an audit done, and it seems that Carmichael had his hand in the till. To quite an extent it turns out. Several hundred pounds are unaccounted for, and God knows the last time they did any sort of stocktaking. I reckon there are a lot more than your six bottles adrift. Of course, all of that will change now.'

'But how did it happen in the first place?' asked Hardcastle. 'Didn't *anyone* do any checking up?'

Bradford scoffed. 'What, here? Good God, no. The committee was blinded by the old officer-and-gentleman notion. They reckoned that because Carmichael had held a commission, his conduct would be beyond reproach. Well, I can tell you this much, Inspector, there are a few rogues among the commissioned ranks of both the army and the navy. But not the Royal Marines,' he added with a laugh.

'Not that any of that concerns me, of course, Captain,' said Hardcastle. 'Obviously the club can't bring charges against the deceased Captain Carmichael, but there might be some others involved.'

'Ah, I see you found out that Carmichael wasn't a major, then,' said Bradford.

'So did Briggs, him what was murdered, and that's why Briggs was able to do as he liked here. And Briggs got Hicks a job too, even though he'd been in prison three times before.'

'Good God Almighty!' exclaimed Bradford. 'What a bloody mess. I didn't know any of that, Inspector.' He stubbed out his cigarette in a brass ashtray. 'But you suggested there were some others involved.'

'When I arrested Hicks, he said three others were stealing, and mentioned the head steward, Wilson – the chap who came in just now – Barnes and Sergeant-porter Lucas, but that may have been spite on Hicks's part because he was unlucky enough to get himself nicked.'

'Maybe, but I wouldn't be surprised if there were a few more rogues here,' said the ex-Royal Marine pensively, 'and I'm not only talking about the staff. Anyway, thanks for the tip, Inspector. I shall certainly keep a weather-eye lifting. What this place really needs is a sergeant-major,' he muttered as an afterthought.

'Of course, my only concern is the murder of Joseph Briggs,' said Hardcastle, and went on to relate what he knew so far, including how the missing crowbar was last seen in Captain Leighton's room, and that Leighton had claimed to have thrown it into the corridor.

'Mmm! Leighton, yes, Madras Light Infantry,' said Bradford, in such a way that Hardcastle surmised he was not much impressed with Leighton or his regiment. 'I'll keep my ear to the ground, Inspector, and if I learn anything, you'll be the first to know.' He paused. 'In fact, you'll be the *only* one to know.'

'We also know that Briggs was procuring women for at least two members of Kendall's, Captain.'

'Was he, by Jove?' Bradford smiled. 'Who were they?'

'Carmichael was one,' said Hardcastle, taking a sip of his whisky, 'and the other was Horace Davenport. There could have been more, I suppose, but all of that's between you and me.'

'Of course, my dear fellow,' murmured Bradford as he stroked his moustache. 'I've only been here forty-eight hours, Inspector, but I've learned quite a lot in that time. Can't beat a bit of intelligence work before you start chucking your weight about. Davenport, eh? Bit of an odd fellow is that one.'

'In what way?' asked Hardcastle, his interest aroused.

'Short of cash, don't you know. Always playing cards but,

from what I hear, not often winning. And he's run up quite a bar bill. Not the done thing. Don't know why Carmichael didn't have a word in his ear.' Bradford raised an eyebrow. 'You interested in the chap, then?'

'I'm interested in everyone until they're eliminated, Captain.' And so far, Hardcastle thought, they were doing a good job of eliminating themselves. Carmichael and Briggs were dead, Jed Parsons had run, and Polly Francis seemed to be making a determined effort not to be found.

An air of tension seemed to pervade the whole of Whitehall on Friday, and rumours were rife about the increasing possibility of war.

On the corner of Parliament Square, a placard announced that Russia had mobilized, and the boy selling the *Evening Standard* was handing them out as fast as he could take a news-hungry public's money. More officers were entering and leaving the Admiralty and the War Office than Hardcastle could recall ever having seen before. And, following the end of a trial mobilization, the fleet had been kept at Portland, its dispersal peremptorily halted the previous Sunday by the First Sea Lord. It was a decision promptly supported by the First Lord of the Admiralty, a rising politician named Winston Churchill.

'Beginning to look as though you might be right about a war, Marriott,' said Hardcastle when he arrived at the office. 'But we've still got a murder to solve.'

'D'you think it could've been down to Carmichael, sir,' asked Marriott, 'despite the thumbprint not having been his? He seems to have had a good reason for topping Briggs, what with him putting the pressure on Carmichael over his dodgy background.'

'I'd thought of that,' said Hardcastle, 'but why? Carmichael must've known that Briggs would never blow the gaff or there'd be no more profit in it for him.'

'Yes, but maybe Carmichael was fed up with being buggered about by Briggs, sir, and decided to put a stop to it once and for all.'

'You might be right, Marriott, but I'm more interested in Jed Parsons. I still can't work out why he run. I reckon the most he'd've got was a month in clink. Maybe even a fine. No, there's more to that fellow than meets the eye. He's got something to say, you mark my words, and that little trollop Polly Francis will have to do some smart talking when we manage to lay hands on her.' Hardcastle stood up. 'But right now, I think we'll pay a visit to that upstanding gentleman Mr Horace Davenport. See if we can't shake the ghost into him.'

'But what about, sir?'

'How about an unpaid bill at the Royal Hotel in Buckingham Gate, eh, Marriott?'

Hardcastle had to knock several times before the door of 17 Broad Street was eventually opened. And then, to his surprise, it was not a maid who appeared, but an elegantly dressed woman who, Hardcastle surmised, was in her mid-thirties.

'Yes?' Even more strange was that the woman opened the door only a fraction, as if expecting unwelcome visitors.

'I'm looking for Mr Horace Davenport, madam,' said Hardcastle. 'I'm a police officer.'

'He's not at home.' But the woman's lie was immediately negated by a male voice asking who was at the door. 'Oh, you'd better come in,' she said resignedly.

Horace Davenport was a dapper man in his early forties, a shade over five feet eight inches in height, and wearing a grey, single-breasted lounge suit in a light worsted cloth. But Hardcastle's quick glance of appraisal noted that it was show-ing signs of wear, particularly at the cuffs and turn-ups. And he wondered if Mrs Davenport's furtive reaction to his arrival was because she was expecting a debt collector.

'I'm Divisional Detective Inspector Hardcastle of the Whitehall Division,' Hardcastle announced, 'and this is Detective Sergeant Marriott.'

'Ah, I've heard your name mentioned at Kendall's, Inspector,' said Davenport, as he conducted the two police-men into the drawing room and invited them to take a seat. 'Aren't you investigating the murder of that poor fellow who worked there?'

'Joseph Briggs,' said Hardcastle. 'That I am, sir, and I'm wondering if you can assist me. It's a complicated business 'and my most recent enquiries have taken me to the Royal Hotel in Buckingham Gate.' He was not at all interested in helping Donaldson, the manager of the Royal, to recover the money owed to him, but that statement would, he hoped, have the effect of unnerving Davenport.

And as Hardcastle had anticipated, it immediately caused concern to register on Davenport's face. 'Well, I don't know anything about that,' he said hurriedly, and turned to his wife. 'I doubt that you'll be interested in all this, my dear,' he said. 'But perhaps the inspector would like a cup of tea.'

'Thank you, very kind, I'm sure,' murmured Hardcastle. There was nothing that he wanted less at the moment than a cup of tea, but he recognized the device as a means of excluding Mrs Davenport from the conversation. He had been tempted, impishly, to say that he did not want any tea, but realized that he was likely to get more from Davenport if the man's wife was absent from the room.

'It's the maid's day off today,' said Davenport without conviction.

'Information has been laid,' Hardcastle began portentously, as if legal proceedings had already begun, 'that last Saturday evening, the twenty-fifth of July, a man fitting your description took a room at the Royal Hotel in Buckingham Gate. That man later left without paying.'

Davenport puffed himself up with indignation. 'If I may say so, Inspector, that is a scurrilous allegation. Why on earth should you imagine it was me? I shall institute proceedings for defamation the moment I see my solicitor. Who told you this?'

'The prostitute who was with you at the hotel, Mr Davenport,' said Hardcastle quietly, 'and who later gave me your name and address. She's not too happy with you. Apart from welshing on the hotel, it seems you never paid her the dues you owed her, and she got saddled with paying the cab an' all. It's no wonder she peached on you.'

'Oh God!' Davenport leaned forward and covered his face with his hands. He stayed like that for a moment or two before recovering and looking up again. 'Leaving the hotel without paying was an oversight, Inspector,' he said lamely.

'Was using the name Carmichael an oversight too, Mr

Davenport?' asked Marriott, at last entering into the conversation.

'What are you talking about?' snapped Davenport, seeming to notice Marriott for the first time.

'We've interviewed the manager of the hotel and the dolly who was with you, and they both came up with the same tale.' Marriott relaxed against the cushions of the sofa. 'Except that the girl told us that you claimed to have forgotten your wallet.'

'Well, I *had* forgotten it,' said Davenport, rapidly clutching at that rather unstable straw.

'I was rather surprised to find you at home of a Friday morning, Mr Davenport. Don't you work?'

'I own a small manufacturing company, Inspector,' said Davenport, his tone lightening at the change in the conversation. 'It's based in Surbiton. Up and coming place, Surbiton, you know. Of course, Kingston refused to have the main-line railway running through it, but Surbiton accepted with alacrity.' He gabbled on, doubtless hoping that the return of his wife would stem any further embarrassing questions.

Hardcastle stood up. 'I daresay we'll need to talk to you again at some time, sir,' he said. 'But if I were you, I'd settle up with the Royal Hotel before they start proceedings. But more important, I should think, would be to pay the young lady you was with last Saturday. You see, sir, they usually have men who look out for them, so to speak, and they can cut up a bit rough if their girls don't get their money.' At the door to the drawing room, he paused. 'Do apologize to your lady wife that we wasn't able to stay for tea.'

'That's given him a dose of the shakes, I wouldn't wonder, Marriott,' said Hardcastle as they walked towards Carnaby Street in search of a cab.

'Reckon he had something to do with Briggs's death, sir?'

'You know me, Marriott, never cross anyone off my list, but I think he's just a loser. All that old madam about it being the maid's day off. I don't reckon they've got a maid. And notice his suit, did you? No, he's skint. Too much playing pontoon down the club has cleaned him out, and that's why he's run up a bar bill, like as not. But he's still trying to keep up appearances. Anyway, I think I'll have him watched for a bit. Put Catto on it, and that new chap.'

'Kimber, sir?'

'Kimber, yes, that's the fellow.' Hardcastle waved his umbrella at a passing cab. 'New Scotland Yard, cabbie,' he said. 'Tell 'em Cannon Row and half the time you'll finish up at Cannon Street in the City, Marriott.'

'Yes, I know, sir,' said Marriott wearily.

By the time Hardcastle and Marriott reached the police station, the newsboys' placards had changed yet again. And this time, the boys were shouting it aloud: '*Grave crisis. Austria mobilizes. Cabinet meets to discuss Belgium – official.*'

To Marriott's astonishment, Hardcastle announced that he was having an early night, and told him to do the same.

'I'm taking Mrs H. to the theatre, Marriott.'

'Anything good, sir?'

'I hope so,' said Hardcastle. 'It's something called *Pygmalion* at His Majesty's.'

'Oh, I've heard that's very good, sir. It's by Bernard Shaw, the Irish playwright. Mrs Patrick Campbell's in it.'

Hardcastle grunted an acknowledgement. He was not very keen on the theatre himself, but had bowed to Alice Hardcastle's oft-expressed desire to 'have supper up west and see a good play'.

'I'll see you in the morning then, Marriott.'

'Very good, sir.'

'And my respects to Mrs Marriott.'

'Thank you, sir.'

During the interval of the play which, Hardcastle had to admit, he found entertaining, he and Alice adjourned to the crush bar for a drink. It was just as Hardcastle was taking the head off a rather inferior glass of beer that he spotted Horace Davenport on the other side of the room.

Davenport was in the company of a very attractive woman, elegantly attired in a gold brocade dress, her hair exquisitely coifed, high on her head. The woman's swanlike neck was encircled by a string of pearls.

Alice Hardcastle's gaze followed that of her husband. 'She

won't have paid less than four pounds for that dress, Ernie,' she said.

'I wasn't looking at her so much as him, Lally. I called at his house today in connection with this murder I'm looking into. And that woman over there ain't the wife he had when I saw him this morning. And knowing what I know about him, she likely paid for the tickets an' all.'

Sixteen

When Hardcastle arrived at the police station on Saturday morning, his first act was to send for Catto and Kimber.

'You know Horace Davenport, don't you, Catto? The man who went to the Royal Hotel last Saturday with a prostitute. You followed him back to his place in Broad Street.'

'Yes, sir.'

'Right. You and Kimber get yourselves up there this evening—' Hardcastle paused. 'No, on second thoughts, get up there straight away. Horace Davenport has got a fancy woman and I want—'

'D'you mean Queenie Hicks, sir?' asked Catto unwisely.

'No, I don't mean Queenie Hicks, Catto,' said Hardcastle sharply. 'He welshed on her last time and she won't be falling for it again. I'm talking about the woman he was with last night at the theatre. All dolled up like the barber's cat, she was. And she ain't his wife Rose, because I've met her. So, wherever Davenport goes, you go an' all, the pair of you. Got it?'

'Yes, sir,' said Catto as he and Kimber turned to leave.

'I haven't finished yet, Catto. If he meets up with this woman, I want you to follow her and find out who she is and where she lives.' Hardcastle gave the detectives a detailed description of the woman he had seen at His Majesty's Theatre the previous evening, and finished with his customary threat: 'And if Davenport or his bit of fluff spots you, I'll have your guts for garters. Both of you.'

'Yes, sir,' chorused the two detectives.

Once Catto and Kimber had left, Hardcastle crossed to the main CID room. 'Wood, a moment of your time,' he said, beckoning to the sergeant who was sitting at the far end.

Detective Sergeant Wood followed Hardcastle back to his office.

'Yes, sir?'

'Yesterday morning, Wood, me and Sergeant Marriott had a bit of a chat with Horace Davenport at his place in Broad Street. He gave me some cock and bull yarn about owning some sort of factory in Surbiton. Know where Surbiton is?'

'Yes, sir.'

'Good. Well, get down there a bit *tout de suite* and see what you can find out about this business of his. And on your way out,' continued Hardcastle, implying that Wood should waste no time in carrying out his enquiry, 'tell Sergeant Marriott to come in when he's free.'

'He's out at the moment, sir, but I'll leave word you want to see him.'

'Where's he gone?'

'Wellington Barracks, sir.'

'What in blue blazes is he doing there? I know he thinks there's going to be a war, but he ain't gone to join up, I hope.'

'No, sir.' Wood smiled. 'Something to do with a man claiming to be a Grenadier officer who got arrested in Windsor last night, sir. Seems he was a con man, but the Berkshire Constabulary want enquiries made.'

It was gone noon when Marriott reported to Hardcastle.

'Sorted out your Grenadier, Marriott?'

'Yes, sir, they'd never heard of him. Seems this bloke was trying it on at one of the hotels. Usual old tale. Reckoned he'd forgotten his money, but as he was an officer in the Guards, et cetera . . .'

Hardcastle laughed. 'Name wasn't Davenport by any chance, was it?'

'No, sir,' said Marriott. 'By the way, how was the theatre last night, sir? Did you and Mrs H. enjoy the play?'

'Yes, not bad, Marriott, not bad, but not as interesting as what happened in the interval.' And Hardcastle related how he had seen Davenport in the company of a woman who was not his wife. 'I've put Catto and Kimber on to it, and I've sent Wood down to Surbiton to see if he can find this factory of Davenport's. If it exists.'

'D'you fancy Davenport for this topping, sir?'

'You know me, Marriott, I reckon everyone till I've ruled 'em out,' said Hardcastle, not for the first time.

'Incidentally, have you heard that Germany's declared war on Russia, sir?' Marriott asked. 'Caused a bit of a stir in the City, by all accounts.'

'What sort of a stir, Marriott? Bit of a riot, is it? All gone mad up there, have they?' Hardcastle remained sceptical about the possibility of war, despite the majority of the population now believing it to be inevitable. In fact, far from being dismayed by the prospect, some of the more bellicose Britons seemed to be welcoming the opportunity of joining up 'to give the Hun a bloody nose'. On several occasions over the past few days, policemen from Cannon Row police station had been forced to scatter crowds outside Buckingham Palace vociferously demanding war with Germany.

'Just another excuse for milling it with the police, I suppose, sir,' said Marriott. And with the Royal Palaces, Parliament, Downing Street, Whitehall and Trafalgar Square all lying within A Division's boundaries, its officers were more than familiar with demonstrating mobs. 'There's a rumour going round that the bank rate's gone up to ten per cent, too,' he continued, 'and someone said the Stock Exchange has shut its doors.'

'All my eye and Betty Martin,' exclaimed Hardcastle dismissively.

'They're saying there's a queue a mile long outside the Bank of England in Threadneedle Street, sir, all demanding gold in exchange for their banknotes.'

'They'll be lucky,' said Hardcastle with a scornful laugh.

'That they will, sir,' said Marriott. 'They're not only refusing, but the bank's issuing pound notes instead of sovereigns, and there's talk of them printing a ten-shilling note, too.'

'It's all panic, Marriott. Nothing will come of it, you mark my words.'

But something did come of it. Three days later, Great Britain was plunged into a war of attrition that was to last four years and a hundred days, a war that would leave over eight million dead, and more than twenty million wounded.

Even so tough a taskmaster as Hardcastle was surprised at the speed with which Sergeant Wood and Detective Constables Catto and Kimber completed the tasks that had been set them. Wood was the first to report.

'This factory of Davenport's, sir,' he began.

'What about it?'

'Don't exist, sir, at least not any more. I made a few enquiries at the local nick and it seems that Davenport stopped trading there about two months ago.' Wood grinned. 'On account of it having burned down, sir. Well, sort of.'

'Oh dear!' said Hardcastle. 'What did he do at this factory of his?'

'He was in business making concertinas. Sold 'em at about two pounds each.'

Hardcastle let out a derisory laugh. 'He don't seem like the sort of cove who'd be making squeeze-boxes to me, Wood. Don't exactly fit in with his image, I'd've thought. So what happened?'

'The tale is that he was getting undercut by the Germans, sir. Apparently you can get a half-decent German concertina in Gamages for about ten bob. And so he went out of business. But shortly after that, his factory caught fire and burned down. The local gossip is that the insurance company refused to pay out. They reckon it wasn't accidental.'

'Can't say I'm surprised, Wood. Are the local CID looking into this suspicious fire, then?'

'They did make a few enquiries, sir, but they couldn't find anything that would point to Davenport having started it.'

'They ain't looking hard enough,' grumbled Hardcastle.

'Anyway, sir, it's between Davenport and the insurers now.'

'Looks like our Mr Davenport ain't having a lot of luck lately, don't it, Wood?' said Hardcastle with a laugh. 'Did I hear Catto's dulcet tones in the corridor just now?'

'Yes, sir. Shall I send him in?'

'Yes, him and Kimber if he's there.'

*　　　*　　　*

146

'Why are you standing there looking like the cat who got the canary, Catto?'

'We found out who she is, sir.' Catto was unable to restrain his pleasure.

'I should hope you have. Out with it, then.'

'About half after midday, sir, er . . .' Mindful of Hardcastle's previous caveat about accurate reporting, Catto paused to consult his pocket book. 'At thirty-three minutes past twelve, sir—'

'Never mind all that mumbo-jumbo, Catto. Get on with it.'

'Yes, sir,' said Catto, now more confused than ever. 'Well, sir, Davenport come out of seventeen Broad Street and went to Kettner's Restaurant in Romilly Street. He walked all the way, sir,' he added in plaintive tones.

'Don't know what you're complaining about, Catto. It ain't much of a stride, and anyway you get a boot allowance. So what happened then?'

'He had lunch, sir.'

Hardcastle raised his eyes to the tobacco-stained ceiling before looking at Catto again. 'Are you going to get to the bottom of this, lad?' He glanced at Kimber. 'Were you there an' all, Kimber?'

'Yes, sir,' said Kimber.

'Well, perhaps you'd better tell the tale.' Hardcastle reached for his pipe. He had a feeling that these two young detectives were going to take some time to spin out their report.

'I went into the restaurant, sir, and asked the head waiter if I could book a table for that evening. While he was writing down my name—'

'You didn't give him your *own* name, did you?' demanded an incredulous Hardcastle.

'No, sir, I gave him a false name. Anyway, while he was putting it in the book, I had a glance across the restaurant. Our man Davenport was in one of those booths they've got there. What the French call *cabinets particuliers*, sir.'

'Don't get clever with me, Kimber.'

'No, sir, sorry, sir. Well, anyway, Davenport was with a woman fitting the description you gave us this morning. And very lovey-dovey they were too. Their heads were close together and they were holding hands.'

'Yes, all right, Kimber, I think I can picture the scene.'

'After they'd finished lunch, sir, Davenport walked back to Broad Street with Henry Catto in tow. The woman hailed a cab and I followed. She paid off the cab in Draycott Place and entered number ten, sir.'

'So who is she, Kimber? Find that out, did you?'

'Yes, sir, I knocked at the door.'

'You did *what*? I told you both not to be seen by Davenport or the woman.' Hardcastle glanced at Catto. 'And you can take that smirk off of your face an' all, Catto. You're the senior man.'

'But I wasn't there, sir,' wailed Catto, the smile vanishing instantly.

'Don't make no difference in my book,' muttered Hardcastle. 'Get on with it, Kimber.'

'Oh, she didn't know I'd been following her, sir. I told her I was a Chelsea police officer and spun her a bit of Fanny Adams about burglars working the neighbourhood and that sort of thing. And to allay any suspicion on her part, I called at one or two other houses, just in case she got chatting to the neighbours. Anyhow, she turned out to be a very friendly woman and she invited me in for a cup of tea.'

'God Almighty!' Hardcastle was beginning to wonder whether he had done the right thing in letting this callow young detective undertake what he had believed was to be a simple observation.

'She told me her name was Veronica Groves and that her husband, who wasn't there at the time, was Major Henry Groves. He's something to do with the army at the Duke of York's Headquarters in King's Road, sir, so she said.'

'Well, I'll go to the foot of our stairs!' exclaimed Hardcastle. 'What sort of house was this one in Draycott Place?'

'Looked expensive, sir, but then it is quite close to Sloane Square. As for Mrs Groves, she's a very attractive woman, and the dress she was wearing must have cost a pretty penny. I should think there's quite a bit of money there. And she was worried about her husband's motor car, too.'

'Car? What car? Why was she worried about it?'

'Well, thinking I was interested in local burglaries and the like, sir, she told me that her husband always parked it in the street. I think she thought it might get stolen. Apparently it's a De Dion Bouton – a French job, sir – and she bought it for him for Christmas.'

'Did she, indeed? I can see I'll have to have a word in Mrs Hardcastle's ear,' muttered the DDI before adding a rare word of praise. 'Good bit of work, Kimber. We'll make a detective of you yet. Now bugger off, the pair of you, and ask Sergeant Marriott to come in.'

'Did they have any luck, sir?' asked Marriott, closing the door of the DDI's office.

'That young Kimber's coming on a treat, Marriott. It turns out that Davenport's fancy woman is the wife of Major Henry Groves. There, what d'you think about that?'

'Wasn't he one of those who was in the smoking room at Kendall's the night of Briggs's murder, sir?'

'It'll be a bit of a bloody coincidence if he ain't the same, Marriott. I doubt we'd have two Major Henry Groveses knocking about in this investigation.'

'But does it have anything to do with Briggs's murder, sir?'

'I don't know, Marriott, but it seems a bit odd. Every way we turn, we fetch up back at Kendall's.'

'Yes, but that is where Briggs worked, after all, sir.'

Hardcastle stood up, knocked out his pipe in the ashtray and reached for his bowler hat and umbrella. 'Well, there's bugger-all more we can do tonight, so I reckon we'll have an early night. See you on Monday.'

'Er, Monday's a bank holiday, sir,' Marriott said hesitantly, wondering whether Hardcastle intended to work through it.

'So it is, Marriott, so it is. In that case I'll see you on Tuesday. Unless something crops up in the meantime.'

Sunday followed the usual pattern of all Hardcastle Sundays. The only variation concerned Gerald Plover, Kitty Hardcastle's latest 'crush' – who worked in her office and whom Hardcastle had condemned as a feckless youth.

Tearfully, Kitty complained that he should have been taking her for a walk that afternoon, but, as a member of the Territorial Force, had been mobilized and ordered to report to his local drill hall. There he had been handed three shillings advance of pay and a railway warrant to the Royal Engineers depot at Chatham.

149

Kitty never saw Gerald Plover again. A week later he was in France. One month later he was dead.

All week, Alice Hardcastle had been badgering her husband to take the family to the August Bank Holiday fair on Hampstead Heath. Hardcastle, however, was in no mood for a long bus journey on one of his rare days off.

'I'm staying put, Lally,' he said. 'With all that's going on, I might get called back to the station.'

'Well, if you're not here, they can't call you, can they, Ernie?' said the frustrated Alice. 'We never seem to go out these days, and the way things is going on, it might be quite a while before we ever do again. I mean, if young Gerald's been called back, they must be taking it serious.'

But even though Kitty, Maud and young Walter – especially young Walter – sided with their mother, Hardcastle would not be moved from his decision.

And in a sense, Hardcastle was proved right. Just before midday the following day, he was surprised to hear the shout of a newsboy outside the house. It was unusual for the evening paper to be published that early in the day, especially on a Bank Holiday Monday.

'Oi!' shouted Hardcastle as he sped into the street. 'Let's have one of those, lad.'

The newsboy turned. 'Special edition, guv'nor,' he said, and pulled a copy of *The Star* from beneath his arm.

Hardcastle took it and handed the boy a penny.

'Ain't got no change, mister.'

'Don't try that on with me, lad.' Hardcastle took back the penny and gave the boy a halfpenny. 'There, now you'll have change for your next customer, won't you?' he said.

Scanning the paper as he went back indoors, he was amazed at the news it contained.

'Has something happened?' asked Mrs Hardcastle innocently, expecting to hear of some great tragedy, and recalling how the loss of the *Titanic* had gripped the nation only two years previously.

'Looks like it, Lally,' said Hardcastle, still reading the paper as he sat down in his armchair. 'Germany's invaded Luxembourg. The Royal Navy and the Territorial Force has been mobilized. Well, we knew that,' he said, glancing up. 'Kitty told us. It seems that that scoundrel Keir Hardie's been stirring things up with a so-called peace rally on Trafalgar Square, so it says here. And the traffic's been held up in Whitehall by crowds waiting for news from Ten Downing Street.' He folded the paper and handed it to his wife. 'That'll mean a load of pickpockets in the charge room, very likely.'

'Can't you ever think of anything but your wretched police force?' said Alice, turning the pages to see what her stars foretold.

'That wretched police force, as you call it, my girl,' said Hardcastle, 'is what puts the food on our table.'

'That settles it,' said Alice curtly. 'If there's going to be a war, me and the children's going to the fair on Hampstead Heath.' Despite their ages, she still referred to them as children. 'It might be the last chance we get for a bit of fun. And if you want to sit here and sulk, Ernest Hardcastle, that's your business.'

Hardcastle had been persuaded by the events of the past two days finally to join the majority view that war was coming, and arrived at his office earlier than usual on the Tuesday morning.

Marriott was waiting outside his chief's office. 'It's on, sir,' he said excitedly.

'What's on, Marriott?' asked Hardcastle irritably. 'I had to fight my way through a bloody mob to get into the nick just now. I don't know what the Uniforms think they're doing. It's a damned disgrace. If it had happened when I was a PC, the guv'nor we had then would have played merry hell.'

'It's war, sir,' said Marriott.

'So I've heard,' said Hardcastle drily, as he hung up his bowler hat and umbrella. 'But the British Army's the finest in the world. They'll soon sort the buggers out.'

'The government sent an ultimatum to the Germans last night telling them to withdraw from Belgium, or else,' Marriott continued, refusing to be deprived of sharing his momentous news. 'But they didn't, so the King's issued a proclamation and we've declared war on the Hun.' He seemed almost pleased.

But then so did a lot of others. It was only later, when the first terrible casualty figures started to filter through, that the awful truth of what war actually meant began to register. For the time being, there was a widely held belief that it would all be over by Christmas.

'That's all very well, Marriott,' said Hardcastle, 'but we're getting bogged down with this murder. If we don't get our skates on, all our suspects will be on their way to join the army. The station officer was just telling me that there's a queue outside the recruiting office in Great Scotland Yard that stretches round the corner and halfway up Whitehall.'

'Polly Francis got herself nicked last night, sir.'

'Why the hell didn't you tell me before, Marriott? That's a sight more important than all this war nonsense. Where?'

'Swallow Street, sir.'

'Cheeky little hussy,' said Hardcastle. 'Just round the corner from the nick. Hawking her mutton was she?'

'Not exactly, sir. She got nicked for attempted larceny of a watch from a gent who thought she was up for it.'

'Court?' asked Hardcastle tersely.

'Great Marlborough Street this morning, ten o'clock, sir.'

Seventeen

The entrance hall of the court at Great Marlborough Street was crowded, the hubbub of conversation dominated by that day's declaration of war. But Hardcastle and Marriott made their way swiftly through the mass to the door, guarded by a policeman, that led to the warrant office at the end of the cell passage.

'Polly Francis, Sergeant,' Hardcastle said, having first told the man who he was.

The warrant officer glanced at the register that would soon make its way into the courtroom. 'Attempted larceny, Swallow Street, sir,' he said, looking up.

'Where's the arresting officer?' asked Marriott.

'In the corridor, sir. I'll get him for you.'

The policeman who had arrested Polly was in his forties and wore Boer War medal ribbons on his tunic. 'PC Ford, 127 C Division, sir, attached to Vine Street,' he said.

'This knock-off of yours, Ford. Polly Francis. Much in it?'

'It was just after eleven o'clock last night, sir. I'd come out of the nick and was walking through Swallow Street to take up my beat in Regent Street. I saw this gent in conversation with Francis – she was obviously whoring, sir – but when he spotted me, he shouted something like "She's trying to steal my watch, Constable". So I arrested her, sir.'

'What about the man? Here this morning, is he?'

'No, sir. Said he wanted to leave it to the police.'

'Pleading, is she?' What Hardcastle meant, and the PC understood, was whether she intended to plead guilty.

'No, sir. She said she was going for a not guilty. Her story is that he'd started talking to her and wanted to get his end away. But I s'pose that when he saw me, he changed his tune and give me this tale about his watch.'

'Well, don't try too hard, Ford. I fancy her in connection with a murder and I'd rather have her out than doing time in Holloway. All right?'

'Anything you say, sir. Personally, I think it's a bit thin anyway.'

'What court are you in?'

'Number One, sir.'

Hardcastle and Marriott next made their way to the chambers of the magistrate who was to try Polly Francis.

'Good morning, Mr Hardcastle.' The magistrate beamed at the DDI. 'Don't often see you here these days.'

'Indeed not, sir,' said Hardcastle.

'Is it a warrant you're wanting?' The magistrate gazed expectantly at the two detectives.

'A little more delicate than that, sir, in a manner of speaking.'

'What then?' The magistrate took out his watch and glanced at it, implying that he would shortly be taking his seat in Number One Court.

'The case of Polly Francis, sir. Arrested last night in Swallow Street. Attempted larceny of a watch.'

'I'll have to take your word for it,' said the magistrate. 'I haven't seen the register yet. Anyhow, what about her?'

Hardcastle explained as briefly as possible about the murder of Joseph Briggs. 'I think she might well be involved, sir, if not as the actual murderess, certainly as a material witness.'

'Yes, that's all very well, Inspector, but it has nothing to do with the charge before the court, does it?'

'No, sir, but I think she might have vital information, and if you could see your way clear to not giving her a custodial sentence, so to speak, it would help me greatly in my enquiries not to have her in Holloway.'

The magistrate smiled. 'I'll see what I can do, Mr Hardcastle. Is she entering a plea, do you know?'

'I understand from the arresting officer that she means to plead not guilty, sir.'

'That should make it easier to arrange then, Inspector,' said the magistrate.

Polly Francis did indeed enter a plea of not guilty. Following the intentionally lukewarm evidence of PC Ford, the magistrate found the case 'not proved', and acquitted her. But in so doing, he emphasized that no fault could be ascribed to the arresting officer. 'The constable had no alternative but to act upon the complaint he had received,' he said. 'But the complainant,' he added acerbically, 'chose not to attend court to give evidence. And without it, I am ill-disposed to convict.'

However, Polly Francis's jubilation at her acquittal quickly turned to dismay when she was confronted by Hardcastle and Marriott in the echoing antechamber of the court. Quickly realizing that there was nowhere to run, she smiled weakly. 'Oh, hello, Inspector,' she said.

'Ah, so you remember me,' said Hardcastle. 'You and me's going to have a little chat, my girl.'

'What about?' Polly glanced around furtively.

'About Joe Briggs. Who did you think I was talking about, the Kaiser?'

'Well, I ain't got no time now.'

'You can either come to Cannon Row police station with Sergeant Marriott and me, nice and quiet, or I'll nick you and *take* you there in a Black Annie. It's up to you.'

154

With a sigh, Polly allowed herself to be escorted out to the street where Hardcastle hailed a cab.

'Where have you been since you quit Flo Winston's whore-house, Polly?' asked Hardcastle, once the three of them were settled in the interview room at the police station.

'Round and about.'

Hardcastle leaned forward. 'Ever done time, Polly?' he asked, well knowing that she had only one previous convic-tion, and that for the minor offence of soliciting prostitution.

'No, course I ain't.'

'Well, if you carry on coming the old madam with me, you're likely to cop some bird-lime in Holloway,' said Hardcastle. 'The lady screws up there would love to get their hands on a pretty young thing like you, I can tell you.'

'Here, for Christ's sake,' squealed Polly. She had heard about the harridans who staffed the notorious women's prison in North London, and what they got up to with the young girls in their charge. 'I ain't done nothing wrong. That geezer what reckoned I was trying to nick his watch was after a bit of fanny. But the minute he spied that copper he starts holler-ing I was trying to nick his kettle. Like as not he's got a missus some place and didn't want to get nicked hisself.'

'I'm not talking about you trying to pinch a watch,' said Hardcastle. 'Anyway, you got away with it.'

'I should bleedin' think so, an' all,' protested Polly.

'No, my girl, I'm thinking more of you maybe topping Joe Briggs.'

'For Gawd's sake, mister, you don't think I had anything to do with that, do you?' Polly stared at Hardcastle, white-faced. She had heard stories about unscrupulous policemen putting innocent people in prison. 'We was going to get spliced, me and Joe.'

'So you said, Polly, so you said.' Hardcastle pushed a sheet of paper towards the girl. 'How's your handwriting?'

'Here, what is all this?'

Reaching into his inside pocket, Hardcastle withdrew the screwed-up letter that Marriott had found under Briggs's bed in his room at the Rising Sun. 'Write this down, Polly.' He handed the girl a pencil and began to dictate. '"I know what

155

your game is, so you'd better come across with the cash or you know what'll happen.'"

Laboriously, and licking the pencil several times, Polly Francis did as Hardcastle told her.

When she had finished, Hardcastle took the sheet of paper and studied it before pushing it, and the letter, along the table to Marriott. 'What d'you think?' he asked. 'The same?'

It took only the briefest of glances for Marriott to agree. 'It's the same hand, sir, without a doubt,' he said.

'Right, my girl,' said Hardcastle sternly. 'You're in a lot of trouble.'

'Watcha mean? I ain't done nothing.'

'This letter' – Hardcastle tapped the one found in Briggs's room – 'was written by you. So who was you blackmailing, eh? Joe Briggs, was it?'

'No, course not. Like I said, we was—'

'Save it, Polly. You were on the game and Joe was pimping for you. And that's it and all about it. You were no more going to marry him than you were going to get wed to Sergeant Marriott here.'

Polly cast a yearning eye in Marriott's direction. 'Chance'd be a fine thing,' she said impishly. 'But I was never blackmailing no one.'

'How come you wrote this letter then?'

'It was for Joe.'

'What d'you mean, it was for Joe? And I'm warning you, Polly, I don't want any more lies.'

'Joe was putting the black on someone, and he got me to write the letters, see. He said as how if he wrote 'em, they might get recognized.'

'So how come this one was found screwed up in Joe's room at the Rising Sun?'

'He didn't like it. Wanted to change the words, see. So he screwed that one up and chucked it on the floor. Then he made me write another one.'

'And who was he sending these letters to?'

'I dunno. He wouldn't never tell me.'

'How many did you write altogether?'

Polly gave the question some thought before answering. 'About five, I s'pose,' she said eventually.

'Did he say why he wrote them, or why he got you to write them?'

'I told you that, mister. He was putting the black on someone.'

'Yes, but what for? Was it money?'

'Oh, I see. Yeah. So he said.'

'And how much was he copping for this little game of his?'

'Dunno. He wouldn't tell me that neither.'

'But he gave you some money for your trouble, didn't he?'

'Yeah. He give me a sovereign or two from time to time.'

'For writing the letters?'

'Yeah, course.'

'Well, that makes you as guilty as Joe. And blackmail can score you fourteen years in chokey.'

Polly began to shake, and her face drained of colour yet again. 'But I never knew what he was up to.'

'You just said you did.'

'But he said that if I never done what he asked, he'd stripe me. Or worse. Honest, mister, I was scared stiff of him.'

Hardcastle thought that was probably true. 'You never worked at the Albert in Victoria Street, did you, Polly?'

'Yeah, I—'

'It's no good lying, my girl. I know the guv'nor there, and he's never heard of you. What's more, if he ever comes across you, he's likely to get a bit nasty that you was going about saying he let you use his rooms for screwing. That'd make him a brothel-keeper, see, and he could lose his licence. Not very pleased with you at all, he ain't.'

Polly stared at Hardcastle but said nothing.

'So why were you hanging about in Palmer Street next to the Albert the night Joe was killed?'

'I was waiting to meet someone.'

'But it wasn't Joe Briggs, was it?'

'No.'

'So who was it? Major Carmichael?'

'Who's that?'

'Come off it, Polly,' said Marriott. 'A week ago last Saturday you spent four hours in his house at twenty-seven Clarges Street.'

'So what?'

'So, what were you doing hanging about outside the Albert at eleven o'clock on the night Joe Briggs was murdered?'

'Joe had fixed me up,' said Polly miserably.

'Who with?'

'A gent from the club.'

'And did he turn up, this mysterious man?'

'Nah, he never showed up.'

'What was his name, this man you were supposed to meet?'

Polly was clearly agonizing over whether to reveal the name of one of her clients, and there was a long pause before she answered. But eventually she did. 'He was called Henry,' she said. 'Henry Groves.'

Concealing his surprise at this latest twist, but only with difficulty, Hardcastle asked, 'Had you seen this man Groves before?'

'Yeah, couple of times.'

'And where did you go with him?'

'He'd got rooms across the road at Artillery Mansions. We'd meet outside the Albert, up the side, like I said, and then he'd sneak me into his place. He had to watch out in case the porter was still about, see.'

'Never mind the porter,' said Hardcastle. 'What about his wife?'

'Henry reckoned she never knew nothing about that place. He's got a house some place else where he lives with her.'

'And presumably you spent the night with him?' Marriott put in.

'Yeah, course. Well, there ain't nothing wrong in that, is there?' Polly demanded truculently.

'Was it always that late at night, when you met him?'

'Yeah. He had a wife, see.' Polly smiled at Marriott. 'Well, most of 'em have, but she was away them nights.'

While Marriott had been talking to the young prostitute, Hardcastle had been thinking over the implications of Groves's association with Polly Francis and Briggs's part in it. 'Did you ever talk to this Groves about Joe?' he asked.

'Yeah, sometimes.'

'And did you tell him you were scared of Briggs?'

'I might've done.' Polly was plainly reluctant to discuss her pimp, even though he was now dead.

'And what did Groves have to say about it?'

'Nothing much, but he seemed a bit cross that I was getting treated that way.'

'D'you think it was Groves who Briggs was blackmailing?'

'I dunno, mister. Like I said, Joe never told me who he was sending the letters to.'

'Where are you living now, Polly?' Hardcastle asked.

'I ain't saying.' It appeared that Polly Francis still had a little spirit left.

'You can either tell me, my girl,' said Hardcastle, 'or I'll lock you up here until I've found Joe Briggs's killer.'

'Perkins Rents, opposite the Elephant pub.'

'Right, well, just to make sure, I'll send you back there with one of my officers. I suppose Jed Parsons ain't there, by any chance, is he?'

'No, he ain't.'

'Any idea where he's run to?'

'No, and I don't give a fig neither.'

'D'you know why he's run?'

There was a further pause while Polly thought over the implications of informing on Parsons. But eventually she yielded.

'You know when you turned over the pub, the day you nicked him?'

'What about it?'

'Well, you never went down the cellar.'

'And what would I have found if I had?'

'He's a fence. He's got all sorts of nicked stuff down there. Been at it for years.'

Once DC Wilmot had returned to Cannon Row and reported that Polly Francis was indeed living in a room over a shop in Perkins Rents – and that there was no sign of Parsons having been there – Hardcastle announced his intention of speaking to Major Henry Groves. And of doing so at the Duke of York's Headquarters in King's Road, Chelsea.

In peacetime, the gate of the barracks had been guarded by a soldier attired in a red tunic, blue trousers and a regimental dress-cap, and with a cane tucked beneath his left arm. But now, with the outbreak of war, he had been replaced by a sentry in khaki service dress, complete with puttees, rifle and fixed bayonet.

'Must be expecting an invasion,' muttered Hardcastle as he and Marriott approached the gate.

The youthful sentry stepped in front of the two detectives and swung his rifle to the high port. 'Halt, who goes there?' he demanded.

The DDI smiled at the soldier's strict adherence to his orders. 'Divisional Detective Inspector Hardcastle, Metropolitan Police,' he said.

'Report to the guardroom, sir,' said the sentry, resuming his former position.

After some form filling, and a certain amount of stamping and shouting on the part of the military, Hardcastle and Marriott were eventually escorted to the office occupied by Major Henry Groves.

Groves, immaculate in uniform, a crown at each cuff, was studying a wall map when the two detectives were shown in.

'And what can I do for you, gentlemen?' he enquired, once Hardcastle had introduced himself. He waved a hand at some hard-backed chairs. 'Some soldier in trouble, is he?'

'You're a member of Kendall's, I believe, Major,' said Hardcastle.

'Yes, but what's that got to do with—?'

'I'm investigating the murder of Joseph Briggs, and I understand that you were in the club on the night he was killed.'

'I'm in the club most evenings, Inspector,' said Groves curtly.

'Was Briggs blackmailing you?' Hardcastle had decided that there was little point in wasting his time or Groves's in skirting around the issue.

'What a preposterous suggestion. Do you imagine for one moment that a club servant employed by Kendall's would do such a thing, or get away with it if he did? In any case, what could he possibly want to blackmail me about?'

'Polly Francis,' said Hardcastle, and was pleased to see a distinct tightening of Groves's jaw muscles.

'What on earth are you talking about, man?' Groves glanced around the office, his eyes darting everywhere but upon Hardcastle's face.

'I'm told you met her on several occasions by the Albert pub in Victoria Street and took her to your rooms at Artillery Mansions where she stayed the night.'

Placing a hand on the corner of his desk, Groves sank into his chair, a stunned look on his face. 'I've never heard such tommy-rot.'

Hardcastle deliberately let out an audible sigh. 'Major, I don't have time to waste, and I don't suppose you do neither, what with the war an' all, but since I started this investigation, I've had all sorts of people followed. And Polly Francis was one of 'em.' He had no intention of telling Groves that it was Polly herself who had told the police about her trysts with the major.

Groves leaned across his desk and took a cigarette from a box, but did not offer it to either of the policemen. 'I don't really see what that has to do with the murder of Briggs,' he said eventually, gazing at Hardcastle through a haze of smoke.

'Perhaps you don't, Major, but I do. Polly Francis wasn't the only one Briggs was pimping for, and you weren't her only client, neither. Nor was you the only member of Kendall's taking advantage of Briggs's whores.'

Groves wrinkled his nose at Hardcastle's distasteful description of the woman with whom he had shared a bed, even though he knew that was all she was. 'What d'you mean by that?'

'What I mean, Major, is that Polly Francis wasn't only having a screw with you, she was doing it with Carmichael.'

'What, the club secretary?'

'Yes,' said Hardcastle, 'or the late club secretary to be precise.'

'Good God!' Groves's shoulders slumped, presumably at the revelation that he had shared Polly's favours with, of all people, a *quartermaster* officer. Since Carmichael's suicide, his scurrilous background had become common gossip in the club.

'Now, if I can get back to what I come here to talk to you about, was Briggs putting the black on you?' asked Hardcastle again.

'Certainly not. Why on earth should he do that? I've no skeletons in my cupboard, Inspector, no secrets to hide.'

161

'What about your wife?'

'My *wife*?' Groves seemed startled by the question.

'Don't take me for a plodding fool, Major Groves. Yes, your wife Veronica who lives with you at ten Draycott Place, not far from here.'

'Have you been following me, Inspector?' demanded Groves indignantly.

'Why should I do that?' asked Hardcastle, thinking it unnecessary to explain that it was the major's wife who had been tailed.

'Well, I must say you seem to know a lot about me.'

'I know a lot about the members of Kendall's, Major, and I ain't too happy about what I've learned of some of 'em.'

Groves was now unsure just how much Hardcastle did know. 'I suppose I'd better come clean, Inspector,' he said with a sigh, 'although I'm damned if I know how it will help you find the murderer of this man Briggs.'

'I'd be obliged if you was to let me be the judge of that, Major.'

'My wife and I tend to live separate lives, Inspector. She goes her way and I go mine, if you see what I mean.'

'Yes, I think I do.'

'We continue to live under the same roof, but the army rather frowns on its officers getting divorced.'

'Am I to take it that while you're giving Polly Francis a seeing-to, your wife's out on the town herself?'

Groves frowned. As one more accustomed to the euphemisms of the officers' mess, he found Hardcastle's directness disconcerting. 'I suppose that sums it up, Inspector,' he said.

'To get back to the night Briggs was murdered. I was told that you was in the smoking room with Lord Slade, Colonel Fitzpatrick and the chairman, Sir John Webster. And that you left at one o'clock in the morning and went to Sir John's flat in Albany where you stayed until about ten past two. Is that correct?'

'Absolutely, Inspector. I must congratulate you on your recall.'

'It's not that clever, Major,' said Hardcastle, 'I wrote it down. But did anyone else join you?'

162

'Er, yes, I believe Horry Davenport came in at about half past eleven. Mumbled something about having had a bad night at cards, sat down and had a drink.'

'And what time did he leave?'

'I've no idea, Inspector. I didn't see the going of him.'

Hardcastle stood up. 'Thank you, Major,' he said. 'I may have to speak to you again at some time.'

'You'd better be quick, Inspector,' said Groves with a satisfied laugh, 'we're under orders to embark for France. Probably as early as this coming Friday.'

'Well, Marriott, we didn't learn much we didn't know already.'

'Telling the truth, was he, sir? About not being blackmailed, I mean.'

'Buggered if I know, Marriott. Probably not. If Briggs had fixed Groves up with Polly, knowing that he'd got a missus, he could've been blacking him. What Groves was saying about his missus and him going their separate ways could all have been eyewash. They're all devious buggers these Kendall's folk, and Briggs could've had a nice little racket going there. Pick a married bloke in the club, fix him up with a bit of crackling and then put the black on.' Hardcastle paused to chuckle. 'But I'm wondering who's getting the best end of the deal between Major Groves and his missus. Polly Francis is probably the better tumble out of the two.'

'Yes, sir, but Veronica Groves is the one with the money, so I reckon it's Horace Davenport.'

Eighteen

'If Groves didn't turn up for his meeting with Polly Francis, sir,' said Marriott as he and Hardcastle approached Kendall's, 'it means that either of them could have done for Briggs.'

Hardcastle shook his head. 'You're forgetting that Groves

was with Slade, Webster and Fitzpatrick that night, Marriott,' he said. 'But Polly Francis don't have an alibi.'

'Then why did she tell us she was outside the Albert between eleven and half past, sir? She could have said she was anywhere. Jed Parsons for one would've lied for her.'

'Unless she *did* do for Briggs, Marriott, but wanted to lay it on Groves. For all we know, the major could have got one of Briggs's threatening letters and told her about it. But she wasn't to know that Groves was at the club that night with three other witnesses of standing.'

As they entered the clubhouse, Sergeant-porter Lucas looked up. 'If you're wanting Captain Bradford, sir, he's gone,' he said.

'Gone? Gone where?'

'Been recalled to the Colours, sir. Left for Pompey this morning. Captain Reilly's gone too. And I daresay there'll be a few others before the week's out.'

'Who's the secretary now, then?'

'We haven't got one, sir. The chairman's looking after anything that has to be done in that regard.'

'No matter,' said Hardcastle. 'It's you I wanted to talk to, Mr Lucas. Who deals with the mail when it arrives here?'

'I do, sir. We have six deliveries a day, the first one at six in the morning – George Hicks used to look after that one, of course – and the last is at about half past seven in the evening. And I put the letters in this rack here.' Lucas pointed to a stylish mahogany framework of pigeon-holes behind his counter. 'And I hands 'em to the members as they come in.'

Producing the letter he had found in Briggs's room, Hardcastle smoothed it out and placed it on the counter. 'Have a look at that, Mr Lucas.'

The sergeant-porter studied the letter closely and let out a low whistle. 'Blimey, that's a bit strong, sir. Who got that?'

'I was hoping you might tell me,' said Hardcastle.

Lucas looked up, an expression of alarm on his face. 'I don't know nothing about that, sir.'

'I'm not suggesting you do, but have you ever seen any writing like that on the envelopes of letters that arrived here?' Hardcastle knew that Briggs had taken the trouble to get Polly to write the letters in order not to compromise himself and, despite her denial, assumed that she had addressed the envelopes as well.

Running a hand round his chin, Lucas pondered the question for a few moments. 'Come to think of it, sir, I might've done. At least, up to about a fortnight ago. There was one or two for Major Groves, and about three for Mr Davenport. Oh, and Mr Hunt got some and so did Mr Dawson.'

'When did these letters start coming, Mr Lucas? Can you remember that?'

Lucas pursed his lips. 'As far as I can recall, about six months ago. Then they was spread over, like.'

'Well, for a start, I'll need to speak to Hunt and Dawson,' said Hardcastle. 'Wouldn't happen to be here at the moment, would they?'

'I don't think so, sir, but if you have a word with Sir John, he might be able to help.'

'Where is he?'

'He's probably in the secretary's office at the moment,' said Lucas. 'Go on through.'

'Where's your lad?' asked Hardcastle, looking around the lobby for the page-boy who was usually stationed there.

'Went up the Tower of London this morning, sir, put his age up and enlisted in the Royal Fusiliers.'

When Hardcastle and Marriott entered the secretary's office, Sir John Webster was sitting behind the desk once occupied by Clive Carmichael and latterly by Captain Bradford.

'Ah, Inspector.' Webster stood up and shook hands with the two detectives. 'Not looking for a job by any chance, are you?' he asked with a smile. 'We're in desperate need of a new secretary.'

'I'm a bit busy at the moment, Sir John.' Hardcastle smiled too. 'Still trying to find who killed Briggs.'

Webster waved the two policemen to chairs. 'One of many,' he said gloomily.

'One of many?' echoed Hardcastle.

'There's going to be a lot more killed before this war's finished, Inspector. All this silly talk about it being over by Christmas is nonsense. When you've been in the army, as I have, you know damned well that fighting's a tough, slow business. Costly, too, in terms of lives. And this war's going to be long and hard. It'll be years not months before we beat the Hun, I can assure you of that.'

'Yes, well, be that as it may, sir, I still have to find Briggs's murderer. Or murderess.'

Sir John stared at Hardcastle with a penetrating gaze. 'You think it might have been a woman?' he asked.

'It's a possibility I'm considering, Sir John. I'm far from satisfied that I should only be looking at a man. However, there are two of your members that I need to speak to.'

'Who are they?'

Hardcastle glanced down at his pocket book. 'Messrs Hunt and Dawson.'

'What, in connection with the murder?' There was good reason for Webster not wanting to believe that Hardcastle was concentrating on members of Kendall's as possible suspects.

Hardcastle extracted the letter from his pocket. 'When we searched Briggs's room at the Rising Sun public house, we found this, Sir John,' he said, handing it to the chairman.

Webster clipped his pince-nez to his nose and adjusted them slightly before studying the document. 'What on earth does it mean, Inspector?' he asked, handing it back. 'What does it have to do with Kendall's?'

'I believe that at least four members of this club received letters like this,' said Hardcastle, as he returned it to his pocket. 'And that's a very good reason for one of them murdering whoever sent them.'

'Good God Almighty!' exclaimed Webster, leaning forward and sweeping off his pince-nez. 'But why? Why should someone want to threaten anyone here? And *who* would do such a thing?'

'The last is easy to answer, Sir John. We know who was sending them. It was Briggs.'

'I don't believe it,' muttered Webster, but it was more a pious hope than a reflection of his true feeling. 'Why would Briggs do a thing like that?'

'He was a pimp,' said Hardcastle bluntly.

'A what, Inspector? I'm sorry, I don't quite—'

'I mean he was controlling a small number of prostitutes, Sir John. And as far as I can see, he was fixing up certain of your members – but only the married ones – with these girls, and then blackmailing them, probably threatening to tell their wives. Or even to tell you, I suppose, thinking that a scandal of that sort would get 'em expelled from the club.'

'Damn right it would,' said Webster vehemently. 'My God, what a disgraceful business. And you think that Hunt and Dawson might be involved?'

'Not only Hunt and Dawson, Sir John, but Major Groves and Mr Davenport, too.'

'But how do you know?'

'I've been speaking to Lucas and he tells me that over a period of time letters of that sort have been arriving at the club for those four, and that he's fairly sure that the handwriting on the envelopes matches the writing in the letter I just showed you.'

Webster appeared relieved by that. 'But that's rather tenuous, surely, Inspector.'

'Possibly, sir, yes,' said Hardcastle, 'but it's something Sergeant Marriott and me's obliged to follow up.'

'Of course, of course,' murmured Webster. 'I just hope you're wrong though.'

'If I may speak in confidence, Sir John . . .?' Hardcastle raised an eyebrow.

'Certainly you may, Inspector.'

'It's already been confirmed to my satisfaction that Major Groves is conducting an affair with a prostitute who I know was put in touch with him by Briggs—'

'Hell and tommy!' exclaimed Webster. 'Henry Groves? Surely not. He's one of my closest friends, Inspector. In fact, he's a frequent visitor to my place at Albany. Well, I told you that he was there the night of Briggs's murder. He couldn't possibly have had anything to do with it.' The chairman shook his head in disbelief. 'But carrying on with a prostitute. He's got a lovely wife, you know. Veronica Groves is a most attractive girl. Been here on ladies' nights, too,' he added, as though that, of itself, was a warranty of impeccable conduct on her husband's part.

'That marriage ain't all it might seem, Sir John. According to my officers, Mrs Groves appears to be carrying on an affair with Mr Davenport. In fact, I saw the two of them myself at His Majesty's Theatre last Friday evening.'

Sir John Webster appeared to have exhausted his stock of

expletives and, saying nothing, leaned back in his chair and gazed at the ceiling.

But just as he thought that there could be nothing more damaging to emerge, Hardcastle added to his anguish. 'I also have reason to believe that Davenport is fast approaching bankruptcy.'

'What?' Webster sat up sharply.

Hardcastle repeated what he had learned from Captain Bradford about Davenport's outstanding bar bill.

'Yes, I know about that, but what else is there?' asked Webster, devoutly hoping that there would not be any more.

Hardcastle recounted what Wood had learned about the collapse of Davenport's concertina business at Surbiton.

'D'you mean the damned man was engaged in trade?' That revelation appeared to upset the chairman more than the suggestion that members of Kendall's were consorting with women of doubtful repute. Or even that they were allowing it to become public knowledge.

'It appears so, Sir John.'

'*Concertinas!*' Webster shook his head. He could not recall ever having met anyone who manufactured concertinas. And to discover that such a man was a member of his own club was just too much for him to stomach. 'How the hell did he secure membership, I wonder? I shall have to look into that, see who put him up.' He looked directly at Hardcastle. 'There'll have to be an extraordinary general meeting,' he said. 'The fellow will have to go.'

'I'd rather you left that until I've finished my enquiries, Sir John.'

For a moment, Webster looked as though he might refuse, but then he nodded. 'Very well, Inspector. So be it.'

'My immediate job is to get in touch with Hunt and Dawson, Sir John. I'd be obliged if you'd give me their addresses.'

'It's not the policy of the club to—'

'We're talking about a murder here, Sir John,' said Hardcastle firmly. 'Either I see them at their homes or I post uniformed officers here until they arrive, and then I arrest them and take them in for questioning.'

The prospect of the unwelcome publicity that would be generated by such a course of action, on top of what he had just learned, was too much for Webster. He rose from his chair and took the register of members from the top of a low cupboard. Quickly scribbling down the details on a slip of paper, he handed it over.

'One other thing that may be of interest to you, Sir John,' said Marriott, while Hardcastle was studying the addresses of Hunt and Dawson, 'Carmichael—'

'Don't talk to me about that rogue,' snapped Webster. 'I'm not likely to forget what your inspector told me about the man's disreputable background. Damned if I know how the wretched fellow was taken on. My predecessor appointed him, you know. Dead now, of course,' he added, as though that had been some condign punishment for inefficiency imposed by the Almighty.

Marriott smiled. 'I was going to say that Carmichael was also taking advantage of at least two of Briggs's whores.'

'For once, I'm not surprised, Sergeant,' Webster said.

'Hunt lives in Weymouth Street, Marriott, off of Portland Place, and this fellow Dawson's got a place in Eccleston Mews.' Hardcastle sighed and glanced at his watch as they left the club. 'I s'pose this evening's the best time to pay 'em a visit.'

'What about their wives, sir?' asked Marriott.

'That's their problem, Marriott,' said Hardcastle scornfully.

'I wondered when you chaps would show up,' said Geoffrey Hunt, as he invited Hardcastle and Marriott into his drawing room. 'I suppose it's about that rascal Briggs.'

'Yes, sir, it is,' said Hardcastle, gazing enviously at the room's rich furnishings.

'Fire away then, although I don't know how I can help you.'

Once again, Hardcastle produced the letter found in Briggs's room at the Rising Sun. 'Have you ever received a letter like this, Mr Hunt?' he asked.

Hunt examined the letter and then laughed. 'Yes, I certainly got one and the writing was a bit like that.'

'And what did you do about it, sir?'

'First of all I showed it to my wife, and then I threw it away.'

'*You showed it to your wife, sir?*' Hardcastle had not expected that reply.

'Why not, Inspector? We both had a good laugh about it. To be honest, I thought it was one of the members playing a trick.'

'Did you ever consort with one of Briggs's prostitutes?'

'Good God, no. Whatever makes you think that?'

'The letter was sent by Briggs, Mr Hunt, and he was in the habit of fixing up certain members of Kendall's with a prostitute.'

'Well I'll be damned!' Hunt mulled over that piece of information before continuing. 'Then that all makes sense. As a matter of fact, Briggs did approach me in the club one night, very discreetly, and said that he knew a young lady who'd be willing to, how shall I put it, "entertain" me.'

'What did you say to that, sir?'

'I laughed and asked him to tell me more. Didn't mean a word of it, of course, but the next night he told me that a young lady called Barbara would be waiting for me outside Buckingham Palace the following evening at seven o'clock. The rest, he said, was up to me.'

'And did you meet her?'

'Good heavens, no. But the very next day I got this letter – at the club – demanding ten pounds or the writer would tell my wife that I'd been seeing this floozy.'

'Did the letter say how you were to pay this money, Mr Hunt?'

'Oh yes. It said that I would be contacted.' Hunt laughed. 'All very mysterious. Anyway, a couple of nights later I was approached by a woman, obviously a tart, in the street right outside here, and she said that I owed her ten pounds. That was how she put it, anyway.'

'What did you do, sir?' asked Hardcastle.

'I told her to clear off or I'd have her put in charge.'

'And she went, I suppose.'

'Like the bloody wind, Inspector,' said Hunt, laughing again.

'Did you think to report it to the police?'

'No. As I said just now, I thought it was one of the members having a joke.'

'Can you describe this woman, Mr Hunt?' asked Marriott, taking out his pocket book.

'I think so,' said Hunt, and gave a good description of a woman who could have been either Polly Francis or Queenie Hicks.

*   *   *

The detectives' visit to Victor Dawson was even less productive.

'Yes, Inspector, Briggs did arrange a woman for me. A rather comely young wench by the name of Queenie.'

'And did you see her, sir?' asked Hardcastle.

'Yes, rather. Met her outside Buckingham Palace and took her to the Royal Hotel in Buckingham Gate. I treated her to dinner in the brasserie and spent the night with her. Bloody good she was, too.'

'I see,' said Hardcastle, somewhat taken aback by Dawson's frank admission. 'And did you later get a threatening letter?'

'Yes, I did. But how did you know that?'

'Written in a hand like this?' Again Hardcastle produced the letter.

'Yes, I'm pretty sure that was the handwriting. It was sent to the club.'

'And did someone approach you for money after you got the letter?'

'Yes. Some woman I'd never seen before turned up out there' – Dawson waved a hand towards the window of his sitting room – 'and said she wanted ten pounds to keep quiet about Queenie or my wife would get to hear of it.'

'What did you do?'

'Told her to bugger off.'

'And did she go?'

'Yes, after a minute or two. She said I hadn't heard the last of it. Something like that. So I told her that I was going to call a policeman, and if she were still there by the time I'd found one, I'd have her arrested. That settled it. She cleared off, and I never heard anything about it again.'

'Did you see Queenie again?'

'Two or three times,' said Dawson.

'Didn't your wife have something to say about all this?'

Dawson threw back his head and laughed uproariously. 'That's the funny part of it all, Inspector,' he said. 'I don't have a wife. She died ten years ago.'

'I suppose you don't still have that letter, sir, do you?'

'Yes, I have, Inspector. As a matter of fact, I was thinking of having it framed. Hold on and I'll get it for you.'

Moments later, Dawson returned to the room and handed

171

the letter over, together with the envelope in which it had arrived at Kendall's.

'I'll keep this if I may, sir,' said Hardcastle. 'For the moment.'

'Of course,' said Dawson, 'but I would like it back. I think I *will* have it framed.'

'This woman who threatened you in the street, sir,' said Marriott. 'Can you tell me what she looked like?'

The woman Dawson described could, like Hunt's description, have been either Queenie Hicks or Polly Francis. But as Dawson knew Queenie well, it was most likely to have been Polly Francis.

'Briggs didn't have much luck with those two, did he, Marriott?' said Hardcastle when the two of them were finally back at Cannon Row police station. He took off his shoes and began to massage his feet.

'It looks as though Polly Francis was much more involved in this than she let on, sir. Having written the envelopes as well as the letters.'

'Of course she was, Marriott, but she wasn't going to tell us any more than she had to. We'll have her in again and give her a good talking to, before we charge her with blackmail, that is. In the meantime, we'll have a walk round to the Rising Sun. I'm anxious to know if anyone there's heard from our friend Jed Parsons. That carney little bugger's up to something, you mark my words, Marriott.'

Acting on the information that Polly Francis had given Hardcastle, Detective Sergeant Wood had been sent to search the cellar of the Rising Sun. And although some stolen property had been discovered there, Hardcastle was convinced that there was another, more serious, reason for Parsons to have disappeared. Perhaps even the murder of Joseph Briggs.

'Where's Jed Parsons?' asked Hardcastle when he and Marriott entered the saloon bar. Not that he had any hope of finding the missing landlord there.

'No idea, guv'nor,' said a barman who appeared to be running the pub in the absence of Parsons. Hardcastle had not seen the man before, and presumed that the brewery had put him in rather than lose trade. As Parsons had not been convicted of keeping a brothel in the Rising Sun, the licensing justices had not removed his licence. As far as the law was concerned, he was just missing. The reason did not, at the moment, concern them.

'I suppose you can manage to pull a couple of pints of best, can you?'

'Yes, guv'nor,' said the barman, promptly filling two glass tankards. 'That'll be a tanner.'

Hardcastle made no attempt to pay. 'D'you know me?' he asked.

'No, mate,' said the barman. 'Why? You an actor or something?'

Hardcastle leaned across the bar. 'I'm Divisional Detective Inspector Hardcastle and I'm in charge of the CID on this manor. And you'd do well to remember that, my lad.'

'Oh, sorry, sir. Pleased to meet you,' said the barman lamely, and made no further attempt to extract money from Hardcastle.

'Where's Queenie Hicks? She here tonight?'

'No, guv'nor, she's packed it in.'

'What, for the night?'

'No, for good.'

'And what about Barbara Burrows?'

'Yeah, she's here somewhere, guv'nor. Want to speak to her?'

When Barbara Burrows appeared, Hardcastle beckoned her to the far end of the bar, out of earshot of the other customers.

'What d'you know about a man called Geoffrey Hunt?' he asked.

'Here, what is all this?' asked Barbara, looking around nervously.

'I know what your game is, Barbara,' said Hardcastle, 'and right now I don't give a fig what you've been up to, but this is important. Did you ever meet Hunt? Outside Buckingham Palace, say?'

'What if I did?'

'I'm dealing with a murder, Barbara. I don't care about your whoring.'

'Yeah, I did meet him. A couple of months ago it was.'

'And what happened?'

Barbara gave a coarse laugh. 'What d'you think happened?

173

He bedded me, that's what. It's what I was there for. Took me to the Royal in Buck Gate.'

'Just the once?'

Barbara thought about that. 'Nah, three times altogether, I think it was.'

Nineteen

First thing on Wednesday morning, while the rest of the country was still acclimatizing itself to the fact that it was at war, Hardcastle decided that he would have to resolve the Briggs enquiry very soon or half his suspects would have disappeared to France. And if Sir John Webster's gloomy predictions were to be believed, they might not return.

'We'll start with Queenie Hicks, if we can find her, Marriott, and then we'll pay Mr Geoffrey Hunt another visit,' said Hardcastle as he counted off his suspects on his fingers. 'If he thinks he can pull the wool over Ernie Hardcastle's eyes, he's got another think coming. And then there's Polly Francis, and we'll catch Major Groves again before he pushes off to the war.'

'Hello, Mr Hardcastle,' said Queenie Hicks cheerfully, as she opened the door of her flat over the boot makers in Broadway. Although it was only ten o'clock in the morning – early by prostitutes' standards – she was not only up and about, but was wearing an expensive, green silk day-dress.

'I hear you've given up working at the Rising Sun,' said Hardcastle as he and Marriott followed the girl upstairs to the sitting room.

'I've come into money,' said Queenie as she sat down and carefully arranged the skirt of her dress.

'Looks like it,' said Hardcastle, appraising her outfit. 'Where did this money come from?'

'From Major Carmichael. Some posh gent come round here from his solicitors a few days ago, and said as how the major had left me his house in Clarges Street in his will *and* five hundred quid. Course, he said I'd have to wait a bit to lay me hands on it 'cos it had to go through pro . . .' Queenie stumbled over the word. 'Pro something.'

'Probate,' said Marriott.

'Yeah, that's right. Probate. That's what he said.'

'And what are you going to do with five hundred pounds and a big house in Clarges Street, my girl?' asked Hardcastle.

'Enjoy meself,' said Queenie, a broad smile spreading across her face. 'You never know, I might even marry a lord.'

'Yes, you might at that,' said Hardcastle. 'Funnier things have happened. So why did Carmichael leave you his house and all his money?'

''Cos there weren't no one else. He told me once he ain't got no relations or nothing. He was a dear man, was Clive.' An expression of wistful sadness momentarily crossed Queenie's face.

'Yes, well when you've come down to earth, Queenie, I've got a few questions to ask you.'

'Fire away,' said Queenie, refusing to be depressed by the arrival of the police.

'Do you know a man called Geoffrey Hunt, lives in Weymouth Street?'

'Never heard of him.'

'So you didn't go round there a few weeks back saying that he owed you ten pounds?'

'Why should he owe me? I don't know him.'

'You never turned a trick for him?'

'No, never, and I'll tell you this, Mr Hardcastle, I ain't turning no more. Not now I'm a lady with money and a big house. That's why I give up working at the Rising Sun.' Queenie glanced across at the dirty windows of the room. 'Cor!' she said. 'Ain't I the lucky one.'

'I didn't think it'd be her, Marriott,' said Hardcastle as the two of them crossed Victoria Street towards Perkins Rents where Polly Francis lived over a shop.

Unlike Queenie Hicks, Polly had been in bed when the

police hammered three or four times on her door, and it was several minutes before she appeared. Tired and dishevelled, she wore a faded and worn dressing gown, and her usually well-coifed auburn hair hung about her shoulders in rat's-tails.

'Gawd blimey, what d'you want now?' she asked, opening the door wide.

'A serious talk with you, my girl,' said Hardcastle, pushing past her.

The single room Polly occupied was in disarray, and redolent with some stale odour. The bed was unmade – not surprising given that she had just that moment tumbled out of it – and there were clothes piled on the only chair in the room. The dressing table was littered with pots and jars. But she made no excuses for the disorder, and sat down on the end of the bed. 'Watcha want then?'

'You told me that you didn't know who Joe Briggs sent them letters to, the ones you obligingly wrote for him.'

'I didn't know.'

'Don't lie to me, girl,' said Hardcastle, 'because I know you also addressed the envelopes. The letters have been identified, see. So, as you addressed 'em, you must have known who got 'em and where they was sent to.'

'Joe made me do it,' whined Polly.

'That's your bad luck then, ain't it? Because you're going down for blackmail.'

'I tell you, he made me,' Polly implored.

'I don't believe a word of that. In fact, I think it was all your own idea. Joe Briggs never had anything to do with it, did he? And what's more, you wrote this letter' – once again Hardcastle produced the missive found in Briggs's room – 'because you were threatening him an' all. You knew about his shady past and you was going to peach on him to Kendall's if he didn't keep dishing out the cash.'

Polly leaped up from the bed, her face working with anguish. 'It ain't true,' she pleaded. 'Honest, mister, he made me.'

'We'll see what the judge at the Old Bailey has to say about that, Polly, because it looks to me as though it was your little scheme, and nothing to do with Joe. And even if he did put you up to it, you're what's called an accessory before the fact, what with writing the letters.'

176

Polly put her face in her hands. 'I couldn't help it,' she said between sobs. 'You've got to believe me, mister.'

'And another thing,' Hardcastle persisted. 'You went to see a Geoffrey Hunt who lives in Weymouth Street, and Victor Dawson in Eccleston Mews. And you demanded ten pounds from them. Demanded it with menaces as the lawyers call it.'

'It was Joe's idea to have me collect the cash from 'em,' said Polly, tears coursing unchecked down her face. 'He said he'd stripe me if I never done what he wanted.'

Hardcastle was inclined to believe her, certain that the unscrupulous Briggs was a bully, and quite capable of terrorizing a girl like Polly.

'Now then,' he continued, 'this Major Groves . . .'

'What about him?'

'You reckoned he was supposed to meet you the night Joe Briggs was killed. Is that true?'

'Course it is. You don't think I was standing up a draughty alleyway at eleven o'clock at night freezing me arse off just to see if there was a new moon, do you?'

'I shall be speaking to him, Polly, and I shall ask him.'

'You ask away then, 'cos that's where he told me to be. And then he was going to take me across Artillery Mansions, like I said before. I was bleedin' fed up when he never come, I can tell you.'

Hardcastle decided not to arrest Polly Francis immediately, even though he had sufficient evidence to sustain a charge. But, as he had told the Marlborough Street magistrate, it was likely to be more helpful to his enquiries if she was not caught up in the judicial system yet.

'Don't you think of running away, my girl,' said Hardcastle, turning towards the door, 'because if you do, I shall swear out a warrant for your arrest. And that warrant will be addressed to each and every constable of the Metropolitan Police Force. And there's twenty thousand of 'em.'

But Polly Francis did run. It was only much later that Hardcastle learned that she had taken a job with the Navy and Army Canteen Board and been shipped off to France to serve 'tea and wads' to the troops. She was never heard of again.

*　　　*　　　*

'This murder's getting to be a right bugger's muddle and no mistake,' said Hardcastle, as he and Marriott alighted from a cab outside the Duke of York's Headquarters in King's Road. Waiting until his sergeant had paid the driver, he marched towards the gate, hardly pausing as he waved his warrant card at the bemused sentry.

Hardcastle and Marriott crossed the corner of the barrack square where a group of men in civilian clothes were attempting to do arms drill with broomsticks.

Major Groves was not at all pleased to see the two detectives again. 'I'm extremely busy, Inspector,' he said. 'The battalion embarks for France the day after tomorrow. You've no idea what that entails.'

'I shan't keep you a moment, Major,' said Hardcastle. 'Just one question.'

'Which is?'

'Did you arrange to meet Polly Francis at eleven o'clock on the evening of Tuesday the fourteenth of July?'

Groves thumbed through his desk diary. 'No, certainly not. I'd agreed to have dinner at the club that night with Colonel Fitzpatrick, and afterwards we played a few frames of slush.'

'Of what?'

'Slush is what the army calls snooker, Inspector,' said Groves with a superior smile.

'So there's no truth in Polly Francis's statement that she hung about for half an hour outside the Albert pub in Victoria Street waiting for you to cart her off to bed, just across the road?'

'Not on that occasion, no.'

'Does your wife know about your little love-nest at Artillery Mansions, Major?'

'This has nothing to do with my wife, Inspector, and I'd be obliged if you left her out of it.'

'I may have to interview her, Major,' said Hardcastle mildly, 'in connection with another matter.'

'What other matter?' demanded Groves.

'Her association with Horace Davenport.'

'What on earth are you talking about?'

'It seems she's in the habit of dining with Mr Davenport, and going to the theatre with him.'

'That's a damned lie,' bellowed Groves.

'I saw the two of them together at His Majesty's last Friday, Major. The play was called *Pygmalion*, it's about a flower-girl – bit like Polly Francis, I s'pose – what this professor turns into a lady.'

'I am familiar with the play, Inspector,' snapped Groves.

'And two of my officers saw the pair of 'em having lunch at Kettner's the following day.'

Major Groves slumped visibly, and ran a hand through his thinning hair. 'I know,' he said. 'And there's something else you should be aware of. She ran off with him yesterday. I presume it was him, anyway. She took my car, too, and I've no idea where she's gone.'

'That'd be the car she gave you for a Christmas box, I suppose.'

'How did you know that?' demanded Groves.

'As I said the last time I was here, Major, I know a lot about the members of Kendall's and their wives, and when I'm investigating a murder I make it my business to find out what they've been up to.'

'Well, I hope you find her, Inspector,' said Groves wearily. 'As I said earlier, I'm off to France on Friday, and I some-how doubt I shall ever see her again.' But Groves was not to know just how accurate that forecast was to be.

'How did you know that she and Davenport were carrying on?'

'She made no secret of it, Inspector. In fact, she taunted me with it. I think she was sick of being married to a soldier, and wanted to see more of the high life as she called it. My orders for France were the last straw, I rather fancy.'

'She won't see much gaiety with Davenport,' said Hardcastle. 'He's stony broke.'

'Yes,' said Groves, 'but my wife isn't. She inherited a substantial sum of money from her father, and no doubt Davenport was aware of that. And intends to spend it for her,' he added bitterly.

'Perhaps that's why he gave up making concertinas, Major,' said Hardcastle mischievously.

'*Concertinas?*' exclaimed Groves. 'Good God Almighty!'

*   *   *

From Chelsea, Hardcastle and Marriott made their way directly to Geoffrey Hunt's house in Weymouth Street.

'Inspector, you're here again. Come in, come in.'

'I don't enjoy people trying to make a monkey out of me, Mr Hunt,' said Hardcastle. 'And when it happens I'm quite likely to charge 'em with obstructing police in the execution of their duty.'

'Now, look here—'

'No, you look here, Mr Hunt. I'm sick and tired of people jigging me about. I'm investigating a murder, and when people tells me lies I get to thinking they might have done it, see.'

'I really don't know what you're talking about, Inspector.'

'I'm talking about Joseph Briggs. And I'm talking about Barbara Burrows, the prostitute you met outside Buckingham Palace three times and took to the Royal Hotel where you bedded her. And when another woman – her name's Polly Francis – came here and demanded ten pounds, you give it to her. That's what I'm talking about . . . *Mister* Hunt.'

'For God's sake keep your voice down, Inspector,' said the alarmed Hunt. 'My wife's in the next room.'

'We can always carry on this conversation at Marylebone Lane police station if you'd rather,' said Hardcastle, who was fast losing patience.

'Look, I'm sorry I misled you, Inspector,' said Hunt, now more contrite than hitherto, 'but I'm not proud of having done what I did. It was damned foolish.'

'Not half as foolish as putting a stop to the blackmail by murdering the man who was sending the threatening letters.'

'For God's sake, Inspector, I wouldn't do anything as crazy as that.'

'Persuade me you didn't then,' said Hardcastle.

'What d'you want me to say?' Hunt was becoming extremely anguished now. That he might be hanged seemed to have concentrated his mind.

'For a start you can tell me where you were the night of Wednesday the fifteenth of July.' Hardcastle knew what other members of Kendall's had told him, but he had now reached the point where he trusted none of them. And that included the chairman, Sir John Webster.

Hunt sank into an armchair, and belatedly indicated that

Hardcastle and Marriott should sit down as well. But Hardcastle remained standing. 'Well?'

'I'm trying to think, Inspector. Ah, yes, I know. I was at the club.'

'And is there someone who can vouch for that?'

'I suppose so. A Wednesday, you say. Oh, just a minute, yes, of course. I was playing cards. We always have a hand of *vingt-et-un* on a Wednesday.'

'Who else was playing?'

'The usual four: Victor Dawson, Horry Davenport, Peter Reilly and me.'

'I've been told that Mr Davenport didn't have too good an evening.'

'He never did, Inspector. I've never seen a man lose so consistently at cards. By about eleven o'clock he was cleaned out and left the room to have a drink.'

'Can you be more specific about the time, Mr Hunt?'

'Not really, no. I seem to recall we stopped for a minute or two and Paddy Reilly went out and got us each a brandy. What happens is that the smoking-room steward goes off at—'

'I know all about the chits,' said Hardcastle.

'What time did you leave the club, Mr Hunt?' asked Marriott, opening his pocket book to the page where he had recorded the departure times of Hunt and the others.

'I think we carried on until about ten to one,' Hunt said, switching his gaze to the sergeant, 'and then Victor and I went home. Paddy Reilly went upstairs, of course. He lives in the club, or did. I understand he's gone off to the war now.'

'And you'd be prepared to swear to that, would you?'

'It's quite true, Inspector,' said Hunt.

'As true as you never having bedded one of Briggs's whores, I suppose,' said Hardcastle caustically as he turned to leave.

'I think that shook him up a bit, Marriott,' said Hardcastle.

'But d'you think he's telling the truth, sir?'

'I reckon so, but if his missus was listening at the door, I reckon our Mr Hunt's getting a right earwigging now,' said Hardcastle, and laughed as he hailed a cab.

It was a tearful Rose Davenport who answered the door of

181

17 Broad Street. 'Have you found him?' she asked, recognizing the two policemen who had called previously.

'Found who, madam?' asked Hardcastle, raising his hat as he affected innocence in the matter of the missing Horace Davenport.

'My husband, of course. Isn't that what you've come about?'

'Perhaps we'd better come in, madam,' said Hardcastle.

'He disappeared yesterday, Inspector,' said Rose Davenport as she led the detectives into the sitting room. 'Do sit down, please.'

'Perhaps you'd explain, Mrs Davenport. The reason for me coming here the other day was to clear up one or two points about the murder.'

'Murder! What murder? I don't know what you're talking about.'

'The smoking-room steward at Kendall's, Joseph Briggs, was murdered a fortnight ago, madam, in St James's Park, and Mr Davenport was one of those in the club at about the time it occurred.'

'But surely you can't think that Horace—'

Hardcastle held up a placating hand. 'I was merely trying to establish when Briggs left the premises, madam. I've spoken to all the members who was there that night.'

'Oh, I see.' Rose appeared relieved by that.

'Now then, what's this about your husband disappearing? Yesterday, I think you said.'

'He never said a word. I'd taken a walk down to Bourne and Hollingsworth, the drapers in Oxford Street, to get one or two things.' Rose Davenport raised a handkerchief to her eye. 'But they said they'd closed our account until we'd paid what we owed. Oh, it's all too dreadful, Inspector,' she said as a solitary sob caught in her throat. 'It's all Horace's fault. It's the gambling, you know.'

'I'm sorry to hear that, Mrs Davenport, but what about your husband going missing?'

'That's what I was going to say. When I got home at about eleven o'clock he'd gone. I looked in his bedroom and he'd taken most of his things.'

'Did he leave a note, anything that might tell you where he'd gone?'

'No, nothing,' said the distraught woman.

'Why had your account at Bourne and Hollingsworth not been paid, Mrs Davenport?' asked Marriott.

'It was the factory.'

'What was?' Marriott knew what DS Wood had discovered from his trip to Surbiton, but wanted to hear what Davenport had told his wife.

'Horace had a very good business going in Surbiton, making concertinas. And with the war coming, he was sure that he could switch over to producing something for the war effort. He was certain that there was something he could manufacture, and he hoped to make quite a lot of money. But one night the factory caught fire. The insurance people went down and inspected it, but they said it had been started deliberately and they refused to pay out.'

'When did this happen?'

'About two months ago, the beginning of June, I think.'

'And your husband had no idea how the fire started?' asked Hardcastle.

'No. He seemed to think that someone had a grudge against him and that they set fire to it out of spite.'

'Did he suggest anyone, a disgruntled employee that he'd sacked, perhaps?'

'No. As far as I know his staff had been with him for quite a long time. Years, I think. He hadn't sacked anyone in ages.' And then Rose Davenport broke down completely, her tears flowing freely. 'And now we're penniless,' she mumbled.

Twenty

Hardcastle sat behind his desk mulling over what he and Marriott had learned the previous day.

'There's something a bit funny going on here, Marriott.'

'Are you thinking what I'm thinking, sir?'

'If I knew what you was thinking, Marriott, I might be able to answer that,' observed Hardcastle drily.

'D'you think it might have been Briggs who burned down Davenport's factory, sir?'

'Possibly, Marriott, possibly,' said Hardcastle. 'If Briggs was sweating Davenport and Davenport wouldn't pay, or if his missus is to be believed, *couldn't* pay, Briggs might have decided to teach him a lesson.'

'To encourage the others, sir?'

Hardcastle shook his head. 'I don't think he was that clever. Anyway, I want to do some checking on exactly when Davenport left the club the night of the murder. Get Wood and . . . no, on second thoughts, get Kimber. He's got his head screwed on the right way has that lad. And it strikes me he's got a bit of education an' all.'

'Sir?' Within minutes of being summoned, Kimber presented himself in the DDI's office.

'Know where Kendall's is, lad?'

'Yes, sir.'

'Good. Get up there and talk to these people.' Hardcastle took the list of names from Marriott and handed it to the young DC. 'Speak to each of them and find out the exact times they saw each other, because I'm thinking that one of 'em might have topped Briggs.'

'You *do*, sir?' asked Kimber enthusiastically.

'Yes, I do. Quite a few of the members up there got black-mail letters from Briggs, even though they was written by Polly Francis, and in my book that's a good enough reason to do for him.' Hardcastle paused, thinking that he owed Kimber an explanation. 'You see, lad, Briggs had a group of whores what he was hiring out to the members up there and when they took the bait, so to speak, he put the black on 'em, on account of 'em being married. 'Cept for Dawson. Briggs come a bit unstuck there. But step careful, lad. They're a funny lot of buggers up there.'

Once Kimber had departed, delighted that his new assign-ment was more interesting than those he had been given previ-ously, Hardcastle turned to Marriott again. 'I don't somehow think this running away of Davenport's is going to last too long, m'boy,' he said, lapsing into one of his rare moments of infor-mality and, at the same time, indicating that Marriott should sit down. 'I wouldn't mind putting a quid on Veronica Groves

throwing Davenport over, once she finds out that he's only interested in spending her cash. Get hold of Catto and Wilmot and
tell 'em to sit on the Davenports' place in Broad Street, discreet
like, and see if the bugger comes back. I want to have a chat
with him about this here concertina factory of his.'

'But we know it was burned down, guv'nor,' said Marriott.

'Aye, we do, m'boy, but I'm interested in knowing *who*
burned it down. And I'm thinking that Master Davenport might
know. It could've been Briggs, but on the other hand, he might
have sent Polly down there to do the deed. There again, being
stony, Davenport might have done it himself.'

When Kimber returned after lunch he was somewhat apprehensive. 'I'm afraid I didn't do too well, sir,' he began.

'Tell me what you've got, then, lad.'

'Lord Slade hasn't been in for some time, sir. The sergeant-
porter said he'd been taken ill and they think it's unlikely he'll
survive the week. As for the chairman, Sir John, he wasn't
too sure about the times, but reckons that Davenport came
into the smoking room at *about* twenty past eleven, maybe
half past.'

'Interesting,' said Hardcastle thoughtfully. 'When I spoke
to him, he said he couldn't remember.'

'Major Groves is off to France tomorrow with the British
Expeditionary Force and he—'

'Don't worry about Groves, Kimber. I've dealt with him.'
Although as he said it, Hardcastle was unsure whether he had
finished dealing with him.

'But Colonel Fitzpatrick said that Davenport came into the
smoking room at somewhere about half past eleven, but he didn't
seem too sure. They were all a bit offhanded, sir. Most of them
were talking about the war, and didn't seem too keen on being
interrupted. They had maps spread out on the snooker table.'

'I didn't see any snooker table, did you, Marriott?'

'No, sir.'

'Er, it was in the snooker room, sir,' said Kimber.

'Would be, I suppose,' muttered Hardcastle. 'Of course,'
he said, 'come to think of it, Major Groves mentioned it.'

'Captain Reilly's already left for the war, sir, and Mr Dawson
wasn't there, neither was Mr Hunt. As for Mr Davenport, sir,

no one seems to know where he's gone. Someone suggested he might have joined up.'

Hardcastle chuckled. 'I doubt it, lad,' he said. 'And his missus don't know where he's gone, neither, and nor do I, but I'll wager he's tucked up in bed somewhere with Mrs Major Groves. Never mind, you've done the best you can.'

'There was something else, sir,' said Kimber diffidently.

'What?'

'While I was there, sir, I thought I'd have a look round. They were all too occupied with the war to notice me wandering about the place.'

'Yes?'

'You know when you go into the smoking room, through the double doors from the lobby . . .'

'What about it?'

'Well, sir, there's a door on the other side that leads into the dining room. And the card room leads off that. But opposite *that* door there's another door from the card room that goes into a corridor.'

'I hope you're going to get to the point of this, Kimber,' said Hardcastle.

'Yes, sir. Turning left out the card room, there are two doors off the corridor into the smoking room direct. But if you turn right, there's a back door that leads to the rear of the premises and straight into St James's Square. According to Lucas, that's the door the staff use when they're coming and going.'

'Now ain't that interesting, Marriott,' said Hardcastle, turning to his sergeant.

'I'm sorry, sir. I thought it might be useful.' Kimber was convinced that the DDI was being sarcastic.

'Oh, it is, lad,' said Hardcastle. 'You've done a good job there. Off you go.'

'Is that relevant, sir?' asked Marriott.

'It could be,' mused Hardcastle. 'I think we'll have another word with Mr Dawson – he's more reliable than that Hunt – and see if he can remember what time Davenport left the card room.'

When Dawson answered the door of his house in Eccleston Mews, he was in shirtsleeves and his waistcoat was unbuttoned.

'Ah, Inspector, you've caught me in the middle of packing.'

'Are you going away then, sir?' Hardcastle, his eyes narrowing, wondered if Dawson was fleeing from justice.

'Joining up,' Dawson said. 'I told you that my wife died ten years ago, so there's nothing to keep me here. I went down to the War Office yesterday and they're prepared to grant me a commission in the East Surreys.'

'Very good,' said Hardcastle, 'but I should keep your head down, if I was you.'

Dawson laughed. 'Don't worry about that, Inspector,' he said. 'However, what can I do for you?'

'When we last spoke, Mr Dawson, I forgot to ask you an important question.'

'And what was that?'

'On the night of Wednesday the fifteenth of July, you and Mr Hunt and Mr Davenport were playing cards with Captain Reilly. Is that correct?'

'Probably.' Dawson looked puzzled by the question. 'We play cards most nights.'

'It was the night Briggs was murdered, sir,' said Hardcastle.

'Ah, of course. Yes, that's right. We were playing pontoon.'

'I believe that Mr Davenport left early on account of him having lost a bit heavy.'

'He lost heavily more times than not, Inspector,' said Dawson with a laugh. 'What about it?'

'What time did he leave the card room?'

For a moment or two Dawson scratched thoughtfully at his chin. Eventually he said, 'About quarter to eleven, I think. He said he was cleaned out and was going to have a drink in the smoking room.'

'Which door did he go out of?' asked Hardcastle.

Dawson laughed. 'Which door? God, I don't know. Just a minute though, now you come to mention it, I think he went out of the door that leads into the corridor. That way you can get to the smoking room without going through the dining room. If any of the members are finishing a late supper they get a bit cross with people traipsing through the dining room.'

'Thank you, sir,' said Hardcastle. 'I think that'll be all.' He paused on the threshold of the sitting room door. 'And like I said, sir, keep your head down over there. Still, it'll all be over by Christmas, so they say.'

'Yes,' said Dawson, 'and I don't want to miss it.'

Hardcastle was seated behind his desk, deep in thought. 'I don't know, Marriott,' he said. 'Now that we know there's a door out of the card room that leads to the corridor and then to the back door of Kendall's, it opens up the field.'

'So who d'you fancy, sir?'

Hardcastle picked up his pipe, stared into the bowl and teased out the dead ash. 'Look at it like this, Marriott. Out of the four who was playing cards in the card room, Captain Reilly was single and lived in the club. I reckon that rules him out. Anyway, he's gone back to the army. That leaves Dawson, Davenport and Hunt. All three of 'em got letters from Briggs, or Polly Francis, and I still ain't certain which of them two was the real blackmailer. So, in my book, it could've been any one of the three.'

'But Dawson doesn't come into it, does he, sir?' asked Marriott.

'No, he's likely in the clear,' said Hardcastle, 'what with being a widower. According to him, he just laughed when Briggs tried to put the bite on him. That leaves Hunt and Davenport. Hunt's a bleedin' liar and Davenport's run off with Veronica Groves.'

'What about Captain Leighton, sir? After all, the crowbar was last seen in his room, and even though he said he'd chucked it out, it was never found till it turned up in the lake.'

'Rank outsider, Marriott. Only just back from India. His wife ain't living in London, but even so I don't think Briggs would have tried it on with him. He'd've found he'd come to the wrong shop and no mistake. I reckon Captain Leighton of the Madras Light Infantry could turn a bit nasty if the mood took him.'

'Be interesting to hear what Davenport's got to say, sir.'

'Yes, it will, Marriott, and I intend to find the bugger pretty soon.'

'And then there's Polly Francis, sir.'

'Ah yes, Polly Francis.' Hardcastle expelled a cloud of tobacco smoke and regarded the cast-iron fireplace as though interested in its construction. 'I ain't ruled her out by a long chalk. She could've done for Briggs. Good strong wench, is that one. And if Briggs was coming it with her a bit too heavy, she might just have taken it into her pretty little head to get rid of him, and put all the blame for the blacking on to him. Nothing to it really. She could've followed him to the bridge in St James's Park, when he's all unsuspecting like, and walloped him across the head with an iron bar. Too easy, Marriott, too easy.'

But at that moment, Catto burst excitedly into Hardcastle's office.

'What's up with you, Catto? Your arse caught fire, has it?'

'No, sir, but—'

'Before you comes in my office, you knocks, Catto, and you waits for the signal to enter. You know that.'

'Yes, sir. Sorry, sir.'

'Right then, what are you all in a two-an'-eight about?'

'It's Davenport, sir. He came home about twenty minutes ago. He was looking a bit ragged an' all.'

'Was he really?' said Hardcastle mildly. 'Well, he's going to look a bit more ragged by the time Sergeant Marriott and me's done with him.' The DDI stood up and took his hat and umbrella from the rack in the corner of his office. 'Come, Marriott.'

Horace Davenport was indeed looking extremely sorry for himself when Rose Davenport showed Hardcastle and Marriott into the sitting room of their house in Broad Street.

'Ah, Inspector.' Davenport looked up listlessly, but did not stand up. His jacket was torn in several places and there was an angry graze down the right-hand side of his face.

'You look as though you've been in the wars,' said Hardcastle as he and Marriott sat down uninvited. 'You ain't been to France already, have you?'

'It was the accident, Inspector.'

'What was?'

'He was in a motor accident, Inspector,' Rose Davenport volunteered.

'Wouldn't happen to have been a De Dion Bouton by any chance, would it?' Hardcastle asked.

Davenport looked up sharply and winced as though he had more injuries than those immediately apparent. 'How did you know that?'

'Because I'm a detective, Mr Davenport, and I'm paid to

find things out. And I can tell you this: Major Groves ain't best pleased with you. But you're in luck.'

'I am?' Davenport appeared doubtful, probably imagining that any further luck for which he might qualify could only be bad luck.

'Major Groves is embarking for France tomorrow morning. So he probably ain't got much time to deal with them as pinches his car and his missus. Mind you, I reckon he was more upset about the car than he was about Veronica.'

'What *is* all this about Henry Groves and his wife, Inspector?' Judging from the surprise in her voice, it was apparent that Rose Davenport was very much in the dark about what her husband had been doing for the past two days.

'I'll explain later, dear,' said Davenport hurriedly. 'Why don't you go and fetch us all some whisky?'

'There isn't any whisky, Horace Davenport, as well you know. And there isn't any because we haven't got any money.' And with tears beginning to well up in her eyes, Davenport's wife fled from the room.

'I haven't told her the full story yet,' said Davenport, 'but this accident . . .'

'What about it?'

'We were making for Brighton, Veronica and me – she has a cottage at Rottingdean – and I'm afraid I was driving a bit too fast. We got as far as Streatham Hill when I swerved to miss some fool on a bicycle and hit a tree.'

'And Mrs Groves?'

'I'm afraid she was killed, Inspector,' mumbled Davenport, his chin sinking on to his chest.

'I'm sorry to hear that.' Hardcastle wondered whether it was true, or whether it was a lame attempt to dissuade him from questioning her. But if that was the case, what did Veronica Groves know that Davenport did not want Hardcastle to learn? 'Where is her body?'

Davenport frowned. 'I'm afraid I don't know, Inspector,' he said. 'I was really in no fit state to ask the police where they were taking her when they arrived at the scene of the accident.'

'Never mind, Mr Davenport, we'll easy find out,' said Hardcastle. 'When did this accident happen?'

'The day before yesterday,' said Davenport.

'Is that a fact?' Hardcastle stared suspiciously at Davenport. 'Given that you only come home about an hour ago, where have you been since then?'

'In hospital. I was knocked unconscious, and they kept me in until this morning. They said it was shock.'

'No doubt you're on the mend now,' said Hardcastle, not really caring whether he was or not, 'although I have to say they didn't do too good a job dressing that wound you've got on your face. But in the meantime, I've a question to ask you about the night Briggs was murdered.'

'What's that?'

'What time did you leave the club?'

'Good heavens, I don't know. Probably about one in the morning.'

'I've been told that you were playing cards, and that you lost quite a bit.'

Davenport smiled weakly. 'Yes, I'm afraid I did.'

'And that you left the game to have a drink in the smoking room. So what time did you leave the card room?'

Affecting an expression of deep thought, Davenport pondered the question for a moment or two. 'Must have been about a quarter to eleven, I suppose, Inspector.'

It did not escape Hardcastle's notice that the time quoted by Davenport was at odds with what other members had stated; apart, that is, from Dawson who had actually confirmed it. 'And you went straight into the smoking room?'

'Of course. But why the interest in when *I* left?'

'I'm not so much interested in when *you* left, Mr Davenport, as what the others were doing,' said Hardcastle, cunningly deflecting the question.

'Oh, I see. I was there with Victor Dawson, Geoffrey Hunt and Peter Reilly. We usually made a four for a hand or two of *vingt-et-un*.'

'And did any of them leave the room around eleven o'clock?'

'I'm not sure. We all went out for a piddle from time to time and I seem to recall that Peter went out to get some drinks. That was probably about eleven. Why?'

'Just getting everything straight in my mind, Mr Davenport,' said Hardcastle, smiling disarmingly. 'Now then, about your factory . . .'

Davenport looked up in surprise. 'What about it?'

'I'm told that you manufactured concertinas there.'

'What of it?'

'And that someone deliberately set fire to it.'

'That's what the insurance people said, but I didn't believe it. I'm going to take them to court over it.'

Hardcastle laughed. 'You haven't got the money to start proceedings, Mr Davenport, and you wouldn't get anywhere, because you know and I know that it was Briggs that set it on fire.'

'What on earth are you talking about, Inspector?' Davenport put on a display of injured innocence. 'That's a preposterous suggestion. Why should Briggs want to do a thing like that?'

'Because he fixed you up with a whore and then threatened to tell your missus and the committee of Kendall's about it, unless you paid up. But you hadn't got any money even then because your business was going under. So he burned down your factory. Either he did or you did.'

'That's absolute nonsense, Inspector.'

'We'll see, Mr Davenport, we'll see,' said Hardcastle, rising to his feet.

'Get on to W Division, Marriott. Urgently. See what they can tell us about this accident on Streatham Hill.'

It was an hour before Marriott was able to report back to Hardcastle that Streatham police station had no record of any accidents involving either a De Dion Bouton or in which a woman had been killed.

'Streatham nick sent a PC round to the Magdalen Hospital in Drewstead Road, too, sir. That's where Davenport would've been taken from Streatham Hill.'

'And?'

'No record of anyone called Davenport being admitted on the date he said the accident happened, sir.'

'I bloody knew it, Marriott,' said Hardcastle, thumping the top of his desk with a clenched fist. 'That bugger's having us on.'

'But why should he do that, sir?'

192

'I don't know, Marriott,' said Hardcastle, 'but I mean to find out, and I mean to do it now. We're going to the Duke of York's Headquarters to see what Major Groves has got to say about it. And if he's buggered off to the war, then we're going to Draycott Place. I've an idea that Veronica Groves is still in the land of the living. What I don't know is why Davenport should be lying about it, because I'm sure he is.'

Twenty-One

It was nearing eight o'clock in the evening when Hardcastle and Marriott arrived at the Duke of York's Headquarters. This time, though, the sentry at the gate was taking the war more seriously than had his colleague of the previous day.

'Halt, who goes there?' he demanded, sweeping his rifle up so that the bayonet pointed menacingly at the DDI.

'Police,' said Hardcastle.

'Got anything to prove that, have you?' the sentry asked, still maintaining his hostile stance.

Hardcastle produced his warrant card and held it up for the soldier to see.

'Report to the guardroom, sir, please,' said the sentry, relaxing.

The sergeant of the guard also demanded to see Hardcastle's identification, but once satisfied, he asked, 'And who do you wish to see, sir?'

'Major Henry Groves, Sergeant.'

'I'm afraid you're out of luck there, sir. He and his battalion entrained for Southampton at sixteen hundred hours today. On their way to the Front.'

'Bugger it,' said Hardcastle.

'Yes, sir,' said the sergeant of the guard.

When the detectives reached Draycott Place, the first thing that caught Hardcastle's eye was a De Dion Bouton parked

193

outside number 10. And it showed no signs of having been involved in an accident, fatal or otherwise.

'I thought as much, Marriott,' said Hardcastle as he hammered on the door.

'Yes?' asked the woman who answered the door.

'Mrs Groves?' queried Hardcastle, even though he recognized her as the woman he had seen at His Majesty's Theatre with Horace Davenport. On closer examination it was apparent that she was an extremely comely woman of about thirty, and it was plain that any man would have been attracted to her.

'Yes, but who—?'

'We're police officers, madam,' said Hardcastle, and introduced himself and Marriott.

'I'm afraid the major's not here, if that's who you were wanting.' Veronica Groves cast an appraising eye at Marriott and smiled.

'No, it's you we'd like a word with, ma'am,' said Hardcastle.

'You'd better come in, then.' Mrs Groves smiled again, and with a rustling of her elegant silk dress, led them into the house.

The drawing room was richly furnished, and it was clear that there was money here, a lot of money. But, as Hardcastle had already learned, the money was Veronica Groves's, not the major's.

'May I offer you gentlemen a drink?' Veronica asked, raising an eyebrow.

'No thank you, ma'am,' said Hardcastle, and he and Marriott waited until she was seated before sitting down themselves.

'I'm rather getting used to having policemen call on me,' said Veronica with a gay little laugh. 'I had a very good-looking young man come here the other day to warn me about burglars.'

'Really?' said Hardcastle. 'Probably from the local station.'

'Yes, he said he was from Chelsea. I take it you're not.'

'No, ma'am, we're from Cannon Row police station, the Whitehall Division.'

'How fascinating. What are you doing here then?'

'Horace Davenport,' said Hardcastle.

'Oh!' Veronica blushed, and taking a small ivory fan from her reticule, flicked it open and began to waft it back and forth in front of her face. 'How awfully embarrassing,' she said and cast yet another shy smile in Marriott's direction.

'I interviewed Mr Davenport earlier today and he told me that you and he had been in an accident.'

'What a silly thing to say. Why on earth should he have told you that?'

'That's what I was hoping you could explain, ma'am,' said Hardcastle. 'He also told me that you had died in the accident.'

'Oh, how awfully horrible of him. I don't know what he could have been thinking.'

'I understand that you and he were running away to Brighton.'

'Hardly running away, Inspector. You did say you were an inspector, didn't you?'

'Yes, ma'am.'

'We were going to the coast for a day or two.'

'And did you get there?'

'Yes, of course we did.' And once again Veronica smiled her ready smile.

Hardcastle wondered how long this cat-and-mouse exchange was going to continue. 'Have you any idea how Mr Davenport was injured, Mrs Groves?'

'Injured? I really have no—'

'Mrs Groves . . .' Hardcastle was beginning to get exasperated. 'When I spoke to Major Groves yesterday, he told me that you'd left him and run away with Mr Davenport, and he seemed to think it was for good.' He sat back in the deep sofa and waited.

'I only met Horace last—'

'Did you enjoy *Pygmalion*, Mrs Groves?'

That took Veronica Groves completely by surprise, but before she had time to recover, Hardcastle spoke again.

'And your lunch at Kettner's?'

The fan began to move more rapidly. 'Oh, this is all too awful,' said Veronica. 'How d'you know so much about us?'

'It seems to me you didn't make much of a secret of it,' commented Hardcastle. 'So where did you and Mr Davenport meet?'

'I'm not sure that's any of your business, Inspector, but it was at a ladies' night at Kendall's.'

That did not surprise Hardcastle. 'Now, would you tell me why you and Davenport went away, and how he got hurt?'

There was a long pause before she answered. 'He said he thought he might be in trouble with the police, Inspector, and he wanted to get away from London for a few days. He said something about his factory having been burned down, and that the police suspected him of having done it himself to recoup the insurance money. He was quite beside himself, saying that he was likely to be made bankrupt and, what was worse, expelled from Kendall's. I'm afraid I rather took pity on him, and lent him some money.'

'And did he say that *he* had burned down his factory, Mrs Groves?'

'Not in as many words, Inspector, no.'

'Did he also tell you he was a gambler?'

'Who . . . Horace? Good heavens no. You must be wrong about that.'

'He lost heavily at *vingt-et-un* almost every night, Mrs Groves. Sometimes as much as twenty-five pounds.'

'What a despicable thing to do.' Veronica was obviously shocked that the man with whom she had been having an affair turned out to be little more than a heartless bounder. And that his only real interest in her was the money she had given him and which he was frittering away at cards.

'What exactly did he tell you about this here factory of his?'

'Just that it had contained some priceless antiques that he was restoring prior to selling them. It seems that it was quite a substantial loss that he suffered.'

'He didn't mention concertinas, then?'

'Concertinas?' Veronica repeated her gay laugh. 'Oh, how absurd.'

'He didn't have any priceless furniture down there, Mrs Groves. He was making concertinas, and got put out of business on account of the Germans undercutting him.'

Veronica Groves snapped shut her fan and held it to her lips, gazing pensively at Hardcastle. 'I don't believe it,' she said. But she did, and now realized that she had been foolish enough to allow herself to be bedded by a concertina maker whose only motive, it appeared, was to acquire as much of her money as he could.

'Did Mr Davenport ever mention being blackmailed?' asked Hardcastle.

196

'*Blackmailed!*' Veronica almost screeched the word. It seemed that there was no end to the string of distasteful revelations being unveiled by this common policeman. 'No, he most certainly did not.'

'So, how did he get hurt?' asked Hardcastle, relentlessly pursuing his original question.

'It was yesterday evening, Inspector.' In view of what she had heard about her lover, or ex-lover as she decided he had just become, Veronica resolved to tell the truth. 'I own a little cottage at Rottingdean, just along from Brighton. I suppose that Henry, my husband, guessed that's where we'd be. He arrived at about eight o'clock and confronted Horace. Thank God we weren't in bed,' she said with uncharacteristic frankness. 'Henry's language was quite disgraceful, but then he is a soldier,' she added, as though that in some way excused his conduct. 'He told Horace that he deserved to be horse-whipped for stealing another man's wife and proceeded to lay into him. There was nothing I could do.'

'And I s'pose the major left then,' said Hardcastle. And when Mrs Groves nodded, he asked, 'Why didn't you go with him? The major I mean.'

'I told him I never wanted to see him again after such an outburst of ungentlemanly behaviour.'

Hardcastle thought that was a bit rich, coming as it did from a self-confessed adulteress. 'And what was his reply?'

'He said it was highly unlikely that I would see him again. I imagine he wanted me to feel sorry for him because he went on to say that he'd probably be dead within the week anyway. He's on his way to France, you see.'

'Yes,' said Hardcastle, 'he left for Southampton at four o'clock today.'

'Did he really?' But Veronica Groves seemed neither to know nor care that her husband was on his way to the Front already.

'On the night of Briggs's murder, Sir John, did Major Groves leave the smoking room at any time between, say, a quarter to eleven and half past?' asked Hardcastle, once he and Marriott had tracked down the chairman of Kendall's.

'You seem to be taking a great interest in what the members

were doing that night, Inspector,' said Webster. 'You're surely not suggesting that any one of them could have had anything to do with that awful business, are you?'

'Privilege don't necessarily rule out murder, Sir John,' said Hardcastle flatly. 'I've known of a few toffs what's taken the eight o'clock walk.'

'Yes, I suppose you must've done.' Webster considered that proposition before answering. 'No, I can't recall that *any* of them left the room between those times. I think I told you that General Slade went home at just after midnight and that Groves and Fitzpatrick came back to Albany with me.'

'So you did, sir,' said Hardcastle.

'Is there a particular reason why you should be interested in Henry Groves?'

'Yes, there is, Sir John, but it's not something I'm willing to reveal right now.' In a moment of rare compassion, Hardcastle had acknowledged that the blustering major was on his way to the fighting and might not return.

'You know, I suppose, that Major Groves has embarked for France.'

'Yes, I do. I spoke to him yesterday and I was told today that he's on his way to Southampton. I also spoke to his wife.'

'Really? I must say, Inspector, that you seem to be making very thorough enquiries.'

Hardcastle smiled. 'I always do when I'm investigating a murder, Sir John.'

By Friday morning, the fervour of war had gripped the streets of London.

Massive crowds lined Birdcage Walk and gathered in Parliament Square to cheer the Grenadier Guards as they marched from Wellington Barracks to Waterloo Station. Women ran into the road and handed bags of sweets and packets of cigarettes to the men, some of whom were lucky enough to have a kiss planted on their cheek, and old soldiers raised their hats to the passing Colours. Small boys, some beating toy drums, wore cocked hats fashioned from newspaper, and strutted beside the troops in an attempt to mimic their disciplined bearing.

But on the corner of Parliament Street there was sobering news.

A paperboy's placard announced the sinking of HMS *Amphion* the previous day with the loss of a hundred and fifty lives.

In Hardcastle's office the sound of the Guards band was muted as it passed along Bridge Street.

'Couple of pieces of good news in this morning's papers, sir,' said Marriott.

'About time,' muttered Hardcastle.

'Mrs Pankhurst's said she's giving up her suffrage movement for the duration of the war, sir, and Fritz is taking a beating from the Belgians at Liège.'

'Yes, and we'll be taking a bit of a trouncing here, Marriott, if we don't soon catch the bugger who did for Briggs. Chief Inspector Ward keeps asking me how we're getting on,' said Hardcastle in a reference to the officer in charge of the Central Office of the CID at Scotland Yard.

'Seems to me that no one quite knows when Davenport was in the card room and when he was in the smoking room, sir.'

'I ain't so worried about him, Marriott,' said Hardcastle. 'It's Major Groves that I'm thinking about. No one seems willing to pin him down neither. Strikes me they're all covering for each other.'

'But Groves wouldn't have been too bothered about Briggs putting the black on him, would he, sir? We know he was carrying on with Polly Francis, but his missus was having a fling with Davenport at the same time. Seems like one-all to me.'

'Ah, but what you don't understand, Marriott, is that people like the major worry themselves to death about getting slung out of their precious club. God knows why, but you heard what Mrs Groves said: that Davenport was in more of a muck-sweat about getting booted out of Kendall's than he was of getting made bankrupt. Well, that's all arse about face if you ask me. I tell you, Marriott, I wouldn't belong to that lot if they was to let me in for nothing.'

'But Groves has gone, sir, so we can't question him again.'

'Yes, more's the pity,' said Hardcastle. 'He's already been proved to be a violent bugger, giving Davenport a good hiding. Not that I blame him for that. But if Briggs threatened to shop him to Webster, he might just have decided to teach him a lesson. And perhaps he went too far.'

'But it's still murder, isn't it, sir?'

'Yes, Marriott, it is. But, be that as it may, it's time we had another word with that lying cove Davenport. Accident be buggered. I wonder what his game is. First though, we'll pay Mr Fitnam a visit and see if we can't get to the bottom of this fire. I ain't too sure that Wood found out all there was to find out.'

Hardcastle was well acquainted with Arthur Fitnam, the DDI of V Division, having served with him at Vine Street some years ago, when they were detective sergeants.

'And what brings you out to the sticks, Ernie?' asked Fitnam.

'I'd hardly call Wandsworth the sticks, Arthur, but I'm interested in a fire at a factory on your bailiwick a few months back. At Surbiton it was.'

Fitnam had no need to refer to a file. 'You're talking about Horace Davenport,' he said. 'A bit of an artful bugger if you ask me, Ernie.'

'What d'you reckon about this fire, then, Arthur?'

'I'm as sure as I can be that he set it,' said Fitnam, 'but we were a bit short of evidence. The fire brigade was no bloody help. Mind you, they was only volunteers. Anyway, what's your interest in him?'

'I'm looking into a murder at a club in Pall Mall,' Hardcastle said.

'Yes, I saw a bit about that in the linen drapers. Nicked anyone yet, have you?'

'No, I ain't, Arthur,' said Hardcastle ruefully, 'and half my bleedin' suspects are buggering off to the war an' all. But Horace Davenport's one of the members there.'

Fitnam laughed. 'Hard old world, ain't it, Ernie?' he observed. 'But d'you fancy this Davenport for it?'

'I've interviewed him a couple of times, but he's only one of half a dozen, including a conniving little whore called Polly Francis.' And Hardcastle went on to tell Fitnam what he knew about the man who not only had succeeded in cuckolding Major Groves, but had also persuaded the major's wife to part with a substantial amount of money to pay his gambling debts. 'Leastways, Arthur, I'm sure it was a fair amount, even though she never said as much.'

Fitnam nodded slowly. 'Well, if you feel like pulling him in again and giving him a bit of a going-over about the fire,

Ernie, it's all right by me,' he said with a chuckle. 'I never mind anyone clearing my books for me.'

'What did the insurance people have to say?'

'I reckon they're better at working out when fires have been set deliberately than the bloody fire brigade,' said Fitnam. 'But all they was able to say was that it was arson, but they couldn't say who, why or how.'

'I've got another theory at the back of my mind,' said Hardcastle, and explained about Briggs's blackmail. 'And Briggs would know a bit about starting fires,' he added. 'He was in the London Fire Brigade for a couple of years. Before he got slung out for kipping on duty.'

'Was Davenport interviewed by your officers, sir?' Marriott asked Fitnam.

'Yes, one of my lads had him in at Surbiton, but Davenport was a smooth bastard by all accounts. Just kept complaining that someone must've had it in for him, but denied having anything to do with it himself.'

'Was there anything left of the factory, sir?' continued Marriott.

'No, Sarge, just ashes. It was burned to the ground.'

'So you've no idea what he kept in the place.'

'According to Davenport it was full of priceless antiques. Hang on a minute.' Fitnam walked across to a filing cabinet and pulled out a thick dossier. 'He reckoned his stock was worth five hundred pounds and claimed it'd cost another two hundred and fifty to rebuild the place. That was a bit much in my view. It was only a wooden hut to start with. However,' he continued, 'my lads made a few enquiries locally and found out that he was making concertinas, but the Germans was undercutting him. Pity he didn't wait. It'll be a long time before we buy any more of Fritz's squeeze-boxes.'

Hardcastle laughed. 'Restoring priceless antiques and selling 'em on was the story he told his lady friend, Arthur.'

'Not surprised,' said Fitnam. 'I had my doubts about that crafty sod right from the start. I suppose I'd better have him in again and let a real detective put him on the grill.'

'I'd like to do that, Arthur, if it's all the same to you.'

'Like I said, Ernie, I never mind someone else clearing my crime book for me.'

*   *   *

201

It was five o'clock that afternoon when Hardcastle and Marriott called once again at 17 Broad Street. And once again it was Rose Davenport who answered the door.

'Is your husband at home, Mrs Davenport?'

'Yes, you'd better come in.' Rose Davenport was looking drawn, and from the redness of her eyes it was fairly clear that she had been crying.

Horace Davenport was looking a little more spruce this time. He wore a different suit and the graze on his face was less angry.

'Oh, it's you, Inspector.' Davenport was standing by the window, a glass of whisky in his hand. Hardcastle wondered where the money had come from to buy it, given that Rose had said only yesterday that they could not afford any.

'This accident of yours, Mr Davenport . . .' began Hardcastle.

'What about it, Inspector?' Davenport raised his chin slightly.

'Don't take me for a fool, Davenport. We've made enquiries and you wasn't in any accident.'

'But I assure you—'

'And we spoke to Mrs Groves yesterday evening. Not only is she alive and unharmed, but she don't know anything about this accident of yours.' Although Hardcastle had to admire the man's constant denial of the truth, he had had enough. 'Horace Davenport,' he said, 'I am arresting you for arson, and attempting to defraud the insurance company that was covering your property.'

'Preposterous!' said Davenport and took another sip of his whisky.

But Rose Davenport, clearly finding this latest twist too much to tolerate, fainted. Davenport, however, seemed not to notice.

Marriott stooped and gently smacked the woman's face while Hardcastle poured her a glass of water from the jug on the drinks table. Moments later she showed signs of reviving, and Marriott helped her to a chair.

But suddenly Rose revealed an inner strength of character that had not hitherto been apparent. 'You disgust me, Horace Davenport,' she screamed. 'I loathe you and I hope you rot in hell.'

'You must excuse my wife,' said Davenport mildly, 'but she's always been somewhat highly strung.'

'Highly strung?' screamed Rose. 'You're a drunk and a womanizer, and you've gambled away all our money. You've invested in stupid business schemes, and you have the gall to criticize me. In fact, Horace, you've done just about everything except an honest day's work.'

Unruffled by his wife's outburst, Davenport held up a hand. 'Do calm yourself, my dear . . .'

But Rose had not finished. 'This house is heavily mortgaged *and* we're behind with the payments, so much so that we're about to be evicted. We owe money to every tradesman in the area and you stand there drinking whisky and tell me to calm myself. I hope they send you to prison for a very long time.'

Twenty-Two

Once the procedures that always follow an arrest had been completed, Horace Davenport was placed in a cell at Cannon Row police station and left there for an hour. Finally, he was taken to the interview room where Hardcastle and Marriott were waiting.

'Now then, Davenport, tell me about these precious antiques what you lost in this fire of yours down at Surbiton.'

'I think I should have a solicitor here, Inspector,' sneered Davenport in supercilious tones.

Hardcastle laughed. 'If you can stump up the cash for a solicitor, I'll get you one,' he said. 'But you know, and I know, that you ain't got two ha'pennies to rub together. And that's a fact. So, let's get down to brass tacks, shall we?'

'I told the police down at Surbiton all there was to tell,' said Davenport, still refusing to be ruffled by Hardcastle's hostile attitude.

'Yes, but what you told 'em was a pack of lies. You never had no antiques down there. You was making concertinas, and you went under because Fritz was seeing you off. Gamages was flogging old square-head's squeeze-boxes for ten bob at

the most, and you couldn't match that, so you burned down
the shed you call a factory and tried it on with the insurance
company. But they wasn't having any, was they?'

'It was Briggs,' Davenport blurted out.

'What was?'

'It was that damned man Briggs who burned the place down,
Inspector.'

'Really?' Hardcastle adopted an air of sarcastic disbelief.
'And why should he do that?'

'He was blackmailing me.'

'Was he now? And what was that all about?'

'He found out that I was seeing Veronica Groves and he
threatened to tell her husband.'

'Her husband already knew,' said Hardcastle, dismissing
that statement with a satisfied smile, 'and that's why he went
down to Rottingdean to give you a hiding.'

'How did you know that?' Davenport sat up sharply.

'Because Veronica Groves told me, and she weren't too
happy about you spending her money on your gambling habit,
nor that you was having a screw with Queenie Hicks.'

'How on earth did Veronica find out about that?' demanded
Davenport.

'I told her.' Hardcastle had not mentioned Queenie to the
major's wife, but saw no reason why he should not discom-
fit Davenport even further.

'You've no right—'

'When I'm investigating a murder, Davenport, I talk to who
I like, ask 'em what I like and tell 'em what I like.'

'Briggs wanted money or he said that he'd tell the committee that I'd been keeping company with Veronica and seeing
Queenie.'

'Ah, now we're getting to it, ain't we?'

'But I hadn't got any money. Quite frankly, Inspector, I'm
on my beam ends.'

'And he didn't believe you, I s'pose.'

'No, he didn't. He threatened to set fire to the factory if I
didn't pay up. And he did set fire to it. He even had the gall
to tell me he had. I know what you said about Henry Groves
being aware that I was seeing his wife, but Briggs knew it
too. I suppose he must've followed me from time to time. But

once the factory had gone, he wanted me to get money from Veronica, otherwise he said he'd tell the major that we were seeing each other. As for Queenie, well he obviously knew about her. He arranged it.'

'I ain't buying it, Davenport,' said Hardcastle. 'You'd gone bust anyway and you burnt the factory down yourself, so's you could get the insurance to pay off Briggs and have a bit to spare. But it all went belly-up on you when the insurance wouldn't pay out.'

'Excuse me, sir.' Detective Sergeant Wood stood in the doorway of the interview room.

'Was he there, Wood?'

'Yes, sir.'

'And?'

'The answer's yes, sir.' Wood stepped across to the table at which Hardcastle was facing his prisoner, and handed the DDI a sheet of paper.

Hardcastle took a moment or two to scan the report that the sergeant had delivered. 'All right, Wood, that's all.'

Hardcastle handed the report to Marriott and then faced Davenport again. 'Now, let's get back to the night Briggs was murdered.'

'I've told you all I can about that, Inspector.'

'No you haven't.'

'I can assure you—'

'You was playing cards that night,' said Hardcastle.

'That's correct.'

'But, as usual, you lost a packet and retired hurt, so to speak. At what time?'

Davenport affected a thoughtful pose, wrinkling his brow as though searching his memory for the answer.

'Must have been about a quarter to eleven, I suppose.'

'How come you remember that so easy, Davenport? It was over three weeks ago. I'd be hard pushed to remember what time I left the office last night, let alone three weeks ago.'

'Well, I'm certain, Inspector.' Davenport, unsure where Hardcastle's line of questioning was leading, began to look decidedly shifty. 'But what's that got to do with the fire at my factory?'

'Nothing, and I ain't in the slightest interested in who set fire to your squeeze-box emporium.'

'Then what on earth am I doing here?' Once again, Davenport's face registered surprise.

'Which door did you go out of when you left the card room that night?'

'Er, I can't recall . . .'

'Strange that, Davenport. You had no trouble remembering the exact time you left, but you don't know which door you went out of. Well, I'll tell you. You went out of the door leading into the corridor. And witnesses will say that you did so at a quarter to eleven. You left the club by the back door and when Briggs come out, on the stroke of eleven, you followed him as far as the bridge over the lake in St James's Park. And when he got to the bridge you hit him over the head with the crowbar what you'd lifted from the club. Then you heaved him over the railings into the lake. Once that was done, you come back by the forward route reversed, as we say in the police, via the back door and into the smoking room. At half past eleven. And there are witnesses to that, an' all. Then you calmly poured yourself a drink, signed a chit – for what that's worth, 'cos you ain't got any cash – and sat down. Then you had a few more drinks and just before one o'clock you buggered off home.'

Davenport stared at Hardcastle in shocked disbelief. 'That's utter nonsense, Inspector,' he said, having eventually collected himself. 'Why should I want to kill Briggs?'

'You've just explained all that, Davenport. He was bleeding you dry, and you said he'd done for your factory. He was buggering up your love life, and even after he was dead, he managed to get you beaten up by Major Groves.'

'Pure speculation,' said Davenport with false confidence. 'You can't prove any of it.'

Although Hardcastle had a certain secret admiration for this man, he knew that he was a born confidence trickster and glib lies came easily to him. 'Ah, but I can.' He took the single sheet of paper back from Marriott. 'I have a report here signed by Detective Inspector Charles Stockley Collins of the Fingerprint Bureau at Scotland Yard. He states that he's examined the crowbar that killed Briggs, and he found a thumbprint on it. He also examined the fingerprints what was taken from you when you got here this evening.'

Davenport shifted uneasily in his chair, but said nothing.

'And he's prepared to give evidence at the Old Bailey that it's your thumbprint on the crowbar.'

'I daresay it is on there, Inspector.' Davenport shook his head wearily. 'But he knew, you see, Inspector. He knew all along.'

'What the blue blazes are you talking about now?'

'It's the officer thing. I'd not been in the army like most of those stuffed shirts had been. No one in that damned club liked me, but they were prepared to take my money at cards. And, it seems, prepared to swear my life away. All because I was engaged in trade, making an honest living. I thought it would help my business to become a member of Kendall's. I must admit that I lied, told them I was a musician, a composer. Well, in a way I was: I made concertinas.' Davenport gave a savage laugh at the thought of having fooled the selection committee. 'But it was only after they'd let me in that they discovered what I really did for a living. They'd've black-balled me if they'd known that to start with, but once I was in they didn't really know how to throw me out.'

Hardcastle chuckled as he tried to picture the reaction of the members of Kendall's when they realized that they had allowed a concertina maker to enter their precious portals.

'But you've seen what a slap-happy place it is,' Davenport continued. 'The accounts are all over the place, people were stealing bottles of whisky and brandy. And I should know: I've not exactly been honest all my life, and I can spot a thief a mile away. Carmichael was on the fiddle, but because he'd been an officer, so he said, they thought he could be trusted. And about once a week someone or other would suggest that I resign. And they weren't very subtle about it, either. Then there was the night that Briggs poured drink over me. I complained to the secretary, but he did nothing about it. Said he'd spoken to the other members who were there, and they'd accused me of being drunk and that I'd spilled the drink myself.'

'How did your thumbprint come to be on the crowbar then?' Hardcastle was extremely sceptical about the story that Davenport was telling. Viewed it as a forlorn attempt to escape from justice.

Davenport laughed. 'I tripped over the bloody thing. I'd arrived at the club early one evening, and I went up to Peter

Reilly's room to see if he was interested in a hand of cards or a frame of snooker, but he wasn't there. Anyway, the crowbar was on the floor just outside that new chap's room. Leighton I think he's called. Snooty sort of chap. Typical Indian Army I should think. Anyway, I picked it up, took it downstairs and left it on Lucas's desk in the lobby.'

'Was Lucas there?'

'No. I don't know where he'd gone, but he does sometimes take a message into the smoking room, if the page isn't there.'

'And that's the last you saw of the crowbar, was it?'

'Yes. I might have mentioned to Lucas later that I'd left it there, but I can't really remember now.'

'Let's start again then. What time did you leave the card room?'

'About a quarter to eleven, Inspector. I went out of the door leading to the corridor and straight into the smoking room. I don't care what time that lot said I got there, but it could only have been a minute later at the most. Half the old buggers were asleep anyway. They wouldn't know what time it was if you stuffed a gold watch up their nose.'

'Who was in the smoking room when you entered?' asked Hardcastle.

'General Slade, Sir John Webster and Colonel Fitzpatrick.'

'What about Major Groves?'

'No, he wasn't there, Inspector. He didn't come in until about half past eleven.'

'We must act quickly, Marriott,' said Hardcastle, 'and we may already be too late. Get on to the Southampton City Police and get them to find out if the bugger's already on a ship for France. And if he is, alert the military at Boulogne and tell them to hold him and send him back. In the meantime, we shall visit Kendall's. With any luck for the last bloody time.'

'I have a serious matter to discuss with you, Sir John, and I must warn you to consider your answers very carefully.' Hardcastle and Marriott seated themselves in the secretary's office where, even at this late hour, Sir John Webster was struggling with unfamiliar paperwork.

'Now look here, Inspector,' Webster began, 'I've been very

tolerant with your constant interruptions, and so, may I say, have the members, but there is a limit.'

'I suggested being careful about what you say because I'm considering the question of criminal conspiracy.'

'Eh?' Webster was surprised by Hardcastle's statement, and his lack of deference. 'What the—?'

'What time did Mr Davenport come into the smoking room from the card room on the night of Joseph Briggs's murder?' And before Webster had time to reply, Hardcastle turned to his sergeant. 'I want you to make careful notes of my questions and Sir John's answers, Marriott.'

'Yes, sir.' Marriott opened his pocket book and rested it on his knee, pencil at the ready.

'I'm sure it was about half past eleven, Inspector.'

'How can you be so sure? Did you look at your watch?'

'No, not exactly, but after the murder, someone said you'd been asking questions about the time and I asked Jimmy Fitzpatrick. Er, Colonel Fitzpatrick, that is.'

'And General Lord Slade? What about him?'

'I'm afraid he was asleep in one of the armchairs,' said Webster and paused, a sad expression on his face. 'I suppose you've heard that he's dead. Died yesterday. Mind you, he'd had a good innings. Over seventy.'

'So it amounts to this,' said Hardcastle. 'The only person who can confirm what time Davenport came into the smoking room is Colonel Fitzpatrick.'

'Yes, I suppose so,' mumbled Webster.

'And what about Major Groves?'

'What about him?' Webster's eyes narrowed.

'What time did he come into the room?'

Webster glanced at Marriott, busily recording everything. 'He was there until about a quarter to eleven. Said he was going off for a bit of supper, and came back at about half past, I suppose, so Fitzpatrick said.'

'What time is supper served?'

'Oh, good Lord!' Webster frowned. 'Only until ten thirty.'

'Then he wouldn't have gone for supper, would he?'

'No, I suppose not. Perhaps he was playing snooker.'

'Yes, maybe,' said Hardcastle pensively. 'Where can I find this Colonel Fitzpatrick?'

209

'I believe he's in the smoking room, Inspector.'

'Go and tell him I want him in here, Marriott,' said Hardcastle. 'And don't mince your words.'

A few moments later the august figure of Colonel James Fitzpatrick, late of the Connaught Rangers, entered the room. His iron-grey moustache dominated a pink face suffused with anger, and his beady little eyes surveyed Hardcastle with ill-disguised contempt.

'What the hell d'you mean by having your damned sergeant drag me in here like some common criminal?' he demanded.

'Why don't you sit down, Colonel?' said Hardcastle mildly.

'I'll stand, thank you.'

'As you wish. The night of Briggs's murder, Colonel . . .'

'What about it?'

'I'll not waste time. When did Major Groves leave the smoking room and when did he return?'

'Dammit, man, how on earth d'you expect me to remember that?'

'It's important, Colonel, and I daresay it's a question that prosecuting counsel will ask you at the Old Bailey. So if I was you, I'd be sure about it. And truthful.'

Fitzpatrick sat down heavily in the only other armchair. 'What's all this business about the Old Bailey?'

'When you were questioned before, you gave answers that don't hang together in view of what I've learned.'

Fitzpatrick let out a deep sigh. 'I don't suppose it matters now,' he said, 'because the fellow's gone off to France.'

'No he hasn't. He's locked up in a cell at Cannon Row police station. But I fancy he'll not be there much longer.'

'I'm talking about Henry Groves, man.'

'At last,' said Hardcastle, and glancing at Marriott, added, 'Keep writing, Marriott.'

'Henry told me he was slipping out to see some filly at about a quarter to eleven. Didn't want anyone to know, of course. But he came back at about half past and said she hadn't turned up. Of course when all this hoo-ha came up about Briggs, he thought it might look a bit suspicious. So he asked me to say that he'd been there all the time.'

'And Davenport?'

'Oh, he came in from the card room at about a quarter to eleven, got himself a drink and sat down by the window. Not a very clubbable sort of chap. Hardly anyone talks to him, you know.'

'So, when Briggs was murdered, you tried to make it look that it was Davenport what was out of the room at the time, and not Groves.'

'Didn't think it mattered,' said Fitzpatrick. 'Fellow's a bounder. In trade, you know. Anyway, it's not one of the club members who killed that bloody man Briggs, is it?'

'That, Colonel, remains to be seen,' said Hardcastle. 'I've obtained a warrant for Major Henry Groves to be arrested at Southampton, or if he's already in France, to be detained there and returned to the jurisdiction.'

'My God!' Sir John Webster leaned forward, a shocked expression on his face. 'You're not suggesting that Henry—?'

'Yes, I am,' said Hardcastle, 'and what's more, if I find evidence that any of the members of this club have been spinning a yarn to cover up for him' – he looked searchingly at each of their faces – 'I shall look forward to making further arrests for conspiracy to commit murder.' He stood up. 'In the meantime, gents, I'll bid you goodnight. Come, Marriott.'

Twenty-Three

The truth of the matter was, that at this stage in his investigation, Hardcastle had insufficient evidence to arrest Groves and had lied to Webster and Fitzpatrick when he said that he had obtained a warrant. He also knew that he had no real evidence to sustain charges of conspiracy against Webster and Fitzpatrick. At least, not yet. But he was determined to charge them with something.

In the meantime, he had spoken to a helpful colonel at the War Office. The colonel had made a discreet and urgent enquiry and was able to tell the DDI that Major Groves's battalion was still at Southampton. The officer also volunteered the information that the unit was under canvas on Chilworth Common and unlikely to embark for France until Monday at the very earliest, and perhaps not even then. The officer had explained that Lord Kitchener, the Secretary of State for War, was adamant that at least two divisions should be kept in England.

First thing on Saturday morning, Hardcastle and Marriott took a train from Waterloo to Southampton. After waiting an inordinate length of time they eventually found a taxi willing to take them from the station to the encampment where Groves's battalion was billeted.

'We might have to gild the lily a bit when we gets there, Marriott,' Hardcastle had confided on the way to Chilworth Common. But even Marriott was surprised at his DDI's outrageous tactics.

Major Henry Groves had a resigned air about him when the detectives were shown into the tent he was using as an office.

'What now, Inspector?' he asked wearily as he tossed a handful of official-looking forms into a wire tray.

'A few questions about the night Joseph Briggs was done in, Major. And before you answer, I have to tell you that I have sworn statements from Sir John Webster and Colonel James Fitzpatrick concerning the matter. What's more, they could be in serious trouble regarding this whole matter. Unfortunately, I couldn't get one from General Lord Slade on account of him having snuffed it.'

Groves did not seem at all distressed at the news of Slade's demise. 'What sort of statements?' he asked.

'Regarding the time you and Horace Davenport went in and out of the smoking room, Major.'

'Oh, I see.' Groves thought about that for a moment or two.

'So, perhaps you'd like to tell me, once again, what your movements was that night.'

'I'd arranged to meet Polly, at about eleven o'clock.'

'Where?' asked Hardcastle sharply.

'Outside the Albert in Victoria Street, but she wasn't there. Once you started asking questions about where everyone was that night, I asked Jimmy Fitzpatrick to cover for me. It would have been a scandal if it had become known that I'd slipped out to meet some damned—'

'Whore,' said Hardcastle brutally.

'Yes, quite so.' Groves brushed at his moustache.

'Pack of lies.'

'I beg your pardon?' snapped Groves furiously.

'When I asked you about that before, you told me that you *hadn't* agreed to meet her. But Polly Francis was there from about eleven to gone half past and you never showed. I've got a sworn statement from her an' all.'

'Then she must be mistaken, Inspector. But more to the point, I don't think anyone would take the word of a common prostitute to that of a commissioned officer in the British Army.' Groves had quickly recovered his customary arrogance and, in a vain attempt to rid himself of this troublesome and somewhat common policeman, he added, 'However, if that's all you wanted to know, Inspector, I'd be grateful if you left me to get on. I have much to do as we're on the point of embarking for France.'

'No you ain't, Major. You won't be going till at least Monday, and probably not then. Seems that Lord Kitchener ain't too keen on sending the *whole* British Army across the water.'

'How the hell d'you know that?' demanded Groves angrily, as he realized that Hardcastle was destroying each of his lies, one after the other.

'The War Office told me,' said Hardcastle smugly. 'And now I'm going to tell you what I've found out so far. At least ten of the members of Kendall's, you included, got letters from Briggs threatening to tell their wives and the committee that you was out whoring unless you stumped up a fair wad of cash. So you volunteered to do him in, and the others said they'd cover for you.' Continuing to guess wildly, he went on. 'And as you was aware the war was looming, so to speak, you took a pace forward like a good volunteer, seeing as how you thought you'd be across in France by the time we got to the nub of it. And I daresay you thought we'd've forgotten all about it by the time this here milling with Fritz was all done and dusted. But you was just a touch too late, Major.'

'I can assure you that you're gravely mistaken, Inspector, and—'

'I ain't finished yet, Major. Webster told me you was going in for supper at a quarter to eleven that night, but they don't serve it after half past ten. When I fronted him with that, he admitted he was lying. And he told me why. And you never played snooker neither, because I've checked.' Again

213

Hardcastle took a guess at what was in all probability the truth. 'And you never met Polly Francis because she said you never and I believe her.' But then Hardcastle took a risk. '*But you was seen, Major,*' he said slowly, implying that Polly had witnessed Groves murdering Briggs.

'Oh!' Groves placed his hands flat on the wooden trestle table and for a moment or two gazed down at them, his closed military mind unable to appreciate that if his crime had been witnessed, Hardcastle would have arrested him three weeks ago. 'That man deserved to die,' he said quietly. 'He was ruining people with his threats, financially ruining them, I mean. Something had to be done. But I was the only one with the courage to do it.'

'What did you do with Briggs's wallet, eh?'

'I took it to make it seem like a robbery,' said Groves. The arrogance was gone now, and he realized that all the plotting, and the attempts to delude this stolid policeman, had come to nought. 'I threw it away.'

'The simplest answer to blackmail would have been to go to the police,' said Hardcastle. 'But no, all you high and mighty members of Kendall's couldn't have that sort of scandal in the linen drapers, could you? That'd be too much to bear, a common steward having you lot on toast. And all the tales of your whoring would've come out at the Bailey an' all. So you decided to take the law into your own hands. Well, Major, there's a price to pay for that sort of malarkey, and I've come here to collect, so to speak.' He stood up. 'Henry Groves, I'm arresting you for the wilful murder of Joseph Briggs sometime between eleven o'clock on the night of Tuesday the fourteenth of July 1914 and eight o'clock on the morning of Wednesday the fifteenth.'

'But you can't possibly arrest me, Inspector,' pleaded Groves, 'not now. We're under orders to go to France on active service.'

'Well, they'll just have to manage without you, won't they? I reckon the bold Lord Kitchener's got a few spare majors sculling about.'

On Friday the thirtieth of October 1914 the first battle of Ypres began. It was raining and the wind swept across the inhospitable muddy plains between that little Belgian town and the Messines Ridge that overlooked it, and from where the German army dominated it.

And men were dying.

One of the early dead was a Private Jed Parsons who, rather than face the prospect of prison, had volunteered in the opening stages of the war. But his body was never found and to this day his only memorial is his name carved on the Menin Gate.

Coincidentally, it was on that day also that Kendall's closed its doors for the last time. The disgrace that had followed the arrest of three of its members – one for murder, and two for being accessories after the fact – had resulted in the resignation of so many members, unwilling any more to be associated with it, that it ceased to be viable.

It was windy and raining in Hammersmith that morning too, and from about half past seven a little knot of morbid bystanders, their shoulders hunched against the inclement weather, waited outside Wormwood Scrubs prison.

At a minute to eight, in the condemned cell that lay in the heart of that prison's grim, grey walls, the two warders of the 'death-watch' moved swiftly to the wardrobe and shoved it aside to reveal a door.

The hangman and his assistant stepped into the cell. Quickly pinioning the arms of the prisoner, they hurried him to the execution chamber next door. Once there, the hangman secured the man's ankles and placed a hood over his head. Next, he fitted the noose and tightened the slipknot.

The hangman's assistant pulled the lever and, with a chilling clatter, the trapdoor opened.

From start to finish, the executioners had taken exactly one minute to despatch the condemned man.

At a quarter past eight, a warder appeared through the wicket of the huge prison gates and placed a black-framed notice on a hook.

The ghouls who were waiting outside the prison, much as their forefathers had gathered at Tyburn Tree, surged forward and clustered around the gates to read that sentence of death had been duly carried out.

'Who the hell was Henry Groves anyway?' asked one idler of his neighbour, a man – hands in pockets – wearing an old suit with the collar turned up against the chill wind.

'If you've an hour to spare, I'll tell you,' said Horace Davenport.

Glossary

'A' FROM A BULL'S FOOT, to know: to know nothing.

ALBERT: a watch chain of the type worn by Albert, Prince Consort.

ALL MY EYE AND BETTY MARTIN: nonsense.

ANTECEDENT HISTORY: details of an accused person's address, education and employment, etc.

BAILEY, the: Central Criminal Court, London.

BARNEY: an argument.

BEAK: a magistrate.

BIRD LIME: time (rhyming slang).

BLACK ANNIE or BLACK MARIA: a police or prison van.

BOB: a shilling (now 5p).

BOOZER: a public house.

BRADBURY: a pound note. From Sir John Bradbury, Secretary to the Treasury, who introduced pound notes in 1914 to replace gold sovereigns.

BRIEF, a: a warrant *or* a police warrant card *or* a lawyer.

BROLLY: an umbrella.

BULL AND COW: a row (rhyming slang).

BUSY, a: a detective.

CARNEY: cunning, sly.

CARPET: three months' imprisonment.

CHESTNUTS OUT OF THE FIRE, to pull your: to solve your problem.

CHOKEY: prison.

CID: Criminal Investigation Department.

CIGS: Chief of the Imperial General Staff.

CLINK: prison. Clink Street, London, was the site of an old prison.

CLYDE (*as in* D'YOU THINK I CAME UP THE CLYDE ON A BICYCLE?): to deny that the speaker is a fool.

COLDSTREAMER: a soldier of the Coldstream Guards.

COMMISSIONER'S OFFICE: official title of New Scotland Yard, headquarters of the Metropolitan Police.

COPPER: a policeman.

COPPER-KNOBS: people with auburn hair.

CO-RESPONDENT SHOES: brown & white shoes, reputed to be worn by philanderers.

CRACKLING: an attractive woman.

CRACKSMAN: a safe-breaker.

CULLY: alternative to calling a man 'mate'.

D: a detective.

DDI: Divisional Detective Inspector.

DEKKO: a look (*ex* Hindi).

DICKY BIRD: a word (rhyming slang).

DOGBERRY: a policeman or watchman (*ex* Shakespeare).

DOLLAR: five shillings (25p).

DOOLALLY TAP: of unsound mind (*ex* Hindi).

DOXY: a woman of loose character.

DRUM: a dwelling house.

DSO: Distinguished Service Order.

DUMMY, to throw a: to set a false trail.

EARWIGGING: listening.

EIGHT O'CLOCK WALK, to take the: to be hanged.

EWBANK: proprietary name of an early type of non-electric carpet sweeper.

EYEWASH: nonsense.

FEEL THE COLLAR, to: to make an arrest.

FIVER: five pounds sterling.

FLEET STREET: former centre of the newspaper industry, and still used as a generic term for the Press.

FLIM or FLIMSY: a five-pound note. From the thin paper on which it was originally printed.

FLORIN: two shillings (10p).

FLOUNDER: a cab (rhyming slang: flounder and dab).

FORM: previous convictions.

FOURPENNY CANNON, a: a steak and kidney pie.

FRONT, The: theatre of WWI operations in France and Flanders.

GAMP: an umbrella (from Sarah Gamp in Charles Dickens's *Martin Chuzzlewit*).

GILD THE LILY, to: to exaggerate.

GLIM: a look, a shortening of 'glimpse'.

GREAT SCOTLAND YARD: location of an army recruiting office, not to be confused with New Scotland Yard.

GROWLER: a taxi.

GUV *or* GUV'NOR: informal alternative to 'sir'.

HALF A CROWN *or* HALF A DOLLAR: two shillings and sixpence (12½p).

HAWKING THE MUTTON: leading a life of prostitution.

HOLLOWAY: women's prison in North London.

IRONCLAD: a battleship.

JILDI: quickly (*ex* Hindi).

JOANNA: a piano.

JUDY: a girl.

KC: King's Counsel – a senior barrister.

KETTLE: a pocket watch.

KIP, to have a: to sleep.

KNOCKED OFF: arrested.

LAY-DOWN: a remand in custody.

LINEN DRAPERS: newspapers (rhyming slang).

LONG BOW, to draw the: to exaggerate *or* to tell unbelievable stories.

MAGSMAN: a common thief.

MANOR: a police area.

MBE: Member of the Order of the British Empire.

MC: Military Cross.

MI5: counter-espionage service of the United Kingdom.

MILLING: fighting.

MINCES: eyes (rhyming slang: mince pies).

MONS, to make a: to make a mess of things, as in the disastrous Battle of Mons in 1914.

NAPOO: no good; finished. Bastardization of the French: *il n'y en a plus* (there is none left), usually in answer to a soldier's request for more beer.

NICK: a police station or prison.

NICKED: arrested.

OBE: Officer of the Order of the British Empire.

OLD BAILEY: Central Criminal Court, London.

OLD CONTEMPTIBLES: name assumed by survivors of

the Battle of Mons in response to the Kaiser's condemnation of the British Army as 'a contemptible little army'.

ON THE GAME: leading a life of prostitution.

ON THE SLATE: to be given credit.

ON THE SQUARE: a freemason.

OUT OF THE TOP DRAWER: of a superior class.

PEACH, to: to inform to the police.

PETER JONES: a London department store in Sloane Square, Chelsea.

PIP, SQUEAK AND WILFRED: WWI medals, namely the 1914-15 Star, the British War Medal 1914-18 and the Victory Medal 1914-19, so named after newspaper cartoon characters of the period.

POLICE GAZETTE: official nationwide publication listing wanted persons, etc.

PREVIOUS: prior convictions for crime.

PROVOST, the: military police.

QUID: one pound sterling.

RAINING CATS AND DOGS: raining heavily.

RECEIVER, the: senior Scotland Yard official responsible for the finances of the Metropolitan Police.

RECORD: record of previous convictions.

ROZZER: a policeman.

SAPPERS: the Corps of Royal Engineers (in the singular, a member of that corps).

SAUSAGE AND MASH: cash (rhyming slang).

SCREW: a prison warder.

SCRIMSHANKER: one who evades duty or work.

SELL THE PUP, to: to attempt to deceive.

SEXTON BLAKE: a detective hero of boys' stories.

SHILLING: now 5p.

SILK, a: a King's Counsel (a senior barrister) from the silk gowns they wear.

SKINT: broke.

SKIP *or* SKIPPER: an informal police alternative to station-sergeant, clerk-sergeant and sergeant.

SMACKER, a: a pound sterling *or* a kiss.

SMOKE, the: London.

SNOUT: a police informant.

SOMERSET HOUSE: formerly the records office of births, deaths and marriages for England & Wales.

SOVEREIGN (or SOV): one pound sterling.

SPIT AND A DRAW, to have a: to smoke a cigarette.

STAGE-DOOR JOHNNY: young man frequenting theatres in an attempt to make the acquaintance of actresses.

STONY: broke.

STRETCH, a: one year's imprisonment.

SWADDY: a soldier (*ex* Hindi).

SWEET FANNY ADAMS, to know: to know nothing.

TANNER: sixpence (2½p).

TATLER, THE: a society magazine.

TEA LEAF: a thief (rhyming slang).

TICKETY-BOO: all right, perfect.

TITFER: a hat (rhyming slang: tit for tat).

TOBY: a police area.

TOD (SLOAN), on one's: on one's own (rhyming slang).

TOM: a prostitute.

TOMMING: pursuing a life of prostitution.

TOMMY: a British soldier. From the name Tommy Atkins, used as an example on early army forms.

TOPPED: murdered or hanged.

TOPPING: a murder or hanging.

TROUBLE-AND-STRIFE: wife (rhyming slang).

TUBE: The London Underground railway system.

TUMBLE, a: sexual intercourse.

TWO-AND-EIGHT, in a: in a state (rhyming slang).

UNDERGROUND, The: London Underground railway system.

UP THE SPOUT: pregnant.

VAD: Voluntary Aid Detachment – wartime nursing auxiliaries.

WATCH COMMITTEE: a provincial police authority.

WAR OFFICE: Department of State overseeing the army. (Now a part of the Ministry of Defence.)

WET ONE'S WHISKERS: to take a drink.

WHISTLE: a suit (rhyming slang: whistle and flute).

WHITE-FEATHER JOHNNY: man avoiding military service.